"What is that?"

Far ahead of them, An... out something dark. It looked like it was growing.

Godwin pressed on the gas pedal. His eyes narrowed and he gripped the wheel tighter. "Our turnoff should be coming soon."

"Not soon enough," Annja said. "It's going to be close."

"What is?" Derek asked. "What is that thing ahead of us? What's going on?"

Annja looked at him. "Can't you hear it?"

Derek stopped and sat back in his seat. He closed his eyes and then Annja saw his body stiffen appreciably. His eyes popped open. "Tell me that's not what I think it is."

Annja nodded. "It is."

Godwin pointed up ahead of them. "It's growing."

Annja looked and saw it was true. Shooting down the ice road toward them was a giant fissure of blackness.

The ice road was cracking all around them.

Titles in this series:

ROGUE Angel

Alex Archer

SACRED GROUND

A GOLD EAGLE BOOK FROM
W RLDWIDE ®

TORONTO • NEW YORK • LONDON
AMSTERDAM • PARIS • SYDNEY • HAMBURG
STOCKHOLM • ATHENS • TOKYO • MILAN
MADRID • WARSAW • BUDAPEST • AUCKLAND

Recycling programs
for this product may
not exist in your area.

First edition March 2010

ISBN-13: 978-0-373-62142-2

SACRED GROUND

Special thanks and acknowledgment to
Jon Merz for his contribution to this work.

Printed in U.S.A.

The
LEGEND

...THE ENGLISH COMMANDER TOOK
JOAN'S SWORD AND RAISED IT HIGH.

The broadsword, plain and unadorned,
gleamed in the firelight. He put the tip against
the ground and his foot at the center of the blade.
The broadsword shattered, fragments falling
into the mud. The crowd surged forward,
peasant and soldier, and snatched the shards
from the trampled mud. The commander tossed
the hilt deep into the crowd.
Smoke almost obscured Joan, but she continued
praying till the end, until finally the flames climbed
her body and she sagged against the restraints.

Joan of Arc died that fateful day in France,
but her legend and sword are reborn....

1

Yellowknife, Northwest Territories, Canada

"It's been my experience," Annja Creed said, "that the motives of private industry and those of the public don't usually make for good bedfellows." She reclined a bit farther back into the deep chocolate leather of her armchair and waited for the man sitting across from her to respond.

"That's a pretty narrow way to look at things." Derek Wainman took a sip from a steaming mug of coffee before setting it on the frosted-glass table. "After all, it's in our best interests to work with the public to make sure they don't feel slighted. These are, after all, potential customers."

Annja considered the map in front of her. This time of year, most of the Northwest Territories of Canada was frozen. The arctic tundra was a mass of brittle green amid the snows and winds. She shivered just thinking about how cold it was out there.

But it couldn't be worse than Antarctica, could it? She smiled at the memories of that adventure and then noticed Derek watching.

"You okay?"

"The cold weather makes me reminisce about the other times I've been in the thick of it," she said.

Derek took another sip of his coffee. "That's been quite often, hasn't it?"

Annja looked at him. He smirked and waved his hand.

"Don't be so concerned. We take great pains to find out all we can about people we might be interested in working with. And there's never been anything that the right amount of money can't purchase. Information especially."

Annja smiled. She was one hundred percent positive there was at least one small nugget of intelligence that their money hadn't been able to procure—the presence of the sword that she always carried with her.

"That's a curious grin," Derek said.

Annja made her face expressionless. This guy didn't miss a thing. She'd have to remember that.

"How successful has the mining operation been at Ekati?"

"By all accounts, incredibly so," Derek said. "It's expected to yield five hundred million Canadian dollars a year for the next twenty-five years. Who would have thought that the earth could have such a repository of untapped wealth?"

"I might have," Annja said. "But then, I dig for a living. That kind of knowledge is my thing."

"You like getting dirty," Derek said.

Annja watched his face for any signs that he was already tossing innuendo around. But to his credit, he kept his expression firm and unyielding. No sign of mirth tinged it.

"Getting dirty comes with the territory," she said. "It

can't be helped. And it's only when you're truly down in the thick of it that you find the most precious treasures. So yes, I like getting dirty."

"Where were you before this?"

Annja raised an eyebrow at him. "Now, why would you ask me such a question? After all, I thought you had a complete workup on my recent activities?"

"We do."

"So, what, you want to see if I lie about my whereabouts?"

Derek held up his hand. "Calm down. It was just a friendly question."

Annja looked at the map again. Frozen lakes, frozen rivers, frozen everything. It would be a damned cold jaunt; she knew that.

"Why now?" she asked.

"Excuse me?"

Annja glanced up. "Wouldn't it make more sense to start something like this in the spring?"

Derek smiled. "We're hoping that by the time you get to the site and extricate everything that needs extricating, it will be spring and just in time for us to start our real work."

"Ah, the real work."

Derek leaned forward. "Annja, please make no mistake— while we're committed to helping the Inuit preserve whatever sacred ground they have in this location, our primary emphasis is on profit. We're a private corporation and as such, driven by the ever-present bottom line."

"Hence my original statement about private and public interests not intersecting."

Derek leaned back. "We can help each other."

"How so?"

"By you agreeing to come on board and assist the Inuit elders with their research, we gain a certain degree of sympathy for our corporation. Our public image looks better than if we simply steamrolled in and took what we wanted from the land with little regard to its history."

"Even though that's exactly what you want to do anyway?"

"You don't strike me as being naive, Annja."

"I'm not."

"So you understand the function of our meeting and your employment with us on this matter."

"I'm coming in as a contractor."

"But you work for us."

Annja smiled. "I gathered as much."

"For which you'll be paid quite handsomely. Far more than you make hosting that little show on television."

"Actually, *Chasing History's Monsters* does pretty well in the ratings."

Derek grinned. "Only when your cohost manages to have a well-timed wardrobe malfunction."

"Granted."

"I don't think we'd see such a thing from you, now, would we?"

Annja shot him a look. "I wouldn't hold out any hope."

"Noted."

Annja folded up the map. "How long has this land belonged to this tribe of Inuit?"

"Almost one thousand years."

"You were able to trace it back that far?"

Derek sighed. "It was part of what we had to do in order to make sure that the government was satisfied we did as much as possible to benefit the tribe instead of our own rather money-oriented motives."

"And what have you paid the Inuit?"

"Far more than the land is worth. But I'm not exactly

at liberty to disclose the exact number we eventually settled upon."

"Still," Annja said. "You'll inevitably extract far more than that if your estimates are correct, right?"

"Of course. It wouldn't have been a good investment otherwise. And we most certainly are not in the business of throwing money away."

Annja nodded. "This dig site was a condition of the purchase?"

"The elders insisted on it. They claim a portion of the land—which happens to be exactly where our scientists tell us that the richest veins of kimberlite lie—is an ancient burial site. It has to be moved to a new area that has been consecrated through a variety of rituals and sacred events."

"Kimberlite indicates the presence of diamonds, right?"

Derek grinned. "Yes. It's a type of potassic volcanic rock. It occurs naturally in 'pipes,' or long vertical structures that have the potential to contain diamonds. Our scientists tell me that kimberlite is formed deep within the Earth's mantle, probably between ninety and three hundred miles deep."

"Journey to the Center of the Earth."

"All for a girl's best friend, yes."

"So, why bring me in?"

"We need you to confirm when the land is free of relics and assorted Inuit history. If we didn't have you in there, the Inuit could hold things up indefinitely and claim there was still any number of items that had to be extracted or moved. It could delay our operations for years. And we are definitely in the realm of time is money."

"I see."

"Your job is to get in there, get friendly with the Inuit elders and help them do what they need to do. Move their burial site. Make sure there aren't any relics that need to be dug up and preserved. Do whatever it takes, but within four weeks we want that land free of any Inuit association. Because at the first sign of a thaw— as much as we get up in these parts—we're coming in with the drills."

"And at that point there won't be any second chance for the Inuit."

"None. Once you give us the word or if the four weeks expire first, we're coming in. I don't think anyone could argue we haven't been more than patient."

"I'm sure someone could."

Derek sighed. "True. People are always able to complain when they're not spending one billion dollars of their own money."

"This is a billion-dollar operation?"

Derek smiled. "I never said that if anyone asks."

"All right, then."

Derek finished his coffee and set the empty mug back down on the table. "Do you have any other questions?"

"My payment?"

He nodded. "We wired the first installment directly into your bank account this morning, prior to this meeting."

Annja smiled. "You're awfully confident that I'd take the assignment."

Derek shrugged. "We make a habit of knowing as much as possible about who we deal with ahead of time. I've read all of your files and information. I've watched you for a while on television even. I know you can't resist the pull of a new dig. It's too deeply ingrained in your spirit."

"You calling me an addict?"

Derek smiled. "Are you?"

Annja took a deep breath. "Sure feels that way some-times."

"You say that with a degree of…sadness?"

Annja shook her head. "Not really. I tend to live a lot of my life locked in the past. Memories of what I've done overlapped with the memories I dig through on an almost daily basis. Sometimes it's impossible to see the future."

"Well," Derek said, "I guess I can understand that to some extent."

"Only some?"

"I've never been on an archaeological excursion."

"Make some time," Annja said. "Come and join me on this one."

"I hate the cold," Derek said.

Annja smiled. "You're kidding."

"I wish. It's the one part of this job that I struggle with on a constant basis. If there was any way to do this from the warm beaches of Fiji, I'd be a much happier man."

"I guess not, though, huh?"

"No."

"The rest of my payment will be transferred in four weeks?"

"Or upon completion of the job, whichever comes first. If you finish in two weeks, you get a fifty percent bonus."

Annja leaned back. "Mighty generous of you."

"Not my decision, actually, but I'll pass it on. Remember what I told you, that we're in the time-is-money realm. My bosses want this thing to move ahead quickly. I hope we can count on you."

"If you had any doubts, I wouldn't be here, would I?"

"Nope."

Annja stood. "All right. I'm in."

"Excellent."

"I'll need a week to get my stuff together and gather up what I'll need to make sure I've got the necessary tools—"

"We leave right now."

"Excuse me?"

Derek smiled. "Whatever you need, we can pick up on the way. Inuvik has a number of good locations to pick up supplies."

"I wasn't planning on this happening so quickly."

"But I know for a fact that you always manage to land on your feet, even in the most surprising situations."

Annja frowned. "I don't like working this way."

"Consider it a show of good faith. You indulge us in this little matter and we'll make sure you have whatever it is that you need."

"Okay, but if I don't have my supplies, I walk away and keep the advance."

"Done."

Annja looked at him for a long moment and then nodded. "All right."

Derek held out his hand. "Welcome aboard."

Annja hesitated and then shook his hand. "I hope I meet your expectations accordingly."

"I know you will."

He guided her out of the hotel lobby and toward the front door. Outside, amid the swirling snow, Annja could just make out the blackened windows of a big SUV. Exhaust issued from the tailpipe.

"Been waiting long?"

Derek shrugged. "Things tend to freeze a lot faster up here. We keep engines going when we can."

"How very environmentally friendly of you."

Derek let the barb roll off his back. "Look, Annja, I know you said you tend to live in the past."

"But—?"

"Keep the future in mind. Four weeks, to be exact. That's the maximum amount of time I can allot you in this assignment. Anything more and we come in. And then all of that history—whatever happens to be left—gets ground up under our drill bits."

2

The ride to Inuvik was spent with Annja praying that the heavy tires on the SUV didn't blow out as they drove over portions of highway, sections of hard gravel and even dirt road. She thanked the inventor of shock absorbers many times during the ride, but even still, when she finally arrived at the Inuvik Welcome Center, Annja found herself massaging her buttocks.

Derek didn't look as if he'd fared much better. "The last time I rode up here, it wasn't that bad," he said.

"Maybe you guys could chip in for a highway reconstruction project. Throw a few million at them to pave the entire expanse for the sake of butts everywhere."

Derek laughed. "I'll talk to my superiors about it."

Annja glanced around. Thick snow coated every exterior surface. Her breath seemed to stain the air in front of her face and then drop to the ground already frozen. "Just how cold is it?"

"Right now?"

"Yeah."

"About thirty below."

Annja sighed. Back in the deep freeze. She had visions of her expedition to Antarctica. But that had been to dispute the existence of an alien race. This was far simpler. Her job was to get in and help the local tribe relocate their sacred relics out of the mining company's drill site.

There couldn't be much danger in that, could there?

She grinned in spite of the cold, feeling her skin almost crack as she did so.

Derek noticed the expression on her face and nodded. "Maybe we should get inside."

"Good idea." She glanced back at their driver, who seemed to be paying more attention to the vehicle than to them. She turned and followed Derek inside the welcome center.

She passed a display showing a map of the area. She stopped Derek. "Will we be working out of the town here?"

He shook his head. "Nope. This is just our waypoint. We've got a temporary camp set up closer to the drill site. I mean the future drill site."

"Right now, it's still sacred Inuit land."

"Araktak, to be accurate. They've been around these parts for—"

"A thousand years, you told me." Annja nodded. "I'm sure they've got an incredible history."

Derek frowned. "I wouldn't know. They're not one of the larger tribes in the area. They've remained incredibly independent despite the efforts to unify the smaller tribes into a larger one for the purposes of government help and education. I don't think there's a lot known about them."

"Interesting."

"It might be another coup for you."

Annja frowned. "What's that supposed to mean?"

Derek smiled. "I know you've had a number of interesting discoveries in your time. Things you've had the good fortune to stumble across before anyone else. Perhaps the Araktak can be another jewel in your crown of accomplishments."

"Maybe," Annja said. "I wouldn't be looking at it as a way of one-upping my peers, though."

"Of course not," Derek said. "It would just be another one of those nice things that some people have happen."

Annja frowned as she watched him walk away. What was his deal? She'd noticed he didn't wear a wedding ring and although he seemed young, she could see the first streaks of gray hair marking their invasion at his temple. She estimated he was probably around forty. He seemed in good shape, and despite his avowed hatred of the cold, it hadn't seemed to bother him too much when they'd been outside.

Maybe he's used to it by now, she thought.

The display told Annja that Inuvik was small, only about three thousand people in total. It hadn't been much of anything before 1979, but now it functioned as something of a gateway to the Mackenzie River and beyond into the Beaufort Delta, which bordered the Arctic Ocean.

Derek reappeared behind her. "The main function of the town is to act as a staging area for truckers to haul loads up to the refinery projects on the delta. Once the river freezes, they actually drive across the frozen water to reach their destinations."

Annja frowned. "You're not serious."

"I absolutely am."

Annja shook her head. "You'd never get me driving

over ice like that. One wrong move, if it's not thick enough and you could go right through and never be seen again."

"Very true. Many truckers have lost their lives to it, but then again, up here, it's the only way to get things done."

"I hope you're not going to tell me that the drill site is located anywhere near this frozen river."

Derek smiled. "Would you want to back out if it was?"

"Very possibly."

"And what about all that money?"

"Money's nice. Living is nicer."

Derek grinned. "Well, don't worry about it too much. The drill site lies inland, lucky for you."

Annja heaved a sigh of relief. "Thank God for small favors."

Derek eyed her. "You don't strike me as someone afraid of much, especially a little frozen river."

"The frozen river doesn't scare me," Annja said. "But falling through the ice and drowning does."

Derek waved his hand. "I wouldn't worry about drowning. The moment you hit the ice water, you'd probably go into cardiac arrest anyway."

"Lovely. Thanks for making me feel better."

"My pleasure." He gestured to the room. "Anything else you want to see here?"

"You're finished with whatever we came in for?"

"I simply wanted to introduce you to the town. Figured it would be a nice way to ease you into things."

"Ease me into things." Annja pursed her lips. "You're just full of contradictions, aren't you?"

"How do you figure that?"

"Because you basically kidnapped me earlier at our meeting. And now you're talking about slowing down."

"Well," Derek said. "I was sort of under orders not to

let you back out of the arrangement. Not to give you an opportunity to say no. That kind of thing."

"I see."

"But now that you're here in town, well, it's different, isn't it?"

"If you say so."

Derek checked his watch. "We're not going any farther today anyway."

"So, we'll stay here tonight?"

"Yup. Got us set up with reservations at the town inn. It's just down the street."

"And what time will we be on the road tomorrow."

"Early as we can."

Annja nodded. "All right. Let's go."

Outside the welcome center, the wind had picked up, making Annja's face instantly feel as if it was baked leather. "I'm going to make a moisturizer company rich off of me," she muttered.

Derek smiled. "Believe it or not, you do get used to it."

"If you say so."

They slid back into the vehicle and the driver gunned the engine before shooting down the road. As they drove through the town, Annja spotted a number of kids out walking with their parents.

"It amazes me what human beings can put up with," she said.

"It's just one of those things, right?" Derek said. "If you don't have the option to move elsewhere, you simply adapt. I think it's our greatest strength. It's what will someday enable us to colonize another planet."

"And hopefully treat it better than we've done with this one."

"Ouch."

Annja glanced at him. "Don't worry, I won't get preachy with you."

"Thanks." He shrugged. "It's not like I don't care for the planet. It's just that I've had to reconcile my work with my beliefs."

"And the bank account won, huh?"

"Sure did."

"I'm sure you must sleep easy at night."

"I sleep well knowing I've taken care of my children."

Annja looked back from the window. "You have kids?"

"Two of them. A boy and a girl. Eight and ten. Great kids. They live in California with their mother." He shrugged again. "We're divorced. She didn't approve of my line of work."

"What does she do?"

"She's an advocate for Greenpeace," he said, laughing.

"Wow, how the hell did you two even get together in the first place?"

Derek smiled. "I wasn't always a corporate lackey. Before I sold my soul I was a lobbyist for the environment on Capitol Hill. We met at a luncheon or a dinner or something in Washington. We were young. Idealistic. We had plans at one point to start a utopian community in the Canadian wilderness."

"So, what happened?"

"I came north to scout a location and somehow fell in with the mining corporation. They appreciated my zeal for causes near and dear to my heart. I thought Canada would be the best place to raise our children. The government at the time in the U.S. was something of a joke."

"Your wife didn't want to move to Canada?"

"Nope. Turns out she was still a bit of a patriot. She insisted that we raise the kids in the States."

"And around that time, the corporation got their hooks into you—is that about right?"

"Yes. They offered me a public-relations job helping them get government approval for a project that didn't pan out. I figured they'd let me go once it became obvious that we were digging in the wrong location. But that didn't happen. Instead, they recognized what I'd been able to do for them and they promoted me."

"They must have seen something they liked," Annja said. "One of those lucky breaks in life, huh?"

"Well, it came with a big pay raise and now I get to spend lavishly on my kids, much to the dismay of their mother. But I don't get a lot of time with them, so it's my prerogative to do what I choose with my money. And, like I said, it helps me sleep at night. If anything happens to me, they're set for life."

"I suppose that's what it's all about, huh?"

"Anything for my kids," Derek said. "Absolutely."

Annja nodded and went back to looking out the window. "I wouldn't know about that yet."

"Kids?"

"Yeah. Maybe someday."

"You're attractive. I don't think you'll have a problem finding a husband if that's what you want."

She glanced at him. "Did your files tell you about my personal life, as well?"

Derek grinned. "Our information tends to be very complete. We need an accurate picture if we're going to commit serious money to working with a certain person."

"I'm not sure I'm all that crazy about how much you seem to know about my life."

"It's nothing personal, Annja. We take this approach with everyone we work with. The corporation is very concerned about the people it lets in on its secrets. News of this drill site isn't even something that most people know about. At least not yet. Once we strike pay dirt, it will make headlines."

"There's that much riding on this?"

"Even more," Derek said. "If our figures turn out to be correct, and there's every indication they will, then this mine will make Ekati look like a lemonade stand."

"Colorful."

"We think we could double their annual yield," Derek said. "If not triple it."

"A billion dollars a year." Annja whistled. "That would be impressive."

"With a substantial bonus for everyone involved."

"Even a contractor like me?" Annja asked.

Derek shrugged. "Just do your job and get us the clearance we need from the Araktak elders. At that point, anything's possible. Even for a contractor like you."

Annja nodded. "I'll remember that."

"Please do. But just as certainly remember that you've only got four weeks. After that, no one wins. Least of all you."

3

The SUV came to a stop in front of a long, squat building with a wooden sign twisting about in the stiff wind. Annja could just make out the name of the inn as The Breton. "This is where we're staying?"

Derek nodded. "I imagine it will seem quite luxurious, especially once you see the dig site."

Annja frowned. "I've stayed in worse."

"I'll bet the Philippines jungle was terrible by contrast."

"You know about that, too, huh?" Annja shook her head. "Just know that for all your information, I've still got more than enough secrets to keep myself warm at night."

"I don't doubt that," Derek said. "But we aren't looking to pry all of your secrets out of you. If that was the case, we'd be using something a lot more painful on you." He smiled. "Just joking."

"I'll bet."

Derek opened the door and a brisk gust of wind greeted them as they stepped out of the vehicle. He nodded at their driver. "Godwin will see to our bags. Let's get inside."

Annja glanced at the driver. Godwin? It was an unusual name. She hadn't actually been introduced to the man. But she shrugged and followed Derek inside.

He pushed through the heavy door and a wall of heat met them, scaring off the thunderous cold wind. Derek took a deep breath. "Toasty in here."

The man behind the counter smiled. "Welcome, folks."

Derek smiled. "You've got some reservations for us, I believe. They should be under the name Mr. Smith."

Annja cocked an eyebrow. Derek waved her off and then turned back to the man. "Should be three rooms in total."

The counterman nodded. "Yep, got 'em right here." He winked. "Not like we'd be full up or nothin'. Don't exactly get ourselves a bumper crop of tourists this time of year."

"We'll just be here for the night," Derek said.

"Pushing on in the morning, are you? Fair enough. Just sign in. It's cash only, mind you, so if you've got anything plastic, there's a bank machine down the road at Terry's Trading Post."

Derek pulled out his wallet and fished out several bills. "Cash is fine."

The man took the money and laid three keys down on the counter. "Right, you're all next to each other. Hope you don't mind. It's easier this way to know where you're all at."

Derek handed one of the keys to Annja and turned back to the man. "What's good around here for a meal?"

"We don't have anything fancy."

"I don't care about fancy. Just good."

"Well, then, you can't do any better than the steak house across the street. They do a great porterhouse. Keep a couple of beers on tap, as well. It's a fine meal. Finish it off with a single malt and you'll be back in time for a toasty night here in your bed."

Derek nodded. "Sounds good. Thanks."

"Where's your third party?" the man asked.

The door to the inn banged open and Godwin came through the door carrying an assortment of traveling bags. He looked even taller and more imposing in the close confines of the inn's reception area. And he didn't seem to smile all that much.

"I'll need some clothes," Annja said to Derek. "If you recall, we didn't stop like you promised."

Godwin set down a bag near Annja. "You'll find everything you need in there, Miss Creed."

Annja looked at the bag and then back at Godwin. "My clothes?"

Godwin shrugged. "All new. With the equipment you might need for your work. If there's anything else you require, please let me know and I'll see that you get it as soon as possible."

Annja glanced at Derek. "Is this more of your paid-for information at work?"

He shrugged. "Discerning your size isn't much of a challenge. And we did enough research to know what you'd need. You'll find it all there."

"You must have been incredibly confident that I would agree to work with you."

"I was."

"Are you ever wrong?"

Derek smiled. "Only about my ex-wife."

Annja allowed herself a small grin. "I'm hungry."

Derek nodded. "Let's get changed and meet back here in what—twenty minutes?"

"Sure."

Derek handed the final key to Godwin. "You've secured the vehicle?"

"Yes, sir."

"All right, let's see to our rooms."

They walked down the corridor and one by one they each entered a room.

Annja took a moment to examine her surroundings. The room was small but functional. A single lamp on the bedside table gave off a warm glow of light. The bed was a double, big enough for one but not much more. Annja smiled to herself. As if she'd be getting lucky in a town like this.

She threw her bag on the bed and unzipped it. She pulled out three heavy sweaters, thermal underwear, fleece pants, lined jeans, turtlenecks and then a heavy parka, gloves and a thick woolen hat. Godwin had thoughtfully removed all the tags and stickers that would have marked the clothing as new. Annja couldn't even see where he might have purchased the clothes from, but judging by the feel of them, they were expensive and perfectly suited to the environment she'd be operating in.

Annja stripped off her clothes and dressed in the thermal underwear, turtleneck, jeans and sweater before sliding into the parka. She looked at herself in the mirror and decided that the road hadn't made her look like a total mess, although the cold was already working on her face. She'd need to remedy that before bed tonight.

She sat on the edge of the bed and took out her cell phone and punched in a number back in New York. The phone buzzed three times and then her voice mail at her place in Brooklyn picked up. Annja punched her code in and recorded a message she'd recorded a thousand times before.

"Hi, you've reached Annja Creed. I'm out digging in the dirt somewhere. Leave me a message and I'll call you back once I get home."

She disconnected and checked her watch. Time to go.

Back in the lobby, Godwin was already there, watching the satellite TV in the corner of the room. He looked up as Annja entered and nodded as if confirming something in his mind.

Annja did a quick pirouette as she entered. "You like?"

He almost smiled. "Everything fits you properly. That's good. It means I did my job well."

"Thank you," Annja said. "I was a bit worried when I suddenly found myself employed earlier this afternoon."

"Mr. Wainman was quite explicit in his instructions. I would be upset if something didn't fit you properly. Up here in these parts, proper fit isn't a matter of fashion—it's a matter of survival. If your body heat isn't adequately managed, you'll die from exposure."

"You sound like you know your way around these parts."

"I do. My ancestors have lived in this area for generations. Longer than that even."

"Araktak?"

He nodded. "I'm half. My father married outside the family. It didn't go over so well, but then again, the course of true love never did run smooth. Isn't that what they say?"

"Some of them."

"Well, I've never really belonged to the family. My mother was an outsider, so her blood in mine makes me the same."

"They won't take you in as one of their own?"

"Not the Araktak. They're far too proud to admit a half-breed."

Annja frowned. "Their loss, then. From what I can see, they'd do well to accept you as family. You don't look like you'd accept such discrimination easily."

"I don't."

Derek came into the reception area. "I see your clothes fit you well." He nodded at Godwin. "Excellent job."

Godwin nodded. "Thanks."

"Everyone hungry, then?" Derek asked. "Dinner's on me."

Annja glanced at the counterman, but he was engrossed in the television behind the counter. "Not on the company?" she asked.

Derek frowned. "We think it's best if we don't advertise the fact that we're interested in this particular area."

"But isn't the deal at least somewhat known?"

"Only by those who need to know," Derek said. "And at this point, it's probably better that we don't let anyone else in on our work. People in these parts are naturally suspicious of outsiders."

Annja glanced at Godwin. "Is that true?"

He actually smiled. "Don't know. I'm an outsider myself."

When they left the inn the wind showed no signs of losing strength, and they walked quickly across the street to the steak house.

Another burst of heat greeted them inside. Annja took stock and while the restaurant was really not much more than a glorified bar, the tables and chairs looked comfortable enough.

A burly waitress ushered them into a booth and handed them each a menu. Derek glanced at his.

"I'd like your porterhouse cooked medium rare and a beer."

Annja ordered the same thing and Godwin asked if there was any fish on the menu. When the waitress informed him there wasn't, he settled for the sirloin.

Annja watched her walk away and then glanced at Godwin. "She didn't exactly seem friendly."

"Maybe she can see my mixed heritage. A lot of folks up here don't trust the Inuit. And if she can figure out I'm Araktak, then she'll have even more reason to be suspicious."

"Why so?"

Derek cleared his throat. "Like I mentioned earlier, the Araktak are secretive. They've kept to themselves for hundreds of years. No one knows this land like they do, but they don't often grant an audience to outsiders."

"So how did your company ever get inroads with them?"

"Perseverance," Derek said. "And Godwin."

Annja looked at him. "I thought you said they wouldn't accept you as one of their own."

"They don't. But since I carry my father's name, they had to at least hear me out of respect for his lineage. I acted as the official go-between and got things settled for the company."

"And it's one of the reasons why he'll be your constant companion on this venture," Derek said. "The company wants one of its own on the inside while you work. It's not that we don't trust you. It's that we don't fully trust the Araktak."

"Why not?"

"There have been some power shifts in the tribe. Some of the Araktak want to do away with the old traditions and embrace the new millennium. Others want nothing to do with the modern world and wish to retreat back into even more secrecy."

"And how does everyone feel about the agreement with the company?"

"There's been some…unpleasantness," Derek said.

"What kind of unpleasantness?" Annja asked.

"The last representative we sent had a tough time gaining any type of relationship with the Araktak. They sent him back with a broken arm."

Annja frowned. "And here I thought this wouldn't be dangerous."

Derek shrugged. "It's yet another reason we wanted to

work with you, Annja. Our information tells us that you are more than capable of holding your own in the event of…unpleasantness."

"I suppose you could say that," Annja said. "Although I would much prefer avoiding conflict if possible."

"As would we. But given the tenuous nature of the situation, it would be wise if you were well prepared for any eventuality."

Annja glanced at Godwin. "Is that another reason why you're along on this?"

"Godwin is here to protect the interests of the company. And in this case, you are most definitely an 'interest.'"

"How nice," Annja said. "I hope you won't have to do anything to protect me."

Godwin shrugged. "It's my job to be ready just in case."

"What if *you* need protecting?"

He smirked. "That seems unlikely."

"Been known to happen, though."

Godwin shrugged. "If it happens, then I'll deal with it. But I am much more interested in making sure nothing happens to you. Or the company's position. It's vital that this go through."

Annja watched him for another minute before turning her attention to the beer the waitress had just set down in front of her. She took a sip and as she brought the glass down, something tickled her subconscious. Across from them, she could see two men at the bar taking more than a passing interest in their table.

Godwin might just get a chance to show his skills sooner than he'd thought. Annja smiled and took a sip of her beer. At least some action would get her blood moving.

4

Annja took another sip of her beer. The two men at the bar were growing impatient judging by the way they jostled against the counter. Annja glanced at Godwin. "I think we might be attracting some interest."

Godwin's dark eyes flashed over to the bar and he nodded once. "Sure seem to be."

"Friends of yours?" she asked.

He shook his head. "Nope. But it doesn't matter. They apparently think they know me or know of me. Either way, it could get messy in here."

Derek struggled to hear them over the din. "What are you two babbling about over there?"

Annja smiled. "It seems as though some of Godwin's friends might be looking to join us."

"Friends?"

"It's a loose term." Annja shrugged. "Really depends on how you feel about people who want to break your bones."

Godwin glanced at Derek. "Mr. Wainman, there's a

chance we might have some trouble here very shortly. Whether we want it or not."

Derek frowned. "We haven't even eaten dinner yet."

Annja grinned some more. "I've found these types rarely have a good sense of timing."

Derek looked at Godwin. "Can you handle it?"

"Most certainly."

Annja stretched her arms overhead. "Well, I'm not missing out on the fun."

Godwin shook his head. "It's not your fight."

"It is my prerogative, however," Annja said. "And I need a bit of activity to keep my muscles in shape."

The bigger of the two men came off the bar then, his eyes narrowing as he stared at Godwin. Annja figured he must have weighed over two hundred pounds, given that even the thick shirt he wore couldn't disguise the mass underneath. He had his huge hands tightly squeezed into fists.

Behind him, the smaller man followed, but he was by no means the lesser of the two threats. Annja saw that he kept his right hand tucked in his back pocket. She frowned. A knife. It had to be a knife of some sort.

Great.

The big man managed ten steps before he stopped and pointed a finger at Godwin. "You there. You're Araktak, ain'cha?"

Godwin shrugged. "Part."

"Part? You mean you're a bastard, too? What was it, your mother or your father that couldn't stand to be with his own people?"

"What business is it of yours?"

The big man growled. "I don't like Araktak."

"I'm sure the feeling is mutual."

The big man edged closer. "I don't like them because they stole my land from my family."

Godwin shrugged. "The Araktak have been in this area for the better part of a thousand years. How long has your family been here?"

"Don't matter," the big man said. "They took what didn't belong to them. And my family lost everything thanks to that no-good government being all concerned for the Inuit scum."

Godwin nodded. "Well, you have my sympathies, if it makes any difference to you at all."

"It don't," the big man said. "Because to me, the only good Araktak is a dead Araktak."

Annja sighed. "God should strike down whichever idiot first coined that expression. Only the brainless still use it."

The big man frowned. "Last I checked, this conversation weren't about you, little lady."

Annja laughed. "'Little lady'?"

The big man nodded. "Just keep yer pretty little mouth shut and you won't get hurt."

Annja rose from the table. "And suppose—just suppose—I feel like opening my mouth? What then?"

"Then you get it closed."

Annja smiled widely. She could feel her blood coursing through her as her heart pumped. She flexed her hands, knowing that her energy was cresting.

She glanced back at Godwin, who had moved closer to the edge of the booth seat. She pointed at the smaller of the two men. "Watch out for the blade that guy has in his right back pocket."

Godwin nodded. "Got it."

Annja looked back at the big man. "I'm not going to close my mouth, so I guess you'll just have to do it for me."

The big man frowned. "Fine by me, you dumb bitch."

But as he started forward, Annja jumped, twisting as she did so until her right foot was aimed straight at the big man's chin. She moved so fast that the man didn't have a chance to track her and in the next moment, Annja's foot slammed into the side of his chin with a solid crack.

To his credit, the man didn't go down. He grunted once and then swatted the air where Annja had been, catching her with a backhand fist on the side of her head.

Annja saw stars, but blinked the pain away as she dropped to the ground and rolled to get some distance. The big man came charging forward.

"You think I won't kick a girl's ass? You're about to find out you're very mistaken."

Annja frowned. That kick should have knocked him out. She came up on the balls of her feet and feinted with a jab that the big man fell for. Annja ducked and drove a sharp right hook into his floating ribs.

The thick shirt absorbed most of the impact.

The man brought his hands together and dropped them down on the back of Annja's back. Annja thought she heard a crack but then the floor rushed to greet her.

Not good, she thought. As long as he's standing, this contest isn't going to go well.

She was briefly aware that Godwin had moved to engage the smaller man. The man had a curved knife out in front of him, flashing through the air in vicious swipes.

The big man charged her again. Annja stayed on one knee and as he came in, she pivoted, sweeping her left leg out to attack the back of the big man's knees.

It worked and he lost his balance, going down hard on his butt.

Annja leaped up and brought her elbow down into his

stomach. She heard a rush of air go out of his lungs and the air around her stunk with the smell of liquor. She blanched and rolled away. "Gross."

But even her elbow strike to his stomach didn't stop her opponent, and he rolled over and got to his feet with surprising quickness for someone of his size. He brought his hands together and frowned at Annja.

"Now you've made me mad."

Annja grabbed a chair from the closest table and smashed it over his head as he charged again. The wooden frame splintered nicely over his skull and this time, he went down and stayed down.

Annja took a breath and then checked to make sure he was finally unconscious.

Godwin was still working on getting the edge with his attacker. The smaller man was clearly more skilled than his oafish counterpart. The way he handled the knife told Annja that he'd used it many times in the past, probably with great effect.

He cut the air with short, clipped circles, keeping Godwin at bay. But Annja sensed no impatience in Godwin's body movement. He seemed content to let the smaller man wear himself out.

The man noted that his comrade was down for the count and then made his error. He feinted with a thrust and then jerked it out in a wider arc than he had before. Godwin's eyes twinkled for just a moment and then he pivoted inside the arc, driving his elbow deep into the smaller man's solar plexus. His hands clamped down on the arm wielding the knife, and Annja heard a pop as Godwin dislocated the man's elbow and the knife skittered clear.

The smaller man screamed as Godwin stepped back

and let the now-useless limb drop harmlessly to the smaller man's side.

Godwin stooped and retrieved the knife. He turned it over and frowned. "I haven't seen one like this in a very long time."

Annja walked over to him. "What?"

Godwin showed it to her. The knife seemed to curve closer to the tip, but Annja could also see that the blade had an edge on both sides. It seemed perfect for stabbing through multiple layers and then hooking to inflict grievous injury.

"This is an assassin's weapon," Godwin said.

"Assassin?"

Godwin nodded. "Certain tribes among the Inuit have secret aspects of their tribes. When the white man started encroaching on their lands, some among the tribes resolved to use their skill and cunning to inflict terror among the new settlers."

"Did it work?"

"Not really. The settlers kept coming. It was inevitable, I suppose. But the traditions of the assassins have been passed down regardless. It used to be something much more honorable than it apparently has become."

Godwin looked at the smaller man. "Where did you get this?"

"I won it in a poker game."

"I don't believe that," Annja said. "Judging by how you used it, someone taught you some basics."

"I don't believe it, either," Godwin said. "No assassin would ever let something like this out of his sight. It means too much to them. It's their badge of acceptance within the ranks. However you came to own this blade, it couldn't have been respectable."

The smaller man massaged his arm. "Maybe someone

wants you dead, half-breed. Maybe they want you dead bad enough to send a couple of us at you so they can see what sort of target you'd make."

Godwin glanced at Annja. "What do you think?"

Annja shrugged. "I think you should have knocked him unconscious like I did with his friend. That way, you can just avoid all the useless talk after the fact."

Godwin raised his eyebrows. "Interesting point."

He backhanded the smaller man right between the eyes. There was the briefest moment of shock on the smaller man's face before his eyes rolled back and he dropped to the ground.

Quiet settled in the bar and Godwin looked at Annja. "You're right. That's much better."

From behind the bar, a hulking bear of a man stepped out. Annja spun to meet his advance but he held up his hands. "Excuse me, folks, just need to take the garbage out."

He reached down and scooped up both men and then ran them out the door of the bar. A round of applause went up from the rest of the patrons as the bartender came back inside clapping his hands.

Annja was concerned. "They'll be okay out there in the snow?"

The bartender shrugged. "Not my problem anymore. They attacked two patrons. Whatever happens to them next is their own business. Not mine. Far as I'm concerned, you two did what was necessary. The cops are on their way to collect them."

"Thanks."

He shook his head. "Didn't like them anyway. They've been hanging around here for the last week looking like they were expecting something to happen at any moment. Put a real drag on the place. Hurt my business. Them getting their asses handed to them was long overdue, I'd expect."

"Happy to oblige," Annja said.

The bartender smiled. "I think your dinners'll be right up, so have a seat and I'll send them over."

Annja and Godwin sat down. Derek had worked his way through most of his beer. He hefted his glass at Godwin. "Nicely done."

"Thank you, sir."

Derek turned to Annja. "Nice to see that our information checks out on that front, as well."

Annja frowned. "I hate proving you right."

Derek smiled. "Well, at least we both know that if something happens, you'll be able to take care of it. And if you can't, then Godwin here can be pressed into service, as well."

Annja took a sip of her beer. She also had her sword. Although part of her wondered if perhaps Derek knew something about that, too. The thought did little to comfort her.

5

After a decent sleep, Annja felt ready to get to the dig site at long last. She showered quickly and dressed in insulating clothes before grabbing a quick cup of coffee and a muffin in the reception area. As usual, Godwin was already there, looking more relaxed than he had the previous night in the wake of the discovery of the assassin's dagger.

"Sleep well?" she asked.

He nodded. "Actually, very well. You?"

"I didn't think I'd be able to get warm, but those blankets did the trick. I was out like a light. Probably the postadrenaline dump helped a bit, too."

Godwin nodded. "Derek was right about you."

"Meaning?"

"You've been in a lot of fights."

Annja shrugged. "I get mixed up in a lot of stuff. I'm always interested in things that most normal people wouldn't get into. As a result, knowing how to protect myself is important."

Godwin watched her. "Well, there seems to be a natural sort of grace to you. It's like some kind of second skin. Very relaxed. And you can hold your own."

If only you knew the whole story, Annja thought. Instead, she smiled some more. "Well, thanks."

Derek entered the reception area. "Good morning. Everyone ready to get going?"

Annja nodded. "Yes. How far is the dig site?"

"Probably shouldn't take us much more than two hours to reach it," Derek said. "We'll follow Hendrick's Highway east and then get onto the dirt track. Probably won't be the smoothest sailing at that point, but you'll get used to it."

"Great," Annja said. "More sore-butt syndrome."

"Excuse me," a voice called out.

They turned and saw the counterman gesturing to them. "I couldn't help but overhear. Did you say something about Hendrick's Highway?"

Derek nodded. "We'll be driving it today. We need to reach our other party to the east."

The counterman shook his head. "Well, you won't be going by Hendrick's, that's for sure."

"Why not?"

"It's closed. About twenty miles from here. They had a bad truck rollover last night in the storm. Whole highway is blocked and frozen in. They're saying it could be a couple of days before they get it cleared."

"A couple of days?" Derek shook his head. "That won't work for us. We need to get moving today."

"Where ya heading?"

Derek frowned. "Tokrak."

The counterman smiled. "Well, that's no problem. You can just go the other way."

"What other way?" Annja looked at the counterman. "There's another way to get there?"

"Sure enough," the counterman said. "You just take the ice road."

Annja's stomach dropped. "You mean the river?"

The man smiled and nodded. "The Mackenzie. She'll take you there no problem. Just hang a right at the sign for Erop and follow that east. Should hook up with Hendrick's farther on."

Annja sighed. The last thing she wanted to do was drive over a frozen river. She'd faced plenty of challenges before, but risking life and limb like this just didn't feel right.

"Annja?"

Godwin was staring at her. "You okay?"

"I'm not crazy about the ice-road option," she admitted.

"Only option you've got," the counterman said. "Otherwise, you'll be waiting here for the next few days. And it doesn't look like your boss here is content to do that."

Derek nodded. "He's right, Annja. We've got to get going. Think of it this way—if you don't get to the site, that's the number of days less that you have to get the things done you need to do."

Annja frowned. "Yeah, I know."

She looked at Godwin. "Ever driven it before?"

"Once or twice."

"That fills me with so much confidence."

"Better that than me lying to you."

"Oh, I don't know. Lying wouldn't be such a bad thing in this case."

The counterman finished writing up the receipt for Derek. "Just remember that when you're out there, the big rigs have the right of way. You have to pull over and let them pass. Trust me, you don't want that kind of momentum coming up on your tail, if you get my drift."

"Can't they slow down?" Annja asked.

The counterman shrugged. "Not really a question of slowing down as much as it is about staying ahead of the wave."

"The wave?"

He nodded. "All that weight on the ice creates a wave under the surface that rumbles along under the truck chassis. They have to stay ahead of it as they drive or it can erupt through the ice and you get a trapdoor."

"Gosh this is sounding so fantastic," Annja said. "What's a trapdoor?"

"The ice, she opens up and the truck just disappears. Then the ice floe slides back into place like nothing was ever there. Incredible, really."

"Wonderful," Annja said. "How long will we be on this ice road?"

The counterman shrugged. "I don't know. Maybe an hour. You can't burn like you do on normal roads. But you can go at least forty kilometers an hour."

"That won't be nearly fast enough," Annja said.

"I AM SO NOT HAPPY about this," Annja said. She sat in the front next to Godwin as he drove through Inuvik toward the entrance to the ice road.

"We don't have the luxury of time," Derek said. "Better we go through some discomfort and reach our destination. Otherwise, it's time lost."

"Discomfort is one thing," Annja said. "Falling through some trapdoor and plummeting to our icy death is quite another."

"Relax," Derek said. "The company has a great life insurance policy." He frowned. "Well, it does for Godwin and me. Contractors are—"

"Screwed," Annja said. "Yeah, I gathered that." She nudged Godwin. "I don't want to die in this river, okay?"

He smiled. "I'll do my best."

"Do better or I'll kick your butt."

"Yes, ma'am."

Derek pointed between them. "Is that it?"

Godwin nodded. "Yep, it feels a little weird knowing you're leaving dry land, but then you kind of forget about it."

"Doubtful," Annja said. But she looked out the window as the SUV rolled down the embankment and then the wheels slipped for just a moment before they found purchase on the thick ice. Annja tried to guess how thick it must have been.

"Probably about five feet in some places," Godwin said suddenly. He glanced at Annja and smiled. "Everyone asks the question eventually. I figured I'd beat you to it."

"And the heavy trucks drive on this."

Godwin pointed. "See there? That's one coming right at us."

Annja stared through the windshield at the approaching rig. It was a flatbed and seemed to be carrying something square and huge. "What is that thing?"

"Generator by the look of it," Godwin said. "Probably coming back down from the refinery project on the delta. The government has a few of them up there. I think they're trying to extract petroleum from ice crystals of some sort. Pretty interesting actually."

The rig honked its horn and Godwin waved as the massive truck rolled past them. Annja shuddered, praying that the ice would hold. But then the truck passed them and was gone.

Annja breathed again.

Godwin smiled. "If the ice road wasn't mostly safe, no

one would be allowed to drive out here, Annja. Just relax and try to enjoy the scenery."

"Yeah, sure. I'll do that." She leaned back in the seat. But there wasn't much scenery to look at. Frozen carcasses of pine trees poked out of the snowy white landscape. Rolling hills and mountains of white surrounded the river road, and beyond that there seemed little of interest aside from the occasional sign.

She glanced at the dashboard and saw that Godwin had increased their speed to a little past forty kilometers per hour. "Aren't you going too fast?"

Godwin shook his head. "Smaller truck means we can travel at this clip pretty well. Besides, I know how badly you want to get back onto dry land so I'm doing my best to deliver."

"Thanks."

"No bother."

Derek unfolded a map and pointed out their location to Annja. "We've got maybe twenty miles to go. Maybe thirty minutes more on this."

Annja took a breath. "That's a relief."

Godwin nodded. "I'll get you there in one piece, Annja. I promise you that. Whatever happens from there on out is up to you."

"You say that like you expect something to happen. Everything all right?"

"I'm concerned."

"About what?"

"The assassin's dagger that guy was using. I want to know how he managed to get his hands on something like that."

Derek cleared his throat. "He said he won it in a poker game. Couldn't it have been that innocent?"

"Actually, no. The dagger represents everything to the assassin. There's no way it would have been wagered. And there's no way it would have been given up without a terrible cost."

"You think someone dispatched those guys to warn us?" Annja asked.

"Possibly."

"But about what?"

Godwin shrugged. "Probably the dig site. I'm sure there are quite a few Araktak traditionalists who are not pleased about the prospect of relocating what they consider to be sacred burial grounds, all for the sake of some giant faceless company." He glanced in the rearview mirror. "No offense, Mr. Wainman."

"None taken," Derek said. "This wouldn't be the first time something like this has happened. Although usually we're able to resolve the situations without much difficulty."

Annja glanced in the mirror out of her window. "Holy crap, that's a big truck."

Godwin glanced back. Behind them, a large rig was barreling down on them at a high speed.

Godwin frowned. "He's going way too fast. And with that much weight, he's going to cause problems."

Annja's stomach sunk. "Problems?"

"Just hang on." Godwin put his foot down on the gas pedal and the smaller truck shot forward across the ice road. But the giant truck didn't fade into the distance. It kept coming.

"He's still coming for us," Annja said. She glanced back at Derek. "Would this possibly fall into the category of 'situations'?"

"Possibly," Derek said. He was staring out of the back of the truck. "Can we lose him, Godwin?"

"Doubtful. It's not like there are any side streets or

alleys to duck down around these parts. And he's coming much too fast for me to lose him even if I tried."

"He looks overloaded, even from this distance," Derek said.

Godwin nodded. "He's got too much load on him. Way too much. I don't understand it."

Annja glanced at him. "Unless someone wants that much weight around us."

"You think?"

"I think," Annja said, "that we need to find a way to get off of this road and soon. Otherwise that truck is going to steamroll us into oblivion."

Godwin nodded. "Hang on. I'm going to let him get closer."

"You're what?"

"Just wait and see."

Annja looked out the back window. The truck wasn't even honking its horn at them. Whoever was behind the wheel didn't seem to care that they were a few hundred feet from rolling right over the smaller truck.

"Here he comes!" Annja shouted.

6

Godwin gripped the steering wheel with both hands as he tried to coax any last bit of power out of the SUV. The speedometer cranked slowly higher, but it wouldn't be enough. He glanced at Annja and shook his head. "Any more and we'll spin out and crash."

The front grille of the lumbering rig grew ever larger out of the back window. Annja thought the truck looked like a hungry shark bearing down on a wounded prey. She could hear the engine of the truck surging as it burned more gas and chewed up the ice as it sped toward them.

"Can't we do anything?" Derek asked.

Godwin shrugged. "Like what? It's not like you'll find a cop waiting to bag you for speeding. No one drives this fast out here except for us."

"And him," Annja said. "Except he's driving even faster than we are. How is that possible?"

"Bigger engine," Godwin said. "Plus, he's got cargo that gives him added weight and therefore force."

"Great," Annja said. "And we aren't big enough to slow down that force by much."

Godwin shook his head. "I'm trying to keep us ahead of him, but I think we've got about two minutes before he runs over us."

Derek had the map open on his lap, running his finger over the entire area. "There's got to be something out here we can use."

"I'm open to suggestions, Mr. Wainman," Godwin said.

Annja stabbed at the map. "What's that?"

Derek peered closer. "Looks like a small turnoff, actually. Probably not much more than an uphill slope if these contour lines are accurate."

Annja nodded. "Should be about a mile from here." She glanced at Godwin. "Can we make it?"

"Don't know. I'll try." The truck surged ahead again and Annja felt the whole thing slide for a moment before Godwin steered slightly left and regained control. Behind them, the truck continued to loom large.

Through the bright sunlight, Annja could see the snow scattering in the slipstream of the truck as Godwin tried to pour on more speed. Annja stared out of the windshield, trying to spot the turnoff.

Derek shook his head. "He's gaining on us!"

"We're not going to make it," Godwin said. "There's not enough time."

"We'll make it," Annja said. And then she pointed. "Look!"

A few hundred yards ahead, she could see the turnoff. It was a slope arcing up to the right off the ice road like some sort of higher bank on the frozen river. "Aim for it now, Godwin."

The distance shrank between the huge rig behind them

and the back of the SUV they drove. Godwin grunted as the mighty giant brushed their back bumper and sent them zipping farther ahead.

"Now!"

Godwin jerked the steering wheel and the SUV fishtailed onto the slope, carrying them off the ice road onto the turnoff. He slammed on the brakes and the SUV came to a rest. Behind them, the giant rig let out an angry horn blast and thundered on past them, soon disappearing in the brilliant sunshine.

Godwin took a deep breath and released his hold on the steering wheel. "Well, that was a bit too close for my liking."

Derek clapped him on the shoulder. "That was a great bit of driving, my friend. I'll make sure you're given your due when we get back."

"Thank you," Godwin said. He glanced at Annja. "Are you all right?"

Annja nodded. "I'll be fine as soon as we get the hell off of this ice road and I'm somewhere where I can control my own destiny." She almost chuckled aloud at that thought. She hadn't felt in control of her destiny ever since she'd come into possession of Joan of Arc's mystical sword. But no one else needed to know that.

Derek looked out of the rear window. "The question is, did that big rig leave us or is it waiting somewhere farther down the ice road to ambush us?"

Godwin took the map and studied it. "Well, unfortunately, we're going to have to get back on the road and follow it until our turnoff. There's just no other way to reach the dig site." He glanced at Annja. "I know, I know, I'm not crazy about this, either, but there's no alternative."

Annja nodded. "I know it."

Godwin slid the truck into gear and backed down the

turnoff until they were once again on the road. Then he slid the truck into Drive and started off again. "If it makes you feel any better," he said, "I don't think we'll see that guy again."

"Why not?" Annja said.

Godwin shrugged. "I'm not sure. Just a hunch."

"Your hunches ever pan out?" Annja asked.

Godwin shrugged. "If they did, I would have won the lottery by now and retired to some place warmer than this." He eyed her. "What about yours?"

Annja smiled. "Sometimes."

"And you think that rig is waiting for us?"

Annja looked out of the windshield at the road ahead of them and calmed her breathing. She felt okay. And she thought that perhaps they might get through this part of the journey unscathed now.

"Actually, I think we're good."

Derek heaved a sigh of relief. "Well, that's a twofer, so I'll accept it as gospel now."

Godwin smirked and continued to drive. "Maybe that was another warning for us, huh?"

"Do you really think so?" Annja asked.

He shrugged. "First the assassin's dagger, and then we almost get run over on the ice road. I'd say someone is trying very hard to keep us from reaching our destination, wouldn't you?"

Annja sighed. "Maybe. But it's only because I don't have a better theory at this point."

"Neither do I," Derek said. "But who would be behind it?"

"Traditionalists in the Araktak perhaps," Godwin said. "Maybe they're less keen on seeing this deal go through than we realized."

"Even with all they'd gain from it?" Derek asked.

"Seems to me that would be rather stupid of them. They'd lose out on all of that money."

"To them it's probably not about the money at all," Godwin said. "They'd see this relocation of the ancient burial grounds as an affront to everything their lineage has taught them to hold dear and respect. All the money in the world wouldn't convince them of it being a good idea."

"So, they'll kill instead?" Derek asked.

Godwin nodded. "Some have probably killed for far less than that."

Annja glanced at Godwin, but his face seemed set as he drove farther on the road. She wondered what gave him such intimate insight into the inner working of the Araktak. After all, hadn't he said that they refused to claim him as one of their own?

"Did you have a lot of experience with them growing up?" she asked.

He looked at her. "The Araktak? No. Hardly any at all. We moved pretty much as soon as my father was kicked out of the tribe for marrying outside the clan. We headed south to Toronto and I grew up there. It's a lot warmer. I think it fostered my love of summers."

"So, why do you seem to know so much about the tribe if they never accepted you as one of them?"

"My father," Godwin said. "He told me pretty much everything I'd need to know about them. The history, the traditions, that kind of thing. That's why I was a natural choice for the company to use as its go-between."

"And what was the reception like when you went there the first time?"

"Like the rest of the landscape. Icy and cold."

Annja smiled. "And yet you persevered."

"The Araktak don't exactly live in luxurious surroundings. The kids need schooling. There needs to be a better standard of living. And if they're sitting on a land filled with wealth, then they should have the opportunity to tap into that. If not for them, then at least for the generations that follow them. The deal with the company will enable them to have a great life for their children and children's children. It wasn't a difficult decision for me to make to come on board and help the company out."

"You're helping the Araktak, as well," Annja said.

"Exactly." Godwin shrugged. "When I first visited them, I saw a number of children playing in the snow. But they didn't even have a ball to play with so they were kicking around snowballs. They were amazing kids, but they didn't even have access to the kind of toys most kids do. I guess it made an impression on me."

Derek clapped him on the shoulder again. "Good man. And with the deal we structured for them, their kids will have a great life. Most of the families will be millionaires when this is all over."

"I hope they won't lose their traditions in the process," Annja said. "Because as nice as it is to give someone access to wealth and prosperity, it would be a shame to see an entire race of people lose its way over the lure of cash."

"It's happened before," Godwin said. "I know this. But I also hope the elders of the tribe will be able to exert some degree of control of their people."

"And preserve what they've respected for so long," Annja said. "I guess time will tell for certain, huh?"

"I think it will be fine," Derek said. "We're taking pains to ensure that we don't just come in and destroy their lands. That's why you're here, Annja. With your help, we'll be able to preserve a lot of their memories. And with the company's money, they'll be able to build something to house their legacies in. If that's what they want, of course."

Annja stared out of the window. She wondered if the Araktak would want to leave this land. While she couldn't ever imagine living in such a cold environment, she knew that this was home to the Araktak and their kind. They'd lived here for a thousand years and knew the lands better than anyone. It would be hard to convince them to give it all up.

They drove in silence for a while. Annja stared out of the windshield. Suddenly she twisted in her seat to look out of the rear window.

But there were no trucks barreling down on them this time.

Annja closed her eyes and tried to relax.

She heard it then even before she saw it. She opened her eyes and started to roll down her window.

"What the hell are you doing?" Derek asked.

Annja shushed him and stuck her head out of the window. It was even more audible now. But where was it coming from?

Annja leaned back into the truck. Godwin looked at her. "What is it, Annja? What's the matter?"

"Can't you hear it?"

"Hear what?"

Annja peered through the windshield. Far ahead of them, she thought she could make out something dark. It looked as if it was growing.

"Oh, my God."

Derek leaned over from the backseat. "What is that?"

Godwin pressed on the gas. His eyes narrowed and he gripped the wheel tighter. "Our turnoff should be coming soon."

"Not soon enough," Annja said. "It's going to be close."

"Real close," Godwin said.

"What is?" Derek asked. "What is that thing ahead of us? What's going on?"

Annja looked at him. "Can't you hear it?"

Derek stopped and sat back in his seat. He closed his eyes and then Annja saw his body stiffen appreciably. His eyes popped open. "Tell me that's not what I think it is."

Annja nodded. "It is."

Godwin pointed up ahead of them. "It's growing larger."

Annja looked and saw it was true. Shooting down the ice road at them was a giant fissure of blackness.

The ice road was cracking all around them.

7

"How far?" Annja asked.

Derek studied the map again. "Maybe a mile. I'm not sure."

"Kind of important that we know," Annja said. She peered through the windshield. The fissure seemed to be shooting right at them, but she could see that it was cracking slowly. The speed of their truck made it seem as if it was happening all the faster.

Godwin frowned. "I don't think we'll make it. We're going to have to get off the ice or we'll risk going through it."

"What's the temperature outside right now, I wonder?" Annja asked. "Can we handle the temperature if we have to leave the truck?"

"Doubt it," Godwin said. "We need off this road with the truck."

Annja could see the water sloshing farther ahead as it crept out of the cracks in the ice like some black viscous blood seeping over the ice itself, dragging smaller chunks under.

"Just how good is this truck at four-wheel driving?" she asked.

Godwin grinned. "I think we're going to find out."

Annja nodded. "Do it."

Godwin guided the truck over toward the bank of the ice road, and then Annja felt the tires bite into the frozen tundra and pull them up off the ice. The truck bucked like a wild horse under them as they hit bumps and dips in the landscape.

"Hang on!" Godwin shouted. "It's going to be rough."

Derek pointed back at the ice road. It looks like it's fine about a hundred yards farther on."

Godwin nodded. "We'll have to chance it. If we stay on this stuff, we'll blow the tires and do worse to the engine."

Annja would have preferred to take her chances with the ground, but she could see Godwin's point. The truck was taking terrible damage from the undulating countryside. They had to get back onto the ice.

Then she heard the sudden pop.

She looked at Godwin. He shrugged. "Looks like we lost one of the tires. Maybe two."

Derek pointed. "The ice looks fine up there. Try going back now, Godwin. We can't take this anymore."

Well beyond where the fissure had forced them off the road, the ice looked as solid as it had been before. Godwin aimed the truck and Annja felt it lurch and buck again as they took another hard hit on the underside of the chassis.

And then she felt the vehicle almost skid as it suddenly zoomed back out onto the ice. Godwin fought to control it as the popped tire's rim bit into the ice and cause them to skid wildly. He turned into the skid and then brought the SUV to a halt about a hundred yards farther on.

Annja caught her breath. "This is turning out to be some kind of trip."

Godwin kept the truck idling. "I need to check us out for damage."

He slid out and Annja joined him. Derek unfolded himself from the backseat and followed them around to the back of the truck.

Godwin squatted by the right rear tire and looked at the rim. "Doesn't look like it got bent, fortunately. It should take a new tire from the back okay. The tire's shredded, though. We can't use that anymore."

Annja could see where the rubber of the tire had been cut to ribbons against something out on the landscape. Probably a rock had started the damage, then the punishment the truck took bouncing all over finished off the tire.

The cold wind blew in to greet them. Annja shivered and zipped up her hood. "How long until we can get going again?"

Godwin opened the tailgate and rooted around in the back, finally heaving out the replacement tire. "Maybe twenty minutes."

Derek nodded. "Good. We've got a schedule to keep."

Godwin rolled the tire over and then went back for the jack. He set about getting it into position and then cranked it up. Ever so slowly, the truck frame lifted off the ice road until Godwin judged he had enough room to do his work.

"Annja, can you get the tools from the back?"

Annja fetched the tool bag and then left Godwin alone while she walked around. It was the best way she knew how to stay warm. As long as she kept moving, she figured she'd keep warm.

Well, somewhat warm.

Derek came up next to her and put his hand over his brow, studying the horizon. "I think our turnoff should be only a mile farther on. We're almost there, I'd say."

"So close we could almost walk," Annja said. "Except if we did that, we'd freeze to death from exposure, huh?"

"Yeah. We need the truck. That's for sure."

Annja walked farther up the ice road, studying the ice underneath her feet. It seemed so weird to be standing on the middle of a huge river like the Mackenzie. She could see deep cracks and fissures in the ice, and yet, none of them looked as ferocious as the one had that had forced them off the road.

She wondered what could have caused it. Was it the giant rig from earlier? And if it was, how had it managed to send a fissure rocketing at them like that?

Maybe it was the wave that built up under the ice like the man at the inn had explained to her.

Annja shook her head. If getting there was half the fun, she must have been having the time of her life so far.

She heard Godwin swear and walked back. "You okay?"

He was sucking his thumb. "Yeah, I'm fine. Just been a while since I tried torquing bolts off in the frigid tundra, that's all."

"Let me help," Annja said.

Godwin smiled at her. "You?"

Annja cocked an eyebrow. "Don't even think about saying anything you might really regret."

Godwin held up his hands and stepped back. "Hey, be my guest."

Annja walked over to the shredded tire and picked up the wrench. She clamped it over the closest bolt and then twisted. Godwin was right; the bolt was frozen solid in place on the tire. He joined her and together they were able to loosen the bolt. They worked quickly and removed the remaining bolts from the tire. Then she stepped back and let Godwin take over again. He heaved the tire off and it toppled away. It slid some distance before at last coming to a lopsided stop in the snow.

Derek was still looking at the horizon. Annja approached him. "You all right?"

He nodded. "Thought I heard something."

Annja frowned. "What now?"

He shook his head. "I don't know. Just thought it sounded vaguely familiar."

"In a good way or a bad way?"

Derek shrugged and walked back to the SUV. "Maybe I'm imagining it. I don't know."

Annja watched him go. She smiled. The trip was getting to Derek as much as it was her. Godwin, despite the moments of intensity, seemed all right, all things considered. But then she figured there must have been something about him that kept him pretty even-keeled. She wondered if his father had something to do with it.

Maybe I'll ask him later, she thought.

"Got the tire mounted," Godwin said. "Another five minutes and we'll be on our way again."

Annja smiled. The sooner they got off the ice road and back onto dry land, the happier she'd be. Their brief respite on the shore had shown her how impossible it would be to travel over land unless there was a road.

She started to walk back to the SUV.

And then she stopped.

The sound came to her like a low growl somewhere far off in the distance, lurking at the edges of her subconscious like a bad dream. She turned around and stared off down the ice road.

A black speck stared back at her.

"Guys," she called out. "I think we're going to have some more company."

Derek looked back. "So, I wasn't mistaken."

"Wish you were," Annja said. "But it looks like you weren't."

Derek rushed to assist Godwin. "Better hurry up with that tire. We're going to need to be mobile pretty damned soon."

"If the bolts aren't tightened down just right, the wheel will come off and we'll crash."

Annja stared at the black speck. It was getting larger. Much larger. And she could already tell it was the same giant rig that had nearly run them over before.

She doubted very much that it would let them survive this time.

"How long?" she called out over her shoulder.

"Four minutes," Godwin said. He grunted under the effort to get the bolts fastened.

"We need some time," Derek said. "Can you do something?"

Annja looked at him. "You're kidding, right?"

But something in Derek's eyes told her he wasn't kidding. Not one bit. She frowned. Just how much did he know about her?

Annja looked at the giant rig. It was barreling toward them. It looked as if it had spotted them and seeing them at a complete stop, its front end had zeroed in on their location. It was locked in and nothing could stop it.

Annja walked away from the SUV. She needed some distance from Godwin and Derek if she was going to pull this off without letting everyone know her biggest secret of all.

But would it work?

The giant truck surged closer. Annja could see it looming in front of her. She felt a measure of calm come over her despite the impending doom she faced. If she stayed in position and did nothing, she'd be little more than a smear on the ice road. And soon enough, just a forgotten remnant of the white landscape.

But she had no intention of going so quietly into the night.

She ran away from the SUV, gathering her speed. She could feel the energy from the sword and her connection to it flooding into her body.

Her muscles felt as if they'd been shocked full of juice, as if a huge current of electricity had touched her.

The truck continued to bear down on her position. It looked like a giant seething machine, belching smoke and steam as it tore up the ice road. She could see its tires and the dented red front fender.

I'll have just one chance, she thought. Only one chance to get this right.

She ran harder, feeling the icy cold bite into her lungs and her face. And yet, somehow, the cold temperature fell away, replaced by the sensation of heat spreading all over her body.

Seen from a distance, Annja looked as if she was going to commit suicide by running right at the mighty truck.

One machine.

One human.

I hope this works, Annja thought.

8

As Annja raced toward the speeding truck, she closed her eyes and saw the sword in her mind's eye. She reached into the otherwhere for it, felt her hands close around the hilt and then she opened her eyes again.

The sword was in her hands.

She flipped it over quickly, aiming the tip down below her. She could feel her heart thundering inside her chest. The sword's energy coursed through her entire body, mind and spirit.

She briefly hoped that her action would go unnoticed by Derek and Godwin. Perhaps they wouldn't be able to see the sword.

With no time to worry about it just then, Annja felt her breathing come in fast spurts. She jumped up as high as she could. And then the ground was rushing up at her fast, almost unnaturally fast. And the truck was still rushing at her.

Annja touched down and drove the very point of her sword into the thick ice beneath her. She exhaled with a loud shout as she drove the metal deep into the ice floe.

From somewhere far beneath her, she heard a deep cracking sound issue up from the ice-cold inky depths and then spread out from her sword blade toward the speeding truck.

Annja twisted the sword blade and almost as if in response, the small fissure gaped before her like a hungry maw, eager to feed on whatever stood before it.

In this case, it was the speeding truck.

Annja watched as more ice broke away into the swirling water of the Mackenzie River. Waves sloshed over the floes. And still the fissure spread toward the truck.

The truck had slammed on its brakes, but all that terrible momentum had no place to go except forward and even as the massive beast shuddered and groaned, straining to halt its progress, the same force that had so threatened Annja and the others now carried the truck toward its final destination.

With a creaking finality, the entire chassis slid right into the water before it, sinking imperceptibly fast. In one blink the truck was on the ice and in the next it simply had vanished.

Annja stood there, watching as the waves quickly returned to their normal ebb and flow. Already, at the edges of the breaks and cracks, the water was freezing back over. She figured in another hour, there'd be nothing to even mark the presence of the truck save for some skid marks on the ice leading to the massive hole that had eventually claimed it.

She took one final look at the water and its darkness. It was almost as if it had its own spirit. Was that even possible? She closed her eyes and quickly replaced the sword back where it rested, waiting to be called forth again.

Annja opened her eyes and turned around to head back toward Derek and Godwin. She hoped Godwin had the tire replaced by now.

Derek was standing closer than she expected. He had a smile on his face and didn't seem the least bit embarrassed to be standing so close to her.

Annja stopped.

Derek said nothing, but kept smiling and turned to walk back toward the truck. Annja caught up with him.

"You look like you just ate a canary."

He shrugged. "Better. I just saw something I would never have believed unless I witnessed it with my own two eyes."

"I could offer to pry them out of your head if it helps you forget what you just saw."

He chuckled. "I'd hate for that to happen."

"I'll bet."

"That was something quite impressive."

Annja frowned. "And yet, you don't seem the slightest bit surprised. Why is that?"

Derek shrugged. "Impressed? Yes. Surprised? Nope. But I thought I already explained to you that our information was good."

"You did," Annja said. "I didn't expect that you'd gotten word about my…talent."

"Is that what you choose to call it?" Derek smiled. "I'd call it something utterly amazing."

"Of course you would. Anyone would. Unless they happened to be burdened with the thing." Annja sighed. "How does it work?"

"I don't even know. I'm still working all of its rather unique functions out. Every time I think I know what it's fully capable of, it has this nagging ability to surprise me."

"Well, you just used it to save our lives. So I suppose a hearty thank-you is in order."

"You're welcome. And you can thank me by not mentioning this to anyone else. And if you have to file a report about me, I'd appreciate you stating that the rumor of its existence is just a silly myth. That you saw nothing out of the ordinary during our entire time together."

"Why would you want me to do that?"

Annja stopped him. "Because if there's one thing I definitely do not need, it's any publicity. I'd much prefer to just live my life and do what I do without being sentenced to a freak-show existence for the remainder of my time on the planet."

Derek looked at her and then nodded. "I guess I can understand that. I thought you might be one of these people who would want to milk it for everything it had."

"Not even remotely close."

Derek smiled. "It's cool. Your secret is safe."

"So, who leaked the information to you about it?"

Derek shook his head. "I'm not sure, actually. And before you go accusing me of holding out, I am telling the truth. We gathered our data on you from a variety of sources. Some of it was from reliable outlets, background checks, that type of thing."

"And others?"

"From less tangible sources. We comb the Internet to compile what we hope is an accurate picture of our subjects. Sometimes the material we turn up is decent. Other times it's pretty bogus."

"In this case," Annja said.

Derek nodded. "We got lucky, all right."

"I'd be curious to know where that particular nugget came from. Any chance you keep a record of the Web sites you comb on file somewhere?"

"Yeah," Derek said. "I can hook you up with the information once we're done up here. Consider it a parting bonus if you want."

"Thanks."

"Forget it. Call us even for saving our lives."

"I will."

They walked back to the truck just as Godwin was putting away the tools. He looked up as they approached. "We're all set to go."

Annja sighed. "Good."

Godwin looked out around them. "What happened to the truck?"

"Detour," Annja said. "I don't think we'll be seeing it again."

"Ever," Derek said.

Annja slid into the front seat and closed the door. Godwin and Derek got in a moment later and Godwin gunned the engine and then slid the vehicle into Drive.

He eased the truck forward. Annja pointed out ahead of them. "I'd steer a little bit over to the right if I was you."

"Why so?"

From behind her, she heard Derek say, "I'd do as she suggests, Godwin. Trust me."

Godwin nodded and steered the truck over to the side. But even as they passed the location where the truck had gone through the ice, Annja had trouble seeing where it was exactly. The water had already frozen over and showed little sign that there had been a massive hole there previously.

Annja shuddered. Whatever the case, whoever had been behind the wheel of that truck, they were no longer a threat to them.

And that was fine with her.

Derek had the map open again. He traced his finger along the ice road and then jabbed at a spot on the map. "We should be pretty close, guys."

"The sooner the better," Annja said. "I really don't like

traveling this way. Big trucks that want to run us over, cracks in the ice, and this forever-white landscape. It wears on a person."

"I think it's kind of beautiful," Godwin said. "Of course, I'm a bit biased."

"I thought you hated the cold," Derek said.

"I do. I meant from inside the warm truck it looks kind of beautiful." Godwin grinned. "But I'd still rather live in Hawaii any day of the week."

"We'll keep that in mind in case we open up a diamond mine in Maui," Derek said.

Annja smiled. The rush of tension that had plagued them with the giant truck and the ice fissure seemed to have evaporated. They were left with the feeling that they would soon be off the ice road and back on to firm ground. Frozen though it was.

Annja took a deep breath and tried to relax her body. She closed her eyes and took several deep breaths. She felt good. And she marveled at how warm using the sword had made her. Maybe it was a side benefit of it. Still, she wasn't sure that she'd felt that way when she wielded it back in Antarctica.

Was it possible that the sword was capable of learning?

She frowned. That would mean that it had its own intelligence. And if that was the case, then was Annja ever really in control of it?

Or was she simply being possessed?

That didn't sound particularly enticing to her. Good or evil, possession meant that she didn't have any measure of control.

"You okay?"

Annja snapped her eyes open and glanced at Godwin. "Sorry, must have drifted off there for a moment."

"It happens," he said. "All this white. Snow blindness. It can make you crazy after a bit."

Annja sighed. "Yet you don't seem to be affected by it."

"My father made sure I knew how to deal with it."

"Did he, now?"

"Sure. He taught me a lot of stuff."

"Like how to recognize the assassin's dagger."

Godwin glanced at her. "Yes. That, too."

"Interesting."

"Is it?"

"I think so."

"We all have those aspects of ourselves that seem mysterious to everyone else, but aren't necessarily." Godwin winked at her. "We all have our secrets."

Annja glanced back at Derek, but he was still studying the map. Had he said something to Godwin?

She looked back at Godwin but he was already peering out of the windshield again. "We should be just about there."

Annja followed his gaze. Up ahead she thought she spotted something red amid all the white. "Is that the sign for the turnoff?"

Godwin shrugged. "Could be."

Derek perked up. "Are we there?"

Annja pointed. "That looks like a sign to me. What do you think?"

Derek leaned forward. "Slow down, Godwin. We don't want to miss the turnoff and keep driving for hours on end. I don't think Annja would appreciate that very much, would you?"

"No, I wouldn't."

Godwin slowed the truck even more and then they saw the small piece of plywood tacked to a metal pole jutting out of the snow on the side of the ice road.

"Erop," Annja said. "I guess this is our exit."

Godwin wheeled the truck around and they turned to the right. Annja noticed that the road gradually climbed higher in elevation. She looked at Derek. "Am I right in thinking that we are no longer driving over frozen water?"

He smiled. "You're right. We're on dry ground again. The ice road is a thing of the past."

Annja glanced back at the frozen Mackenzie River and shuddered. She hoped Derek was right—that it really was a thing of the past.

9

Thirty minutes of hard, bumpy driving brought them into the tiny town of Erop, a collection of a few buildings, a gas station and two restaurants. It looked more like a refueling point than anything else, its identity marked by whatever or whoever moved through the place.

"Let me out," Derek said. "If I don't get to a bathroom after all that bladder beating, I'm done for."

Annja could sympathize. The drive to Erop had been a constant bouncing and sinking over a road that could only just be called that. She headed for one of the restaurants while Derek headed for the other. Godwin drove on to the gas station, saying he would fill up and get a replacement tire for the one they'd lost.

Ten minutes later, they were back on their way. Derek bought them all sandwiches, which they gratefully demolished and Erop fell behind them, a slightly pleasant memory for the basic human comfort it had offered up and nothing more.

The road twisted through the frozen countryside and then after another thirty minutes, broke out onto Hendrick's Highway. Godwin gave up a little cheer and steered the truck onto a paved road for the first time that day.

"Hooray," Annja said. "The mark of civilization."

"For someone who spends so much of her time in the past," Derek said, "you sure seem ready to put the past behind you."

"Bad roads are bad roads," Annja said. "And there's nothing of interest to be found on them. Plus, my butt was taking another beating back there."

"Just so long as you don't start thinking that where we're headed is any more civilized, because it's not."

"I realize that," Annja said. "But it doesn't change my mind about being relieved to be off that road."

Godwin grinned. "I feel the same way."

Hendrick's Highway was a two-lane road, and even though the asphalt had seen better days, the stretch proved to be a welcome change from both the ice road and the roller-coaster ride of the road to Erop. The SUV's tires all seemed in decent shape and Godwin had managed to procure a spare tire, just in case they should run into another rock jutting out of the landscape.

Annja felt good for the first time all day. An hour of driving would take them to their turnoff and then they could finally get to where they were going. Getting to the dig site was always the hardest part. Annja could put up with a lot of stuff, but she was often impatient when it came to actually reaching the destination. She liked getting there already.

She didn't kid herself. The events of the morning and the run-in with the giant truck didn't make her feel especially good about what might be waiting ahead. The incident in the steak house was still fresh in her mind and she turned all these events over in her mind, trying to figure out what could be going on in the frozen tundra that surrounded her.

If people weren't happy with what was going on with the Araktak, there'd be no telling what they would do to keep the company from completing its deal with the tribe. That meant Annja might have to use the sword again.

And that was something she didn't really want to do.

Godwin turned the SUV suddenly and looked embarrassed. "Sorry, almost missed the turn."

"You all right? I can take over driving for a while if you want," Annja said.

He shook his head. "It's no problem. I was just yawning, that's all."

Annja glanced behind her but Derek was already dozing. She heard a soft snore come from him and turned back. "Is he a decent guy to work for?"

Godwin shrugged. "Yeah, he's all right. Pretty fair, that sort of thing. It's not my dream job, of course, but it gives me the money to save and put away for when I figure out what I really want to do with my life."

"How old are you?"

"Twenty-eight." He shrugged. "I know. I ought to have a game plan by now, right?"

Annja smiled. "I wasn't going to say that."

He waved his hand. "I've heard so much advice from people urging me to find my way and find it fast. But I guess I'm just not in that big a hurry. I know there's something out there for me, but I haven't really felt a pull toward anything. Weird, right?"

"Well, at least you're working." Annja shrugged. "That's better than what a lot of people in your situation would do."

"Seemed like a good fit," Godwin said. "The company, I mean. And I was intrigued with the idea of going home to my birthplace, so to speak, after being away from it for so long."

"I'll bet," Annja said. "I'm still trying to figure out where it is that I come from. I can appreciate the sentiment."

Godwin smiled. "Lost lambs, huh?"

"Something like that." Annja stared through the windshield, remembering as much as she could about her own childhood. She knew what it felt like not to have that sense of belonging, or some place to call your own. To be able to point at something, even in your mind, and call it home, was a feeling she'd never enjoyed as a child.

Maybe even to this day, she thought. After all, her place in Brooklyn seemed at times to be pretty much a flop pad and nothing else. It was as much its own version of Erop as Annja ducked quickly in and out between digs and trips to other parts of the world.

She wondered if her job as an archaeologist had been predetermined by the fact that she was an orphan and had never known what it was to have a real past. Maybe that's why she spent so much of her own time digging into other people's pasts. Her quest to uncover the truth about ancient civilizations and people was really a mirror of her quest to find out about herself.

And inheriting the sword certainly hadn't helped matters, either. Where once she might have thought it would help to illuminate her past, it now seemed only to further blur it under the fog of uncertainty.

Some day, she thought to herself, I'll figure this all out.

Godwin steered the truck down a smaller road, little better than what they'd driven on to Erop. Annja groaned. "So much for civilization."

"We won't be long on this," he said as he drove around a tree stump jutting out of the road. "The dig site is relatively close."

"What's relative?"

"Twenty minutes, no more."

Annja nodded. Derek was bounced out of his sleep by a sudden dip in the road that caused him to go airborne for a fraction of a second. He sat up and rubbed the top of his head. "Guess we're almost there, huh?"

"Twenty minutes," Annja said. She glanced at Godwin. "No more."

Derek leaned forward with a yawn. "Did you sleep?"

Annja looked at him. "Didn't seem fair to leave Godwin here the only one awake. I know what it's like to drive for a long time with no rest."

"Well, you'll need your rest if you're going to impress the Araktak elders as being suitable for their cause."

"Excuse me?"

Derek smiled. "Think of it as a job interview and you'll be fine."

"What are you talking about?"

Derek leaned back and put his hands behind his head. "They wouldn't accept just anyone for this assignment, you know. They said they would have final say over whomever showed up. I guess they're not particularly crazy about letting an outsider help them relocate their sacred lands."

"Nice to hear about this now, when it's impossible to turn back."

"Wouldn't have done any good to tell you about it before now," Derek said. "The Araktak elders are a notoriously picky bunch. But then I guess that's been a function of their society for some time now, eh, Godwin?"

He shrugged. "This is something of a homecoming for me, as well."

"I thought you mentioned you'd been up here before this, to make way for the company's plans," Annja said.

Godwin nodded. "I was here. But I dealt with a representative for the elders. This time, they're all going to be here. I wouldn't be surprised if they have a smoke lodge all set up and everything."

Annja looked out of the window. She wasn't used to having people question her credentials and qualifications. She was usually begged to come in and frankly she preferred it that way. The interview with Derek had been the first real one she'd been on in a long time.

She wondered why she'd even agreed to this. It wasn't as though this was routine for her. She was taking a leave of absence from her job to handle this. She frowned. Maybe I'm just worried about yet another race of people losing everything they hold dear.

Or maybe it was the sword exerting some unnatural control over her and her decision-making.

Was she here because the sword was demanding she be here?

Annja sighed. "Well, I hope they're not too disappointed." She glanced at Godwin. "How are women treated in the Araktak?"

"Probably the way they are in any other tribe of Inuit." He shook his head. "But I'd be lying if I said I know for certain. My own mother was a white woman, so I can't ever be sure if the way she raised me was the way it works up here."

"Or if they're considered second-class citizens," Annja said.

"We're here," Derek said.

Annja stared out of the windshield. The forest suddenly broke away on either side into a clearing. She could see several rough-hewn huts that looked like a combination of log cabin and wigwam. They were large and sturdy and a great number of pine trees had been felled to make the lodges. Smoke issued from small chimneys at each corner. At least it looks warm inside, Annja thought.

Godwin brought the SUV to a halt and then looked at Annja. "I'm still figuring this out for myself as I go. You aren't alone," he said.

Derek slid out of the truck and walked over to an older man with a weather-beaten face. Annja could see a hundred years' worth of hard living etched across the narrow slits of his eyes. He nodded to Derek and then took him aside to speak in low tones.

Annja glanced at Godwin. "He seems comfortable enough."

Godwin nodded. "That's our main contact. His name is Wishman."

"Is he cool?"

"We'll find out." Godwin nodded for Annja to follow him over to the old man. Annja walked behind Godwin and waited until Godwin had introduced her to Wishman.

Annja smiled. "It's an honor to meet you."

Wishman's eyes probed hers and he said nothing for a long moment. He clasped her hand and then seemed to stare directly into her soul. His dark endless orbs looked like perfect black marbles of onyx.

Finally, he broke contact and pulled back. He turned to Derek and Godwin. "We will talk of this woman in the lodge. The others are waiting."

He turned and walked toward the largest of the buildings. Godwin and Derek followed him. Annja started to walk with them, but then Wishman stopped and turned back to Annja.

"You must stay here until you are called."

Derek shrugged and held up a hand. "Shouldn't take too long," he said. "Just hang out and be cool."

Annja frowned. "Yeah, sure. Whatever."

She watched them go and then the sudden realization that she was all alone washed over her. The camp seemed lonely and without much cause for celebration. Annja suspected the camp was there to make sure that nothing in these lands would be left behind. Perhaps the Araktak had once used this area for something else other than burying people. If so, there would be relics that would need to be cared for and transported to a new place.

Otherwise, the company would destroy them.

Annja took a stroll around the camp. It was utilitarian and nothing more. She saw the latrine and the firewood pile. Each shelter seemed to have its own cooking fire inside where meals would be prepared. Apart from that, she spotted several long axes for chopping wood and little else.

The forest stretched before her and Annja decided a little exercise might be a good thing. She felt a pull toward a certain section and ducked under the frozen pine boughs.

A bit of snow fell on her head as she walked. She crested a small hill and the trees broke apart into another clearing that sloped down and away from her for some distance.

This must be the place, she thought. Already she could feel the tug of something almost otherworldly. The unbroken snowfield before her looked like one continuous blanket of white.

"Beautiful," she said aloud.

And then she heard the terrible growl behind her.

Annja turned slowly to see a massive polar bear rearing back to stand up to its full height. It was only ten feet away from her.

And it didn't look happy.

10

Annja stood motionless as the giant polar bear swayed slightly on its haunches. She could see the sharp teeth in its mouth and the claws of its front legs loomed large in her vision.

How in the world had this bear sneaked up on her? She frowned. She should have known better than to wander around so carelessly.

She stared at the polar bear, willing herself to look right into its eyes. She'd never seen a creature like this up close before. Usually, she saw most of her dangerous animals from behind the safety of iron bars at a zoo. Not having some type of fence between them made Annja's stomach twist into knots.

The polar bear's breath stained the air with mist as it stared at Annja. Clearly, she must have been trespassing on its land. But she was curious. Didn't polar bears usually hunt closer to the water for their diet of fish? Or was this an anomaly of some type?

The bear closed its mouth. Annja wondered if she would need her sword. She could draw it in an instant, but the last thing she wanted to do was kill the bear. Even worse, if the Araktak considered polar bears as sacred animals, she could be committing a grave cultural faux pas. They'd chuck her out of the dig site and all of this would have been for nothing.

And Annja hated wasting time and effort on something only to see it falter.

The polar bear came down off its haunches. Annja relaxed further but kept absolutely still. The bear could easily kill her if she wasn't careful. She had to play this right.

She could hear the bear inhaling and exhaling all around her as it seemed to sniff her scent.

This close, she could smell the bear. It wasn't a good smell by any means and it reminded Annja of a wet dog that hadn't had a bath in weeks. She wrinkled her nose and tried to breathe less.

The polar bear looked up at her again and then sat back, regarding her for some time. Annja spoke soothingly and the bear cocked its head to one side then the other. Maybe, Annja thought, this is something new for it, as well.

The bear pawed at the ground in front of Annja and she looked down. In the snow, the bear's claw had drawn back the blanket of white to reveal the hard dirt underneath. But Annja saw something else.

Blood.

She frowned. The bear pawed at the ground with its claw again and Annja saw a fresh streak near the snow. The bear was injured.

Annja took a deep breath and then knelt down until her head was level with the dirty white creature.

"You've got something in your paw, don't you?" she said soothingly.

The bear cocked its head to one side and let out something that sounded vaguely like a whine. Carefully, Annja reached out with one hand and then the other until she cradled its paw in her hands. Very slowly, she turned it over and then saw the wound.

A piece of metal poked out of the bear's claw, embedded in the soft padded fleshy part. Annja grimaced. It looked like part of a steel arrowhead.

"No wonder you're upset." She bent closer to examine the wound. She could see that there wasn't any sign of infection yet, so it must have only happened recently. Where had the bear managed to get such a thing trapped in its claw?

She didn't think anyone around here would be such a callous hunter as to leave their weapons lying about. But then again, this was a new part of the world to her.

The bear grunted, snapping Annja's attention back to the present. Annja smirked. "Sorry."

The piece of metal looked small, but she could see just enough poking out of the surface of the skin that would give her something to pinch and yank out. She looked up at the bear. "This might hurt. You sure you want me to help you with this?"

The bear whined again. Annja took a deep breath.

She reached into the wound and felt the bear jerk a little as the pain hit. Annja gritted her teeth, pinched at the exposed metal and then, as smoothly as possible, pulled the metal free of the bear's claw.

She fell back in the snow as the bear let out a long howl that made Annja fear for her life again. The bear rolled onto its back and howled over and over again.

Annja got to her feet and the bear growled but then it got

up and walked over some of the untouched snow. Once its wounded paw touched the cold snow, the growling stopped.

Annja nodded. "Feels better, does it?"

The polar bear stalked around for a few more minutes doing what looked to Annja like an attempt to wash the wound the best way it knew how. It was using the snow and its body heat to get water into the cut skin.

After a few minutes, Annja found a log and sat down on it. The piece of metal in her hand really did look like part of an arrowhead. It had the appearance of one of the fancy steel-tip hunting arrows that sporting goods shops sold all over the world for bow hunters.

But who would shoot a polar bear in the paw? Or was that even it? Maybe one of the arrows had fallen or been broken. Perhaps the arrowhead had broken off and had been in the snow. And when the polar bear had come through, its weight had sent the metal into its claw.

The bear wandered over to Annja and sat down next to her, its huge bulk rippling as it did so. Annja spoke quietly. "So, now we're best friends. Is that it?"

The bear grunted and nuzzled Annja's arm. Annja frowned. "When was the last time you had a bath for yourself? Don't take this the wrong way, but lord do you stink to the high heavens."

The bear grunted, heaving deep breaths out on to the frozen ground. Annja smiled and shook her head. Who would have thought she'd be seeing all this beauty while enjoying the company of a creature that could easily kill her?

Life sure threw curveballs.

The bear's head suddenly turned back toward the direction Annja had come from originally.

"Annja?"

The bear growled. Annja patted its head. "Calm down. You don't have to get upset."

Derek, Wishman and Godwin, along with several other men Annja didn't know, broke through to the clearing and all of them stopped instantly. Their sudden appearance made the polar bear growl louder than before.

Annja held up her hand to stop the group of men. "Don't come any closer or he'll get angry."

Derek's eyebrows almost jumped off his head. "You're all right?"

"I'm fine."

Annja saw something like a smile play across Godwin's face. Behind him one of the younger men raised a hunting rifle and was sighting down the barrel.

Wishman saw the rifle and said several quick words that carried a clipped tonality to them. He was commanding the man to put his gun down. With a look of disbelief, the younger man lowered his rifle.

Wishman came forward slightly. He looked at Annja and then at the bear. The bear regarded him but didn't growl this time.

"How did this happen?" Wishman asked.

Annja shrugged. "I went for a walk when you all excluded me from the meeting. I found my way here and the bear surprised me. He was wounded. This was in his paw." She held out her hand and showed the metal arrowhead fragment to Wishman.

He frowned and then stepped back. This time he spoke to the bear and said several things that Annja didn't understand. The bear, however, seemed to and with a single grunt, it took one last look at Annja and then lumbered off, leaving only its tracks in its wake.

"Bye," Annja said.

She looked at Wishman. "Why'd you make him go?"

Wishman shook his head. "He didn't need to stay any longer."

"Says you."

Wishman ignored her and turned to face the group. "You have all seen what has happened here with your own eyes."

The men murmured their agreement. Wishman pointed back at Annja. "The great god Chunok has shown himself to the woman and she has been approved by his presence. She has shown her depth of spirit by caring for the wounded animal."

Derek took a calming breath. "I would have run away screaming."

Wishman nodded. "Many a man would have done just that. She did not. And so she has earned the respect of Chunok. And she has earned my respect, as well."

He turned back to the group and spread his arms. "This woman, this Friend of Bear, shall be welcomed in our camp. She will help us do what must be done to preserve our legacy and sacred traditions. Chunok has sent her to us and we will honor his choice by respecting her."

The men nodded, some of them less so than others, but Annja could see they were all impressed. Looking back on it, Annja was impressed, too. How had she managed to get herself into this situation?

Derek and Godwin came forward. Derek helped Annja to her feet. "How did you do that?"

"I don't know. I just did it."

"Incredible. Simply incredible."

Godwin chuckled. "You certainly gave them something to talk about over the fire tonight."

"How did the meeting go?" she asked.

Godwin shook his head. "There was a lot of outrage that

a woman was coming into their camp. This is something the men consider to be sacred to them only. Women apparently aren't accorded the same respect. Mr. Wainman argued your case, but in the end, it didn't look like it was going to work."

"And you were coming here to tell me it was off?"

Derek nodded. "Yeah. We were going to turn around and head for home only to find you out here doing the whole *Dances with Wolves* thing. Pretty damned impressive. If I didn't know you better, I'd say you might have staged the entire thing."

Annja shook her head. "Yeah, because I routinely try to get deadly animals to come and bother me. You should see my trick with great white sharks. That always leaves them wanting more."

"Well, the most important thing is they've accepted you." Godwin shrugged. "Wishman says you've been chosen by Chunok, who is their most important god, so that's pretty much law now."

"So, I'm good to go?"

"In spades."

"Excellent. Does this mean I have one of those shelters all to myself, you know, being divinely chosen and all?"

Godwin smiled. "Probably not. But I can put in a good word for you about letting you share the communal spittoon."

"Swell."

Derek looked around. "It's beautiful, isn't it? All of this unspoiled nature. Gorgeous."

"Shame it's going to be ruined by the drilling of the mine," Annja said.

Derek sighed. "Sometimes I feel like I've sold my soul to the devil. I used to be a lot more idealistic, I suppose. But then again, I can at least reconcile it by telling myself that you'll help ensure the Araktak find a way to preserve their traditions."

"As long as I do it within four weeks."

"Exactly."

Annja glanced at Godwin. "So, what happens now?"

"Nothing right away. There will be a welcome feast for you tonight. It's in your honor. I believe you made quite an impact on them. Far better than the impact I made when I walked into their lodge."

"Oh?"

"Some of them are quite upset that there's a half-breed in their presence."

"You had nothing to do with your father's decision to leave," Annja said.

Godwin shrugged. "Doesn't matter. I am a reminder of his decision. And rather than let them forget what happened, my mere presence serves to remind them of the clash between the old ways and the new. In a lot of ways it mirrors the situation with the company."

Derek clapped him on the back. "Relax, pal. As long as it works out in our favor, I think you'll be fine, too."

Annja watched them go and then followed them back to the lodges.

11

The fire in the main lodge made the entire place almost too hot. The birch and pine logs crackled and popped amid the orange-and-yellow flames, sending a trail of smoke circling skyward out of the chimney hole.

Annja huddled near the fire, warming herself. She hadn't realized how cold she'd been during her run-in with the polar bear. It was almost as if she'd forgotten about the temperature while she was with the creature.

Wishman sat nearby, watching her closely. She glanced up at him and smiled, but his eyes never blinked.

"You realize that's a little bit unsettling when you do that," she said.

He shrugged. "I am trying to understand you, Friend of Bear."

"You can call me Annja if it makes it easier."

He shook his head. "Chunok brought you to us and to the bear for a reason. It would be disrespectful for me to call you by another name."

"I guess I understand."

Godwin came and sat down nearby. He nudged Annja. "Is he bothering you?" he whispered.

"Only when he stares at me, which seems to be all the time. What's his deal? He said he was trying to understand me."

Godwin nodded. "It's his role within the tribe. He's kind of like the shaman or medicine man if you want to put it into Native American terms."

"And he does what, set the law down or something?"

Godwin frowned. "We don't really have laws per se. We have three ideas that we use as the basis for our system of government, such as it is."

"Like what?"

Godwin scratched a few symbols in the dirt floor. "*Maligait* means things to follow or what must be followed."

"Which I assume means you already have a basic understanding of what that would refer to."

"Sure," Godwin said. He kept writing in the dirt. "Then there's *piqujait,* those things that must be done or things to do."

"And the third?"

"*Tirigusuusiit.* Things that are not done."

"Interesting. And what happens if someone decides they don't want to abide by these ideals?"

"Then people like Wishman are called in to mediate the dispute and try to get the offending party to see the error of their ways."

Annja looked at him. "Otherwise?"

Godwin smirked. "Well, it's not like it was in the old times, now, is it? We're not able to simply condemn someone to die because of their refusal to follow the ways. But there would probably be some sort of punishment. Hell, these days, maybe they'd even banish the offender. Just kick him out of the tribe."

"Does that happen often?"

Godwin shrugged. "Only once as far as I know. When they kicked my father out."

"I thought you said he left."

Godwin shrugged. "That's what he told me as a child. I guess he didn't want his son to be embarrassed for his actions. When I grew older, I had a feeling that he wouldn't have left as much as they would have ex-communicated him for marrying outside the tribe."

"Did Wishman intervene?"

"I don't know," Godwin said. "Possibly. But marriage is a weird thing in Inuit culture. There's a lot of polygamy and even open relationships. Hell, even divorce isn't unheard-of. Of course, this is all in relation to older times. Nowadays, most Inuit do as they see fit. Only the Araktak have really kept a firm hold on their people."

"So, if marriage is so fluid an arrangement, then why did your father pay such a steep price for what he did?"

"He went outside the tribe. That's taboo. Most marriages are arranged and he was supposed to marry the daughter of one of the tribe elders. But it didn't work out that way."

Annja stared into the smoke of the fire, feeling herself grow drowsy. "Tell me about it."

"My father was supposed to go on his journey. When a male in the Araktak comes of age and has absorbed all the teachings, he is supposed to go out on his own and find himself. It's sort of a spiritual journey. They go into the wilds and explore and commune with the spirits."

"I take it the Inuit are very much an animalistic-belief society?"

"Absolutely. We believe that every living thing has a

soul. I think someone once said that we, as a people, survive by eating the souls of others. It's one reason why you'll see so much respect for any animal or thing that we eat. Even when we hunt, there is great tradition and respect accorded to the prey."

"So your father went on his journey."

Godwin nodded. "He traveled for miles across the ice floes, stopping only to hunt for enough food for himself. But one day, his journey was interrupted by a noise he hadn't heard before. And before long he'd tracked the source to a plane that had crashed in the delta."

"An airliner?"

"No, nothing so big. Just a small Cessna or a Piper Cub, I don't remember now. Anyway, there was only one survivor, a woman."

"Your mother," Annja said.

Godwin smiled. "My father couldn't take a chance of moving her because she had a broken leg and to do so would have meant indescribable pain and suffering for her. So instead, he built a shelter for them both and then splinted her leg."

Annja nodded. "Backwoods medicine."

Godwin smiled. "It was, according to my mother, incredibly painful. But my father did what he had to do to make sure she lived. And while she recovered, he set about keeping them fed with all the skills he'd learned from his tribe."

"And obviously, they made it."

"My mother was a fast healer, but even still, they had to weather the winter in the Arctic Circle. If my father hadn't found her when he did, she would have died. As it was, they nearly died that winter anyway. But they survived and as a result of their struggle together, they fell in love."

Annja smiled. "I love a happy ending."

"Well, this one doesn't have one," Godwin said. "Because when my father returned to the tribe with news of all he had endured, he did not receive the welcome he expected. And my mother was never accepted."

"They kicked him out right then?"

Godwin shrugged. "What probably happened was they called a council of elders together to listen and try to explain to my father that he was wrong. He would have been a valuable asset to them with the skills he'd learned and honed during that winter of survival. They wouldn't want to lose him."

"But they did."

"My father was a stubborn man. That's probably one of the things that kept him alive as long as he was. He refused to die. Or give up the woman he loved. And in the end, the tribe had little choice but to banish him forever."

Annja took a breath. "That's an incredible story."

"Welcome to my world. As I said, we moved south and I went to a normal school and had a pretty normal upbringing. Except that all the time I've felt like something's been missing. Some part of myself I never really knew."

"Your family."

"Yeah."

Annja glanced at Wishman but the old man was turned and talking in low tones to another elder of the tribe. She looked back at Godwin. "Do they know who you are?"

"Oh, yeah. The first time I came up here they knew." He smirked. "It's funny, isn't it? You go through life thinking about things in a fairly logical way. Science and all that. And then you see something or something happens that makes you question it all."

"Like them knowing about you?"

"Or wild polar bears nuzzling you. Yeah."

Annja grinned. "Welcome to my world."

Godwin eyed her. "So that kind of thing happens to you often?"

"Well, not often, but frequently enough that I have no idea what kind of personal belief system I have in place now. Every time I try to upgrade it, something happens and I have to make further changes."

"I don't think I've ever heard it described in quite such a clinical fashion before. That really takes the spirituality right out of it, huh?"

"I do the best I can," Annja said. "Doesn't always come across the right way."

Wishman nudged her. "Why do you talk to the outcast?"

Annja frowned. "Because he's my friend."

"He is the son of one who betrayed us. He cannot be trusted."

"That's rubbish," Annja said. "And while I respect your traditions and culture, this is one thing I will not agree with you on. Godwin is not his father. And as such, he should not be held to the same punishment that you held him to. It's not fair."

Wishman shook his head. "What his father did is not done. The son has spoken to you of our belief of *tirigusuu-siit,* yes?"

"He has."

"Then you should know that what his father did falls under that law. He chose to forsake our traditions for the white woman. And we could not convince him to see the error of his ways."

Annja shrugged. "It's love. Who can make matters of the heart follow some unspoken rule like that?"

"We can," Wishman said. "Or else the option is always there for the offender to leave the tribe."

"But you kicked him out."

"Yes. So he would not pollute the others with his twisted ways of doing things."

"I wouldn't call it twisted."

"That is because you are not yet Araktak, Friend of Bear."

Annja looked at him. "'Yet'?"

Wishman nodded. "Chunok has chosen you for a special purpose—to help us preserve our ways amid the modern times."

"So?"

"So his wishes must be abided by or else we risk his wrath. And we will not risk the anger of the gods."

Annja looked back into the fire. "What does that mean? That you'll make me a member of the Araktak?"

"What you would call an honorary member. You are not born into the tribe, so you can never fully be Araktak. But we will make you the closest thing we have to it."

"Does this entail me doing anything…unusual?"

Wishman smiled at her. "One would say that helping a wounded polar bear—a creature that could have easily killed you—is unusual enough. Do you agree?"

"Well, yeah."

Wishman nodded. "So tonight we will have a feast in your honor and we will ask the gods to accept you as one of us. If they agree, then the ceremony will end and we will do what you are here to help us do."

Annja glanced at the scrawled symbols in the dirt. "What happens if the gods don't accept me?"

"That has never happened before."

Annja looked at him. "That's not what I asked you."

Wishman took his hand from his pocket and scattered

bits of bone in the dirt at his feet. He bent lower and studied what looked to Annja to be ancient symbols carved in them.

Annja watched him trace his finger along the symbols, muttering something under his breath. He picked up the bones again and threw them back into the dirt.

Annja cleared her throat. "So, what do they say?"

Wishman held up his hand for another moment and picked up the bones a third time and threw them back down. This time he grunted twice, spoke some more words and then studied the bones carefully.

"Wishman?"

"Friend of Bear, you must learn patience," he said.

Annja nodded. "Yeah, see, that's never really been my strong suit. I can't stand waiting for stuff. Like right now, for example. What you're doing is driving me crazy with questions."

Wishman scooped the bones into his hand and stored them back in the pocket of his coat. He looked at Annja. "Chunok chose you for a reason."

"Okay."

"Everything is as it should be."

"Yeah, but what if it wasn't?"

Wishman shrugged and stood. "Then maybe we would see if the polar bear comes back to kill you."

And then he walked away, leaving Annja to ponder his words.

12

The feast started promptly at sundown. And while Godwin had explained that usually women would cook and take care of the shelters, the men of the Araktak tribe were also expected to be able to cook for themselves during times when they were away. As a result, the Araktak men, particularly the elders, put on a tremendous spread.

Before anyone could eat, Wishman came out before the improvised log tables and seats and lifted his hands overhead. He gave a long prayer in his language and then repeated it in English for the benefit of Annja and Derek.

Finally, he looked around and spoke to the gathered crowd of a dozen. "My friends, we hold this feast to honor the presence of the one Chunok has chosen, Friend of Bear. He has spoken today and came to us in the guise of the mighty polar bear. And this woman befriended him, cared for him and sent him on his way. She showed neither fear nor hesitation and above all the depth of her spirit. For that, we must be thankful that Chunok has sent us one as strong as she."

There was a great deal of nodding and Annja felt as if she was slipping back in time. If it hadn't been for the flannel shirts and jeans on the men, she might have believed this scene was taking place a thousand years before this night.

Wishman looked at Annja. "Friend of Bear, we offer you what we have in the token of friendship of the Araktak. We hope you will use your strength to help us through the times that are coming soon."

Annja bowed her head and then looked back at him. "I am honored by your gesture of kindness."

Wishman nodded and then spoke once more. "Let us feast and give thanks to Chunok that Friend of Bear is among us!"

A great chorus of whoops and cries went up from the Araktak men. Godwin joined them, despite his outsider status. Annja wasn't sure what to make of it all. She wondered if Godwin was trying to prove himself worthy of their acceptance, as well.

Only Derek seemed slightly uncomfortable and Annja found that strange. He'd seemed so at ease earlier on. She wondered if something was bothering him, and if so, what?

Wishman appeared before her and gestured to the long table of food. "Please, you are our honored guest and you must start the feast. Help yourself to whatever you wish."

Annja smiled. "I'm not sure what you've cooked for me."

Wishman took her by the hand and pointed out the walrus meat, the caribou and even some whale blubber. Annja had to resist the urge to reprimand Wishman for the whale blubber and reminded herself that the Inuit still whaled in the Arctic Ocean, although they did it from much smaller ships than the typical harpoon-cannon-wielding floating carnage houses that other nations used.

Annja helped herself to some of the walrus and caribou and then sat down.

Wishman offered her a cup of something warm and strong. Annja drank it and marveled at how fast the obviously alcoholic drink hit her system. She felt entirely relaxed and when she tasted the meat, it only seemed to enhance the drink's effects.

"This is delicious," she said.

Godwin sat next to her. "The Inuit have a high-fat diet with very little in the way of carbohydrates. Surprisingly, it doesn't seem to have an adverse effect on their health."

Annja nodded. "Just like the folks down in Antarctica who have to eat double the number of calories people in temperate climates have to. The body will use it all to make heat. I'm sure it just gets burned through. Just sitting and shivering you can burn through a thousand calories like it's nothing."

"Up here, it is nothing," Godwin said. He glanced at Derek, who was sitting apart from them. "He okay?"

Annja shrugged. "I don't know. I was just wondering that myself. He seems to be thinking about something pretty hard."

"Mr. Wainman?" Godwin called.

Derek looked up and then came over. "Hey."

"You okay?" Annja asked. "Looks like you've got the weight of the world on your shoulders."

Derek shrugged. "Nah, just some minor complications. Nothing too important."

"Really?"

"Well, maybe."

Annja bit into another piece of caribou and chewed slowly. "Have something to drink. It will help calm you down."

Godwin fetched him a mug of the liquor and when

Derek drank it down, he coughed and sputtered as he struggled to swallow it. The action brought a rousing chorus of laughter from Wishman and the others.

"Careful," Wishman said. "That will make you breathe fire."

Annja glanced at him. "Why didn't you warn me about that?"

Wishman shrugged. "You are Friend of Bear. Liquor should not be a challenge for one such as yourself."

"Ah," Annja said. "I got it now."

Derek took another sip and set the mug down. "Wow, that stuff's insane. Any idea what it is?"

"Don't ask," Godwin said. "Just enjoy it."

"That sounds ominous," Annja said. "And just when I was starting to like this feast."

Derek went back to eating and Annja eyed him. "You clammed up again. What gives?"

"I got a text message from the company."

"You got reception all the way out here? That's impressive," Annja said.

Derek shrugged. "Satellite technology."

"So, what did the message say?"

Derek glanced around. "They've expedited things slightly."

"Why?"

"The board wants to get started drilling faster than a month from now. They claim they need the extra time to produce a better return on the investment."

"But you told the Araktak that it would be a month."

Derek looked at her. "And now you know why I'm not exactly a Chatty Cathy right now."

"You're going to have to tell them," Annja said. "Sooner than later, too. If you hold off, they might get upset."

"They're going to be upset anyway," Godwin said. "The Araktak don't like deals being renegotiated without them."

Derek nodded. "Thanks for telling me that, Godwin."

"Sorry, Mr. Wainman."

Derek waved his hand. "Forget it. I didn't mean to snap at you. It's just that we came into this planning one way and now the arrangements have been changed on me. And I have to make sense of them in such a way that our hosts here don't feel like they're being screwed over."

"Are they?" Annja asked.

"No. Well, not really. I hope not at least."

Annja shook her head. "Way to be firm."

"What would you do, *Friend of Bear?*"

Annja elbowed him. "First of all, don't be a wiseass. Secondly, you should just tell them and get it out of the way. They're going to have to know eventually, right?"

"Well, they'll figure it out pretty soon anyway."

"Why is that?"

"Because the company is sending a half-dozen miners up here to begin exploratory coring."

"What? When?"

Derek frowned. "They'll be here tomorrow."

Annja and Godwin stared at him. Godwin shook his head. "Well, that changes things rather drastically."

Annja kept looking at Derek. "Doesn't the company board realize what a precarious situation this places us in? This isn't just about you, you know? Godwin and I are here, as well. What's to stop these guys from just throwing us out of here?"

Derek frowned. "A signed deal. And the fact that the Araktak have already accepted the company's money. We own this land now, not them. We're only giving them this respect as part of the deal."

"If they don't like it, though," Annja said, "can't they claim you violated the terms of the agreement and refuse to cooperate?"

Derek nodded. "They could. But the question is, would they? If they roadblock us, we can have the RCMP up here in a flash. The company has a lot of power and the Canadian government won't be keen to see something stop an operation that could be worth billions."

"This is not going to go over well," Annja said. "And I don't know if I should be sitting next to you."

"What—you don't want to help me?"

Annja took a deep breath. "Buddy, I think you're going to have to be on your own for this one."

Derek looked at Godwin. "You'll get my back if it comes to that?"

Godwin shook his head. "It won't. They might be plenty pissed off at you, but they're not going to stick a knife in you, as much as they might want to. This isn't the old days."

"I wish that made me feel better," Derek said. "But it doesn't."

Wishman came over and knelt in front of Annja. "How does Friend of Bear find the meal?"

"It's fantastic. And the drink is something else."

Wishman offered her another mug of the strange liquor. "This will make it easier for you to rest tonight so that we may have a productive day tomorrow."

Annja glanced at Derek but he looked away. She smiled at Wishman. "Thank you. I feel pretty relaxed already."

Wishman nodded at her plate. "Finish your food so you will have the strength to deal with the cold. The fat on the meat will help you stay warm. And when you are working outside, you must have enough in your belly to stave off the environment."

Annja nodded. "I will. Thank you."

Wishman didn't look at Godwin but glanced at Derek. "What troubles him so much?"

"Bad news," Annja said.

"Annja!" Derek glared at her.

Annja shook her head. "It's like a bandage. Better to just rip it off quick. It might hurt for a moment but then the pain's gone."

"You hope," Derek murmured.

Wishman eyed him. "What bad news do you have to share with us?"

"It's nothing."

Wishman tilted his head. "Friend of Bear says you have bad news. Friend of Bear would not lie."

Derek glared at Annja. "I was trying to come up with a better way of doing this, Annja."

"Yeah, well, sometimes you just have to get it done. Now stand up and tell them what you have to tell them. Keep putting it off and the only person who will look bad is you."

"I hope you're right."

"I think she is," Godwin said.

Wishman kept staring at Derek. "Please tell us this news."

Derek stood and put his plate down. He strode out to the middle of the lodge and cleared his throat. No one quieted down, however, so Wishman raised his hands for quiet and instantly everyone fell silent.

Derek cleared his throat again. "I would first like to thank the Araktak for hosting us here in this incredible land. You have our most sincere gratitude for honoring us with this feast and this fantastic meal. The drink is also quite…potent."

Someone chuckled in the back of the room. But a glance from Wishman silenced him again.

Derek nodded. "I have been informed by my company that they will need things to move a little faster than we had originally allowed for."

Wishman frowned. "The company told us they would give us one month, during which time we might search for relics on this sacred land before you drive your drills into it."

Derek nodded. "Yes, I realize that was what they told you. I was told this, as well, and it is this timetable that I conveyed to Annja—Friend of Bear, as you call her. It was with this timetable that she agreed to help the Araktak."

Wishman frowned. "But?"

"That has changed," Derek said. "The company is sending the first miners to this place tomorrow. They will not start drilling right away, of course."

Angry murmurs filled the room. Wishman urged quiet. "How long will we have?"

Derek shrugged. "Perhaps a few days. Perhaps a week."

All hell broke loose.

13

By the next morning, things had quieted down to an unsettled murmur. Annja came out of the shelter that she shared with Godwin and Derek to find the camp bustling with Araktak men. Some of them were chopping wood for the fires while others had unloaded an array of shovels and picks from the backs of trucks that Annja hadn't even noticed the previous day.

Derek's news of the accelerated schedule had not gone over well, but it was Wishman who finally restored order by reminding them all that they had signed an agreement with the company. Rather than argue about it, the best course of action was simply to accept the idea that things were moving faster. It just meant they had to do their work faster and accomplish what they set out to do.

"Besides," Wishman had said, "Friend of Bear is with us. And Chunok would not have sent her if he was not confident in her abilities."

Annja had frowned. Nothing like having more pressure added to the situation, she thought.

But she knew upon waking that she would have to do her best, if only so that the Araktak people had a legacy to share with future generations.

She wandered over to the main lodge and got some breakfast before stepping back outside. She finished a cup of coffee and saw Godwin coming back through the trees. He'd obviously been out for a walk.

"Good morning," she said.

He nodded. "This really is beautiful country. I can see why the Araktak would claim it as home."

"Sure," Annja said. "But it's part of your land, as well."

Godwin grinned. "Good luck making that argument with the council of elders. My attempts to talk to Wishman have so far met with dismal failure."

"You can't blame him. What with Derek's bombshell last night, they're not necessarily in the right frame of mind to discuss internal politics. And I sensed that Wishman is one of the few holding the Araktak together."

"Meaning what?"

"You mentioned factions before, right? I think you're on the mark there. When Derek unloaded last night, there was some definite dissension in the ranks. Only Wishman was able to keep things from spiraling out of control."

"Pretty good for a crusty old guy."

"Who is a crusty old guy?"

They turned and saw Wishman standing there. His eyes crinkled into something like a playful grin. "Did you have a restful sleep, Friend of Bear?"

"Very much so," Annja said.

"Good morning, Wishman," Godwin said.

Wishman regarded him for a moment and then turned back to Annja. "Are you ready to begin?"

Annja nodded. "The sooner the better. Time is not going to be an ally to us on this day."

"Indeed." Wishman gestured to an Araktak man standing nearby. "This is Nyaktuk. He will be your guide to our burial area. Once you start, he will be in charge of making sure the items uncovered are handled in a respectful manner."

Annja nodded. "Nice to meet you."

Nyaktuk nodded and then eyed Godwin suspiciously. "Does he need to come along with us?"

Annja frowned. "Godwin is indispensable to this dig. He has certain expertise that I require."

Wishman frowned. "Is that so?"

"Yes," Annja said. "It is so. You don't want to hamper me, do you? Wouldn't that be the same as suggesting that your god Chunok had chosen incorrectly?"

Wishman frowned. "The half-breed may accompany you."

Godwin sighed. "I feel like a mutant."

"You are a mutant," Nyaktuk said. He gestured to Annja. "Follow me."

They ducked through the pine trees and covered the ground that Annja had walked right before she met up with the polar bear. Nyaktuk led them up a slight rise in the landscape and then stopped.

"Here."

Annja looked around. "What is *here?*"

Nyaktuk pointed at the ground. "We are standing on the burial mound."

Godwin looked around. "I don't see an opening."

"It hasn't been used in almost one hundred years. The top was covered up with dirt."

Godwin squatted in the deep snow. "It'll take us hours to dig through this, and then we have to crack the frozen dirt covering the mound."

Nyaktuk shook his head. "We'll clear the snow quickly. Then we only need to dig six inches down to find the door that leads to the chamber."

"You're sure it's still structurally sound?" Annja asked. "A hundred years under the ground with melting snow and all could easily rot a wooden door."

"The door is made from whale bone," Nyaktuk said. "It will take centuries for it to decompose."

Annja nodded. "Let's get started, then." She and Godwin headed back to their SUV. Annja took a breath. "I wasn't aware we'd have to dig into the ground."

"Does it make a difference?"

"Well, yeah. Ideally, I'd like to have a ground-sensing radar or sonar that we can use to get a more complete look at what we'll be dealing with under the surface."

Godwin unhitched the tailgate and hauled out a large yellow box. "You mean something like this?"

Annja's face lit up. "Get out!"

Godwin shrugged. "I was told to make sure you had all the necessary tools at your disposal."

"Yeah, but this—"

"I try to plan for anything," Godwin said.

"I'm glad you do," Annja replied. She grabbed a shovel while Godwin hefted the radar unit and they moved back to the burial mound. As they approached, Annja saw Nyaktuk giving the radar unit a baleful look.

"What is that?"

She pointed with her shovel. "Ground-radar unit. It will help us see what's beneath the ground before we dig into it."

"Why would you need such a thing?"

Godwin frowned. "So we don't end up destroying something precious with the shovels. This way, we can see what's down there and make sure we don't dig into a relic. Just the dirt."

Nyaktuk looked unsure of whether the radar would somehow violate the degree of sanctity that surrounded the area, but after a moment of introspection, he nodded. "It is a good idea."

"Show me where the entrance to the burial mound should be," Annja said.

Nyaktuk took his place on top of the hill and measured off with an aged old pine nearby. He mumbled softly to himself, paced back and forth a few times, and then planted himself at what looked like the exact crest of the hill. "Here," he said.

Annja nodded and pulled the unit over to the top of the hill. She looked at Godwin. "Can we set this up right here to give us a reading?"

"Sure. Give me a second and I'll get it going."

She watched him unbundle the unit and set the probes out. The spikes would shoot impulses into the earth and register the return echoes by displaying them on the small screen of the unit. They should be able to see a good picture of what lay below the surface of the burial mound.

"It's really handy you thought to bring this along," Annja said.

Godwin smiled. "I did some research on archaeological digs. It seemed like it might just be a good idea."

"Remind me to mention this to Derek. It's always nice to make sure the boss knows you've done good."

"Thanks. I appreciate that."

Annja hefted the shovel. It had a nice sharp edge to the steel blade, and she started clearing off the snow in a twelve-foot diameter from the top of the hill. The packed snow was tough to move. Nyaktuk disappeared and returned a few minutes later with several other men.

Annja saw they were armed with shovels, as well. Nyaktuk directed them to take up positions around the area and they all started clearing off the top of the hill. Within a few short minutes, they had already reached down to the frozen earth.

Annja looked at the clearing and saw the brown grass and lichens that covered the ground. Somewhere, below the hill, were the bodies and bones of countless members of the Araktak. She would have to proceed very carefully so that as little as possible was disturbed.

She wasn't sure what Wishman would want done with the bones of the deceased. Did he expect her to gather them up for transport to a new burial site? Or would they simply be discarded? Perhaps the Araktak could perform a ceremony that would maintain the dignity of the deceased without having to replant the bones elsewhere.

It was something new for Annja. She'd never taken part in a burial-mound relocation before and she wasn't quite sure what to expect. But as she watched Nyaktuk and the others finish clearing the area, she knew that this was something incredibly important to them. And she appreciated the zeal.

Godwin finished firing up the ground radar and called Annja. "We can start using it now."

Annja helped him move the unit over to the precise location that Nyaktuk had pointed out. "Let's get the probes into the ground here and there and then two more over in that direction so we have a four-point picture of the place."

Godwin drilled holes and then planted the probes so they jutted out of the ground with their points embedded in the frozen earth. Then he resumed his position behind the unit.

"Ready."

Annja nodded. "Go ahead."

She heard the beeps and then she waited. Godwin frowned at the screen.

"Something wrong?" Annja asked.

"I can see the entry door to the mound, but that's it. The radar won't penetrate beyond it for some reason."

Annja frowned. "That's weird."

"I know."

"This ever happen before?"

Godwin looked sheepish. "This is the first time I've ever used one of these things."

"How'd you know how to operate it, then?"

"I read the instruction manual last night before I fell asleep."

Annja smiled. "I see."

"Sorry."

"Don't be." She looked at Nyaktuk. "Can we dig down to the door and open it up? Once we get that clear, we might be in a better position to see what's underneath."

He nodded and instructed his men to dig carefully. They moved into position and started easing up shovelfuls of dirt, pried loose from the frozen earth.

Gradually, they worked through the permafrost. The color of the soil looked very rich, and Annja supposed that the presence of the decomposing bodies in the area would have naturally added nutrients to the soil.

It seemed coldly scientific to put it that way, but everything broke down. Ashes to ashes, she thought.

One of the men struck something hard and he looked up at Nyaktuk. "This is the door."

Nyaktuk stood over him to verify the whale bone and then stepped back to look at Annja. "Still intact."

"Can we pry it up?"

"Yes." He nodded at the man in the hole and then waited. The man used his shovel to pry open the door and then he lifted the entire piece out of the hole.

Annja smelled a bitter scent on the air and had to remind herself that this was a cemetery and that all sorts of things would have decomposed underneath. The air trapped in place by the door would still contain traces of the smells of death.

Nyaktuk helped the man out of the hole and nodded to Annja. "You wish to look in there?"

Annja shook her head. "Not just yet. Let's use the radar to make sure we don't accidentally break something."

Nyaktuk nodded. "I appreciate your concern for our past."

"That's why I'm here, remember?"

Annja motioned for Godwin to reposition the ground probes and he did so. "Ready."

"Do it," Annja said.

Another series of beeps went off and this time Godwin's face showed surprise.

"What now?" Annja asked.

"It's deep," Godwin said. "Really deep. And wide."

Annja looked at the display. "Amazing." She glanced at Nyaktuk. "How deep would these mounds typically be?"

He shrugged. "Not too deep. Why?"

"Because this shaft seems to go straight down. And it keeps going."

Nyaktuk came over to look at the display. "How deep does it go?"

"That's just it," Annja said. "It doesn't seem to end. It keeps going."

"For how far?"

"I don't know," Annja said. "Maybe forever."

14

Godwin stared down the shaft. "You're joking, right? There's no way it could go on that far."

Annja shrugged. "I remember Derek telling me something the other day about kimberlite pipes. That's where the company expects to find its diamonds, right?"

"Yeah. So what?"

"Well, if this burial mound is built on what are basically kimberlite pipes, then they might well run down straight into the Earth's mantle." She shook her head. It seemed almost like something out of a Jules Verne novel, the notion that the burial mound was actually one giant tunnel leading right to the Earth's core. It was too fantastic. And yet, the possibility was staring her right in the face.

"So, where are the burial areas, then?" asked Godwin. "They wouldn't have just tossed bodies into this hole, would they?"

Nyaktuk frowned. "Each body would have had its own resting place, according to tradition and their place within the tribe."

"So you mean the elders would have held a higher place of esteem than a hunter," Annja said.

Nyaktuk nodded. "But only just. Hunters were obviously a highly valued member of the tribe. More likely, women and children and the elderly would have been buried in a less respectful position than the others."

"I don't see any bodies to speak of," Annja said, once again studying the ground-radar display.

"I'd be amazed if you could pick out an actual body on that thing," Godwin said. "They've had a lot of time to settle and get moved around as the landscape has shifted."

Annja nodded. "Good point. But I still ought to be able to see something on this screen. Instead, I see a whole bunch of branches."

"Branches?"

Annja pointed as Godwin came over. "See? There's the main shaft going down at what looks to be about a thirty-degree slope. But then there are whole branches sprouting off like a tree that's been turned upside down."

"Which means what?"

"It means we've got a pretty interesting dig site in front of us. It's a burial mound to be sure. But the shaft's depth and these branches indicate something else entirely."

"You think the Araktak built the burial mound on top of something else that was already here?"

"It's possible. Likely even." Annja frowned. "But what could it be? And why would they have done something like that? It doesn't make a lot of sense."

Nyaktuk scowled at them. "We're wasting time. We should be excavating and helping move the deceased to our storage vehicle."

Annja looked at him. "You have a storage vehicle?"

"We weren't sure what condition the bodies would be

in, so we arranged to have a truck ready to transport the bones to the new site."

"Is the new site close by?"

"It's fifty miles to the east. It's actually closer to where we are concentrated now. In some ways, this will be helpful to us."

"But you don't seem too thrilled with this process in general," Annja said.

"I am helping you because Wishman decrees it. He carries a great deal of respect within the tribe."

"Even if you happen to not agree with his decisions?"

"It is not for me to judge his actions. He is many years my senior in this tribe and has seen many more things than I will likely ever see during my entire lifetime. I follow his commands."

Godwin turned to Annja. "All right, then. If there's nothing else, I suppose he's right. We should get started."

Annja nodded. "I'd like to show this to Derek. He might have some ideas about the unique construction of this area."

"Good idea. I'll stay here with Nyaktuk and get started on the first tombs. Maybe you can go chase him down and bring him back. I think he's still pretty upset about having to tell the bad news last night."

"All right. I'll be back as soon as I can."

Nyaktuk whistled twice and the sharp tones carried out across the area. Within seconds, a half-dozen men came out of the forest, each bearing a long wooden box. Annja watched them file over to the opening of the burial mound. New coffins, she supposed, for the bones of those long since dead.

It didn't make a lot of sense to her. The owners of the bones were probably long past caring about whether they were bagged or boxed, but then again, Annja had seen a lot of respect accorded to the dead in her travels all over the world. The Araktak were just another culture who valued their dead almost as much as their living.

She walked back toward the camp. It was quieter now as more of the men moved to the burial mound to help with the excavation. With their timeline drastically reduced, they would have to move fast.

But even still, Annja wanted to show Derek what she'd found.

She entered her shelter and called his name. "Derek?"

He was sitting on his improvised bed with his head in his hands. He looked up as she came in. "Oh. Hey."

"You look like hell warmed over with a butane torch."

"Thanks. I feel about the same way. Must have been that damned drink I had last night."

"Sure it's not something else?"

"Like what?"

Annja shrugged. "I don't know, like maybe you're feeling bad because you basically reneged on the deal with the Araktak and it hurts your innate sense of honor and compassion?"

He smirked. "Innate sense of honor and compassion? Where'd you get that from?"

"I just made it up, but I think it fits. You're not a bad guy, Derek. You just got stuck being the bad guy this time by your company. And I think you realized something else, that you're just another cog in the machine. You'll get used just like everyone else."

"You included," he said.

"Yep."

"And it doesn't bother you?"

Annja shrugged. "Sure. It's weird for me. I'm not really used to working this way, but at the same time, I made the decision to take their money, so stuff like this comes with the territory."

"I don't know how you're able to maintain such equanimity about this stuff."

"I'm remarkably well adjusted." Annja laughed. "I'm kidding, of course. Trust me, I'm anything but."

"I read the file."

She frowned. "Of course you did. Now, are you going to get up or are you just going to sit here and feel depressed about things and mope around for the rest of the day being completely and totally unproductive despite the deadline?"

"Well, when you put it like that…"

"Yes?"

"Is there any coffee?"

Annja nodded. "Yeah, in the main lodge. And hurry up, too, because we found something interesting."

"Yeah?"

"The burial mound has a shaft that descends at a thirty-degree slope."

"What's so special about that?"

"It keeps going."

"Excuse me?"

"Just what I said. The shaft doesn't appear to stop. Even more interesting, there are branches off of the main shaft."

"What, like other rooms to put the bodies into, that kind of thing?"

Annja shook her head. "I don't think it's that simple."

"Why?"

"Because the branches seem to go for some distance, as well." Annja shook her head. "I've never seen anything like it before. It's weird. And yet there seems to be some sort of reason to it, even if I can't figure out what it is yet."

Derek pulled on his parka and they walked over to the main lodge. "What do you think it might be about?"

"I don't know. But I thought about that kimberlite pipe thing you talked to me about the other day. It occurred to me that this whole area might be almost honeycombed with the things. If we play our cards right, it's possible that you could simply descend into these pipes and do all the mining you need without having to drill all that much more."

Derek's eyes lit up. "That would save the company millions of dollars in time and effort."

"At least," Annja said. "And it's possible. But I want you to see it first before we make the phone call back to your company."

Derek nodded. "Great, let me grab a cup of joe and I'll head on over."

Annja watched him prepare his coffee by dumping a huge lump of sugar into the swirling hot black liquid. He sipped it and recoiled. "Damn, that's hot."

"What time are you expecting the miners?"

"Oh, I don't know. Personally, I sort of hope they get lost and have to come back another time. As soon as they show up, the mood around here is going to go from bad to worse. And I'll be looked at as the bad guy again."

"The Araktak will know it's not you."

"Yeah, but they shoot the messenger around these parts. Not literally, of course, but I still feel like crap for having to do it."

Annja led him back through the trees to the burial mound. She came through the final stretch and saw the wooden boxes being moved around carefully. Godwin and Nyaktuk were delicately placing bones into one of the boxes.

Godwin nodded to her. "Three so far."

"Any idea how many more might be down there?" Derek asked.

"Could be hundreds," Annja said. "The mound is huge and there would seem to be room for a lot more."

"This is just the first branch off the shaft," Godwin said. "We're going to need to string lights to get illumination down there. Things get dark pretty fast and it's not all that open and airy. Claustrophobia will sneak up on you damned quick."

"We will bring the lights," Nyaktuk said. "We have a supply of them."

"You got a generator with them, too?" Derek asked.

Nyaktuk regarded him. "We don't discriminate against technology as a general rule. Only when it threatens our traditions and seeks to corrupt our young people. Only then do we rebel."

"So, you've got a generator?" Annja asked.

"Yes."

Nyaktuk turned back to dig. Annja watched him work the shovel carefully and nodded to Derek. "Over here."

Derek followed her over to the display screen and whistled. "Wow, you weren't kidding."

"You see? It goes down and keeps going. It's possible it continues for a long time. All we can see here is the maximum distance for the display screen. And that's reading at a thousand meters right now."

"Better than half a mile." Derek shook his head. "What would it have taken to tunnel something like this out?"

"Well, that's just it. We don't know if it was tunneled out by the Araktak or whether it's natural."

"Could be a giant earthworm, too." Derek grinned. "I'm kidding."

Annja nodded. "That would be the last thing we need

on this. But I'm puzzled that the shaft goes on for so long. That's what made me think of the kimberlite pipes."

Derek nodded. "I can see why. But the pipes I'm used to seeing aren't anywhere near this large. We call them pipes, yeah, but they're usually much smaller in diameter than this." He pointed at the screen. "I mean, there's room in there for two people to stand side by side."

"Yes."

Derek frowned. "Something like this occurring naturally? I don't know. It just doesn't seem possible."

"And yet," Annja said, "we have the actual thing right in front of us. Kind of hard to argue with the reality of it, huh?"

"Yes." Derek turned and watched Godwin bringing up another bundle of bones. "All of this for the dead."

"There's room enough in there for a mass death incident," Annja said. "But then the question becomes, what could have caused so many people to die so quickly?"

"I've got a bigger question for you," Derek said. "Is what killed them all still lingering? And if so, are we in danger, too?"

"I don't like that question," Annja said. "I don't like it one single bit." And she stared at the entry to the burial mound for a long time.

15

By the end of the first day, Nyaktuk and his men, working in concert with Annja and Godwin, had managed to transfer the remains of almost three dozen separate bodies into wooden coffins and arranged for them to be transported to the new burial ground closer to the permanent Araktak community.

The cold wind swept in over the plain, cresting like a wave as it rushed the burial mound. Annja had spent the majority of the day shivering inside her parka, warmed only temporarily by the steady stream of coffee that flowed from the camp.

Godwin seemed to work hardest of all. He showed no sign of exhaustion, even though Annja had seen him mop his brow covertly and pause here and there to take a deep breath. He refused the coffee that Wishman grudgingly offered him. The action seemed to set the Araktak elder back on his heels, but he simply shrugged and left Godwin to his devices.

Annja suspected he was trying to show them all how much this job meant to him and how serious he was about this part of his ancestry. Godwin would be the first to admit he wasn't pure blood, but neither would he state that he wasn't Araktak.

Annja watched more of the wooden boxes emerge from the burial mound, borne up from the underground chambers by men with blistered hands and dirt-streaked faces. Even in the numbing cold, the men managed to work up a tremendous sweat.

They paused as the sun started to dip closer to the ground. Nyaktuk emerged first from below. He looked weary, but still wore a frown on his face.

"We've had a good day," Annja said.

He shrugged. "There are still many of them down there. It may take us much longer than I thought."

"There are that many bodies?"

He glanced at her. "Haven't you seen them all?"

Annja shook her head. "You haven't let me down there all day. You said that bearing the dead was work only for the Araktak."

Nyaktuk nodded. "The half-breed helps, as well."

"He's part of you and you know it."

Nyaktuk looked thoughtful. "I don't bear him ill will for being the son of a white woman. But he is only now returning to his homeland. What does that say about his spirit when it takes the lure of money to make him acknowledge his true people?"

"It says he was too young to know any better."

"His father was an Araktak warrior. He should have schooled the boy better."

"Kind of hard to do once the tribe has banished you, don't you think?"

"He was given a choice."

Annja smiled. "And you've never fallen in love before? You've never felt the tug on your heart when you look at a special woman? How many other men have had their logic and reasoning destroyed by the emotional urges of their heart?"

"Probably far too many than I could ever conceive," Nyaktuk said. "But it still was not right for his father to take up with the white woman."

"Well, he did. And the child of their union is no longer a child and he wishes to know those to whom he is related. The least you could do is show him some measure of respect. If for no other reason than the hard work he has done today. He hasn't even had a drink of water in hours."

Nyaktuk wiped his face on his sleeve. "We'll see."

More of his men filed out of the mound. They looked exhausted, as well. Godwin came out last. He still wore that grim look of determination, as if the fact that night was approaching was a personal insult to his quest to show the Araktak how much he cared.

"Time for some food," Annja said. "And you need to rest. All of you." She spoke her last words looking at Godwin directly. He turned away.

Nyaktuk said a few words to the men and they walked back toward the camp. Godwin watched them go and then turned to Annja.

"Am I being a fool?"

"I don't know, are you?"

"I just want them to see me for who I am, not as the product of an ancient taboo. But something tells me they'll never change."

"You mentioned the Araktak were among the most secretive of the Inuit. That means they probably don't like the idea of change all that much." Annja smiled. "Still, no one can fail to respect the amount of work you've put in. You've done everything that was asked of you and more today."

"Maybe."

Annja punched him on the shoulder. "Well, you impressed me. Maybe that will count for something."

Godwin looked at her and grinned. In the fading light, he looked almost ghostlike with the dirt obscuring his features. Only his smile remained white against the falling darkness.

Annja laughed. "You look like the Cheshire cat. Your face is a mess."

"I need a shower."

"Good luck finding one back at camp."

Godwin frowned. "I hadn't thought of that. I wonder what the others will do to keep clean."

Nyaktuk and the rest of the men suddenly came back through the pines toward them. Nyaktuk nodded at Godwin.

"You need to bathe."

Godwin smirked. "So do you."

"We intend to. There's a river a mile away. We will go there and wash. Come with us."

Godwin's eyes widened. "The river will be frozen."

One of the men hefted a pickax. Nyaktuk nodded at him. "We will chop our way through to the water that flows beneath it."

"And bathe in the cold water?"

Nyaktuk regarded him. "We seem to be short of hot water at the moment, so yes. On the shore we will build a fire and warm ourselves there after we wash. This is how it is done."

"For Araktak," Godwin said.

Nyaktuk frowned. "For anyone dirty from digging all day long. This is how it is done in this environment."

Annja nudged him forward. "Don't be a snob."

Godwin nodded and looked at Nyaktuk. "Thank you for the offer to join you."

Nyaktuk led the group of men through the clearing and off into another glen farther away. Annja watched them go for several minutes. She smiled and thought that perhaps the Araktak would eventually warm to Godwin. But he would have to continue to work hard to prove to them that he was worthy of their acknowledgment. Still, he'd done well today.

"The idea of a cold bath in a frozen river doesn't exactly make me jump for joy. Hypothermia being what it is and all."

Annja started. Derek stood behind her watching the men troop down the incline that led away from the burial mound.

"You've certainly mastered the art of sneaking up on people in deep snow."

Derek shrugged. "Not exactly deep snow anymore what with all the feet trampling it down all day long. It's actually pretty easy."

"Well, you caught me off guard."

Derek eyed her. "I would have thought it was impossible."

"It's not. Unlikely, maybe. But not impossible."

"Interesting." Derek looked at the mound. "How'd we do today?"

Annja shrugged. "We got a lot of the old dead out of the mound, but Nyaktuk tells me there are still many to go. And I can't really do my thing until the Araktak have finished with the transferring of the dead. It would be a gross injustice if I tried to conduct any research or look for relics while the bones of the dead remain in the mound."

Derek nodded. "So, until they finish with the bodies, you're stuck here doing, well, what, exactly?"

"Morale booster?"

Derek smirked. "Okay. I won't touch that one." He pointed at the ground-radar unit. "That working well?"

"Seems to be."

"Show me the display of the burial mound again."

"Why?"

"I want to see it again."

Annja nodded and set some of the probes into the ground. The machine took a while to heat up in the cold of the coming night air, but then the gentle hum sounded and Annja looked at Derek. "You ready?"

"Sure."

Annja pressed the button and a series of beeps sounded. Slowly, the display screen revealed the shaft going down at the peculiar angle into the burial mound. Derek leaned closer to the screen.

"You weren't kidding about it going on and on, huh?"

"Nope."

He leaned back. "I wonder how far it goes."

Annja shook her head. "Like I said earlier, it's at least a thousand meters. The display screen won't show anything more than that until we take the unit into the burial mound and ping it again."

Derek looked around. "Could we do that now?"

Annja shook her head. "Didn't you just hear me tell you that I can't go in there until they've finished moving the bodies?"

"Yes. I heard you."

"I would assume the same thing applies to you, Derek."

"But wouldn't you like to know what we're dealing with here?"

"Of course. But I'm not in a hurry to throw any respect I earned being Friend of Bear back into their faces. I'd probably have to do battle with some extraterrestrial monster to win back that favor if I shirk it now."

"Well, I'd pay money to see that."

"I'll bet."

Derek looked around. "No one's here. Let's just do it quickly and then we can get back out before they even know we were down there."

Annja shook her head. "I don't think so. And Wishman didn't go with them. He might be old and somewhat tied to his ancient beliefs, but that doesn't make him stupid."

"I never said he was."

Annja sighed. "But you're suggesting we go against what they asked of us just to satisfy our curiosity. I'm not going to participate in that kind of activity. It has the potential to disrupt everything we're working toward here. You should know that. I would have thought a company guy like yourself wouldn't risk it."

Derek took a breath and blew it out. "Yeah, I suppose you're right. I'm too damned curious for my own good sometimes. I see something like this and my mind just grabs at it like some lifeline. I tend to obsess over things in my life, especially things that spark my interest." He smirked. "When I was younger, it was the Loch Ness monster, bigfoot, UFOs, that kind of thing."

"A lot of kids are into that stuff."

Derek shook his head. "Not like I was. I had this old pseudo-storage-file system made from heavy-duty cardboard. It was like a beginner storage unit with drawers. I kept detailed files and personal notes on my thoughts and ideas about all those strange things."

"What'd your parents think about that?"

"My father always told me that I was obsessive. Of

course, I think he knew that it would eventually stop when I started discovering women."

"Was he right?"

"Oh, yes."

Annja nodded. "Well, I'm sure the Loch Ness monster is happy you turned out to be a diamond-mine employee rather than a cryptozoologist, huh?"

Derek grinned. "Probably so, yes."

Annja switched off the radar unit. "So, we're not going into the burial mound. That's settled, right?"

"Yeah, fine," Derek said. "It's too dark and cold out here anyway."

"Good," Annja said. "Weren't you expecting the imminent arrival of some miners today?"

Derek nodded. "Yeah, they haven't arrived yet. I tried them on the radio but got no response."

"Is that normal?"

Derek shrugged. "Radio interference is nothing new up here. The landscape plays hell with radio signals."

"But you got the text from the company via satellite yesterday, right?"

"Yes. But these guys have a standard CB in the truck they're in."

"Mr. Wainman."

They both turned and saw Wishman standing there in the darkness. Annja frowned. He was awfully close to them. Had he been hiding in the darkness listening to their conversations? And if so, for how long? Annja hoped he hadn't heard Derek plotting to get into the burial mound.

Derek kept his face from showing surprise. "Hello, Wishman."

Wishman pointed behind him. "There will be a truck

arriving in the next few minutes. I assume these are the men your company has sent."

"I don't hear anything," Derek said.

"Nevertheless, they will arrive," Wishman replied. And then he walked off into the darkness.

Derek glanced at Annja and then cleared his throat. "Well, I guess we'd better go and see about welcoming them to their new home."

16

As Annja and Derek walked back through the trees, they could already hear the crunching tires of the truck as it drove in over the snow. The headlights bounced and waggled as it maneuvered down the bumpy path. Finally, the truck came to a stop and six men climbed out.

Derek strode over. "Which one of you is Hansen?"

A bulky man zipping up his coat raised his hand. "Here."

Derek nodded and shook his hand. "Glad you guys arrived intact. I tried reaching you on the radio but I got nothing back."

Hansen pointed at the truck. "Damned thing's busted. Not good for anything except listening to static. Trust me, we're damned glad to see the lot of you here. Time was we were getting worried about making it here in time to see where we were going. Any longer and they would have found us frozen solid somewhere out there."

Derek nodded. "Hungry?"

"Famished. We left this morning and haven't stopped but for gas."

"I'm not sure where we're going to be able to put you. The conditions are a little…rustic."

Hansen shrugged. "No matter. We can crash on the floor tonight and get a shelter of our own started tomorrow. As long as you've got a fire going, with some coffee and food, we should be fine."

"Good." Derek smiled. "I'm guessing you'll be in our lodge. Not sure the Araktak will take too kindly to you being in their shelter."

"Sort of a sticky situation here, then, is it?"

Derek shrugged. "We're on tenuous ground perhaps. We have a done deal with these people, but they want time to move their deceased to another area. Headquarters has gone back on that deal somewhat by bringing you guys out well ahead of time. It hasn't gone over swimmingly with them."

Hansen shrugged. "Can't say I blame 'em. I'd be madder than hell if someone tried to change the rules on me midway through the game." He spit a wad of tobacco on the ground. "Not to worry, Mr. Wainman. I'm sure once we get ourselves squared away, these Araktak guys will see me and the boys are pretty much the same as them. We just got a job to do is all."

Annja raised an eyebrow. "That's awfully enlightened of you to say."

Hansen turned as if seeing Annja for the first time. "And just what did you say your name was there again, miss?"

"I didn't," Annja said.

Hansen tucked his chin and grinned. "Pardon me, then."

Derek sighed. "This is Annja Creed, Hansen. She's here on special assignment for the company. Her role is to conduct a search for any relics or lingering items that belong to the Araktak people. She's to help them relocate the sanctity of this land to a new location."

"Never heard of anyone relocating a burial ground," Hansen said. "Of course, that don't mean all that much. People got different ideas on doing things every damned day, right?" He guffawed once and then spit on the ground again.

Annja pointed at the sickly brown stain on the white snow. "You might want to watch out where you spit around here, it being sacred ground and all."

Hansen looked mollified. "Oh, yeah, you're right. Sorry about that, Mr. Wainman. Won't happen again."

"I appreciate that." Derek pointed out the shelter amid the pines. "We're in that lodge there."

Hansen turned back to the five other men and waved them on. "Okay, fellas, let's get our gear inside and rest up." He glanced at Derek. "Where's the chow?"

Derek pointed to the main lodge. "That's where we have dinner, although it's still a bit early. We ate rather after sunset last night."

Hansen shrugged. "We can wait."

Annja watched them troop off toward the shelter. "Our place isn't exactly big enough for that bunch of brutes."

"Brutes?"

Annja smirked. "Well, they are big guys."

"They're miners," Derek said. "Different breed of men. What else would you call a person who willingly descends into the bowels of the earth in order to dig out its most precious treasures?"

"They're like modern-day dwarves," Annja said. "Except for the fact that those guys are pretty big."

"I think they'd like the analogy," Derek said. "To them, the pride is in doing their work and doing it well. The diamond miners of Canada are especially proud of what they do. They don't have the black lung that plagues coal miners, but they do have their own health issues. Still, the promise of that shiny gem makes them work all the harder."

"Even though at the end of the day the treasure goes to the company."

Derek nodded. "True enough."

There was a rush behind them and Nyaktuk led a small group hurrying along the trail. Annja spotted a litter and stepped forward. "What in the world?"

Nyaktuk held up his hand. "Your man got trapped partly under the ice. His foot got wrapped in a vine of some sort. We had to work to free him. But he is in trouble. He is too cold."

They carried the litter past them and Annja could see Godwin's bluish face in the dim light. Piles of clothes had been placed atop him while the other Araktak men walked behind and beside the litter almost nude.

Nyaktuk directed them into the main lodge. Annja and Derek rushed to follow.

Inside, the fire blazed and a wall of heat hit them upon entering. Wishman sat close by stoking the fire to greater heights and intensity than it had been during the feast.

Annja shook her head. How in the world did Wishman manage to be in so many places at almost the same time? They'd only seen him out in the woods a few minutes earlier and yet, here he was back at the fire in the main lodge, adding fuel and seemingly completely unconcerned with anything.

As soon as he saw Godwin's face, however, he moved quickly. He bent closer to Godwin and listened to the scattered breaths that came from him. He looked at Nyaktuk and motioned for them to turn Godwin on his side.

"He has too much water in him. Until it is expelled I can do nothing to draw out the cold."

The men turned Godwin over and Nyaktuk pelted Godwin's back with his hard fists near the shoulder blades. The percussive strikes startled Godwin into a coughing fit that gave way to retching. Finally, he vomited a lot of water that splayed across the dirt floor of the lodge before being absorbed by the soil.

Wishman nodded. "Good. Turn him on his back once more."

This time Wishman listened a second or two longer to Godwin's breathing. He glanced up at Nyaktuk. "The water is gone. The cold remains. He must be warmed by the spirits."

To Annja, this meant little, but Nyaktuk and the men seemed to understand implicitly. They moved Godwin closer to the fire and for the first time Annja noticed a small bed of dense pine boughs on the floor. Godwin's body was lowered gently onto the boughs. Then the men piled their clothes on him again and waited.

Wishman took up a slender wooden pole and began chanting in his own dialect. He sprinkled the air with bits of some powder and then tossed a few different herbs into the blazing hearth. Annja heard the snap and pop of several of them and a delicate scent oozed into the room.

Wishman's voice sallied higher and lower, dancing over tones and rhythms of some ancient origin. Annja found the lull of the strange chanting irresistible. The perfume of herbs that hung in the air called out to her and she felt her eyelids droop before starting again to stay awake.

The fire blazed harder now despite the fact that no one had added any fuel to it or even stoked it. The flames seemed to reach out of the hearth itself toward Godwin's prone figure. They licked toward the pine boughs and then for just an instant, seemed to touch Godwin's body itself. Briefly, Annja could swear that the fire turned a different shade of yellow, but then she blinked and everything seemed to be back to normal.

Wishman's chanting died down into a soft rhyming mumble of syllables and clucks from the back of his mouth. It reminded Annja of the language the bushmen of Africa spoke, but such a thing wasn't possible.

Or was it?

Wishman's voice finally died with a final stroke of the pole he carried and then the fire popped one last time.

Godwin's eyes fluttered and he woke up.

Annja glanced at Derek but he only shrugged, seemingly as confused as she was by the entire ordeal.

Nyaktuk held a bottle of something to Godwin's lips. "Drink this."

Godwin drank from it and coughed instantly. Nyaktuk urged him to drink more and then at last, Godwin was able to do so without choking on it.

Wishman looked at Annja. "Your friend will be fine now, Friend of Bear. Have no more worry about this. Tomorrow he will be in good health again."

"Thank you very much," Annja said.

"It is part of the things that have to be done." Wishman bowed his head once and then smiled at her. "Now you understand a little bit more about us."

Godwin raised himself up on his elbows. "Sorry for the trouble."

Derek waved his hand. "What happened?"

"They cut through the ice on the river and we went in. I ducked under and was trying to get my bearings when my foot touched something. Before I knew it, it felt like I was being pulled under. It was the strangest thing! I panicked and took in a lot of water. If these guys hadn't been there, I would have been a goner."

Godwin reached out to Nyaktuk. "Thank you and all of you for what you've done for me."

Nyaktuk nodded solemnly and then, remembering that he and his men were without their clothes, scrambled to get some on because Annja was present.

She averted her eyes. "Nothing I haven't seen before, guys, really."

But they continued to dress and even Godwin managed to find the strength to do so quickly.

The door to the lodge opened as they were pulling on their pants. Hansen and his crew strode in and stopped short.

Hansen's mouth dropped open. "What in the hell—?"

Derek held up his hand. "Hypothermia treatment. That's all, Hansen."

Hansen chewed his lip. "I've been around the cold a long time, but I ain't seen nothing yet that means a guy's got to get down to his birthday suit to help out another fellow who's cold."

Wishman frowned. "Then you haven't seen all there is to see, young man, have you? These men bore your friend back here using their clothes to help keep him warm. If they had not done so, he should be dead by now."

Hansen chewed his lip some more and finally nodded. "Well, I thank you for that. Just a bit weird opening the door and seeing what looked like an ass party happening, you know?"

Annja had to fight not to smile. "'Ass party'?"

Hansen inclined his head. "Nothin' but ass, Miss Creed."

"Thanks for clarifying that."

"You bet."

Derek cleared his throat. "Wishman, these are the men

from the company that I told you would be coming out here today. They will stay the night in our shelter and then tomorrow build one for themselves."

Hansen nodded. "However, we'd be most thankful if we could partake in some food with you all. We haven't had a bite all day and we're starved."

Wishman's frown finally eased some and he nodded. "Very well. We will eat together and try to make sense of this situation as it has become. We do not wish to upset the company with whom we have bargained. But neither do we wish to see our ancestors defiled ahead of the time we were given to relocate them."

Hansen held up his hand. "Mr. Wishman, if we do our job right, you won't even know we're here."

"Very well." Wishman nodded for the men to assemble the meal. "Come and join us and eat with us."

Annja moved to Godwin's side as he finished buttoning his shirt. "Are you really all right now?" she asked.

He nodded. "I think so. Damned weird thing it was, though. 'Specially when they got me back here."

Derek leaned closer. "Was that all some sort of big show for our benefit?"

Annja shook her head. "Didn't seem to be. And the fact is, Godwin's alive now as a result of something."

"Yeah, but what? Not magic, was it?" Derek asked.

Annja shrugged. "I don't know. I'm pretty skeptical about that kind of thing. But I have seen a lot of unexplained stuff in my travels."

"How's that one rank?" Derek asked.

"Right near the top," Annja said.

17

In the darkness, Annja slept, exhausted by the day's efforts. Her breathing issued smoothly in and out of the black night as the camp lay wrapped in the cold of the land that surrounded them. Every now and again, the gales would cause part of the shelter to flutter in time to the rise and fall of the wind before once again allowing silence to drape itself over the shelter.

Annja's muscles relaxed in time to her breathing, sinking her consciousness ever lower to a state of complete rest. She stayed there, allowing her mind to drift along the dreamscape of swirled memories, vivid imaginings and a cloaked sense of what the future might hold in store for her.

She slept surrounded by an ocean of snores sent forth from the blowholes of the miners who camped on the floor. They'd spent several hours feasting on the meal laid out by the Araktak. Contrary to the discomfort Annja expected the miners to feel when they saw the assortment of game the Araktak ate, the miners embraced the game-filled diet, eating their fill while simultaneously listening as the Araktak warriors regaled them with stories of great hunts, elusive prey and a great narwhal that had become for them, at least for a time, a kind of Moby Dick.

The miners, in turn, told the Araktak fantastic stories of their adventures deep with the earth, spinning tales of passages suddenly collapsing, the rush for fresh air, the panic that ensued and the darkness.

Always, it came back to the darkness.

Their eyes shone as they told of the friends they'd lost to the darkness. To the hardened miners, it was almost like a beast kept at bay only with the help of light. As long as the electricity remained on, the beast was stayed.

But the few who had been trapped during a cave-in and lived to tell the tale spoke of the darkness and its hunger for souls. It preyed on the fear of being robbed of sight. It lapped at the minds of those buried alive, wondering if their rescue would ever come. More than a few had been driven insane by the relentless assault of the darkness on the minds of otherwise sane men.

In the end, Hansen had produced several bottles of Canadian whiskey and passed them around. They had all imbibed the liquid fire, and Annja herself had felt the shivers of the terror that had been sneaking into her own mind felled by the strong drink.

Hansen hefted the bottle at last and spoke only a few words. "To them who walk forever under us."

His men had murmured their agreement and to her surprise, the Araktak had echoed Hansen's solemn salute.

Annja had glanced at Derek, who had chosen not to drink the whiskey, and shot him a look. He only shrugged and then excused himself, saying he was already tired.

The miners and the Araktak men stayed up late. Godwin

and Annja found themselves increasingly cut out of the bond that was forming between the hardened Inuit warriors and the oversize dwarves of deep earth.

Annja helped Godwin back to the shelter and got him into his bed. He still shivered occasionally and as Annja tucked the blankets in around him, he had grabbed her hand.

"I thought I was gone," he said.

Annja nodded. "You almost were. They saved you."

He nodded. "I wonder if that means they'll accept me."

Annja shrugged. "I have no idea. But I wouldn't rush right out again and try to die again. They might pick up on your scheme." She smiled at him. "Get some rest. We've still got a lot of work to get through tomorrow. And knowing them, they'll expect you at peak condition for it."

"Thanks."

Annja crawled to her own bed, noting that Derek was already snoring softly on his side. She frowned. What made him so tired?

But the whiskey had dulled her own senses and as Annja lay deep in the folds of her bedding, she succumbed to the onslaught of sleep. She lengthened her breathing, allowed her eyes to roll back slightly in her head and soon enough was fast asleep.

Until now.

Something sparked inside the dream state she resided in. A brief flash poked out of the muddled land of dreams, pinpoint in its delivery, jabbing her almost fully awake immediately.

But Annja had long ago learned not to sit bolt upright with open eyes. Instead, she stayed perfectly still, keeping her breathing rhythm exactly the same as it had been.

Was she in trouble?

She opened her eyes slowly, accepting the limitations in the almost total darkness of the shelter and the night.

A sudden brief blast of cold wind stole into the shelter and then vanished. Around her, the bodies of the miners shifted in subconscious response, but then returned to normal.

Except for Annja.

Someone had opened the door. But had someone come in? Or had someone left?

She couldn't fathom walking around outside in the middle of the night. Not in this cold. It was almost suicidal. And she'd been in the woods enough to know that at night, it was terribly easy to wander in the wrong direction, lose your way and end up lost and dying from exposure.

She turned over onto her side and scanned the room as much as she could. She counted several distinct breathing patterns emanating from the floor. Six of them to be exact.

So the miners were all accounted for.

Godwin rested in his bed, snoring slightly. She almost smirked. There was no way he'd be going anywhere tonight. He was lucky just to be alive.

Annja snored once, turned over onto her left side and looked at Derek's bed.

She saw the rumple of blankets and his sleeping bag. But the zipper was open and the bed was empty.

Derek was gone.

Annja frowned. What was he up to? And where had he gone?

She thought about earlier this evening when he'd wanted to go into the burial mound and use the ground radar to see farther into the shaft.

Annja sighed. If Wishman caught him doing that, the whole agreement could be jeopardized.

More likely, it would make the somewhat tense conditions around camp more tense. The miners didn't seem to have any problems with the Araktak and vice versa, but Derek, Godwin and Annja were all somewhat less fortunate. Derek and Godwin represented the company. And Annja was a woman. An outsider, as well.

Anything that upset the delicate balance could result in serious repercussions. Wishman didn't look the type to take lightly to stupid moves such as the one Derek might be making right now.

Annja unzipped her own sleeping bag slowly, trying her best to keep the noise at a minimum. She detected no real change in the breathing patterns of the miners. Probably they were being helped to sleep by the whiskey they'd drunk. Their full bellies would have kept them more asleep than awake, as well.

Annja slid out of the bed, carefully picking her way through the maze of arms, legs and bellies. She put her coat on and then right by the door, she pulled her boots on, as well.

She grabbed the door handle and waited until one of the miners closest to her uttered a particularly loud snore. In that second, she shot out of the door, pulling it shut quickly before the cold could rouse any of the men.

Annja squatted outside the door and scanned the darkness. She detected no movement or anything else that would betray the presence of someone out in the night. She tied her boots and then zipped up her coat. She put her hat and gloves on now, as well.

The icy air cut at her face. She felt her sinuses open and then snap shut. She sniffed quietly and the air in front of her clouded as she exhaled.

A brief sickle of moon hung suspended against the black backdrop of sky, shedding just a little illumination across the area. The pines blocked most of it, sucking the light into the black hole of their long shadows.

Where would Derek have gone? Annja wondered. But even as she thought it, she knew too well that he would head right for the burial mound.

The question really was, what should she do?

She could wake Wishman and explain things to him and hope he'd understand. But in doing so, she would no doubt wake the rest of the Araktak men and they would be highly annoyed that Derek had gone where he was not supposed to.

Or she could simply try to get to Derek first and convince him that his idea was a really bad one.

She frowned.

She moved off through the snow, using the already trampled tracks to help muffle the sound of her steps. Fortunately, no new snow had fallen this night, meaning she would not crumple the ice crystals beneath her boots.

She paused at the edge of the trees and looked back at the camp. Nothing stirred in its sleepy grip. Annja took a final look and then pushed through the pines toward the burial mound.

She could smell the delicate scent of pine even in the midst of the frozen world. It reminded her of how much she loved the scent of it around Christmas.

Branches tugged at her sleeves, but Annja lowered herself even more until she cleared them all with ease. Her thighs burned but she was used to the strain on her legs. Being skilled at combat meant that she had strong legs. All the better for some of the crazy maneuvers she'd performed in the past and would no doubt perform in the future.

She came through the trees and saw the burial mound silhouetted against the night sky. She paused and took in

the entire scene. A friend of hers who had served in the
British special forces had once told her that tuning in to a
new environment sometimes meant just sitting still for
twenty minutes and letting your subconscious catalog everything around you.

But the area didn't have any wildlife to speak of. Annja
detected very little in the way of noise or ambient sounds.
Just the cold wind blowing over the plain and through the
trees. The vague rustle of something could be heard, but
nothing human seemed to stir in the dark.

Annja moved closer to the opening of the burial mound.
She could see the twinkle of something inside.

Derek had turned on the lights that the Araktak men had
strung up to help them underground.

What was he looking for?

Annja slid closer to the burial mound opening and could
hear scuffles and movement. Derek was definitely down
inside the shaft. Annja looked up and around.

The ground-radar unit was missing.

One glance at the ground confirmed that it had been
dragged down into the shaft. Annja shook her head. Curiosity was going to get them into serious trouble with the
Araktak tribe.

And all because Derek couldn't wait another day or
two for the transferring to be completed. The idiot.

Annja took a step into the shaft and paused. Should she
go down? It was bad enough that Derek was already inside.
Wishman, if he found out, would be insulted and outraged.

But what about her? She had some degree of status
within the tribe as Friend of Bear. Should she risk that to
make sure Derek didn't blow this entire operation?

How would the Araktak feel about a woman, even Annja,
going into the burial mound without their permission?

She sighed. It was either she go in and stop Derek or stay up here and call him out. In that case, she would probably wake up the Araktak.

And Annja was growing very cold standing out in the night air.

She took another look around. Perhaps Wishman had stationed guards to make sure that no one disturbed the site during the night.

She almost laughed. Who would be able to stand out here in the absolute freezing cold of night and stand guard? Certainly no one she knew of.

All right, then. She nodded. Time to go get him back.

Annja took a step into the shaft of the burial mound.

She promptly felt her feet go out from under her and she slid right down the shaft.

18

Somehow, Annja managed to keep from screaming out in surprise as she slid down the slick tunnel. She came to a rest by bumping into the squat yellow box containing the ground-radar unit and then looked up to see Derek staring down at her.

She grinned. "Hey."

He frowned. "You following me?"

Annja got to her feet and almost slipped again. "I didn't expect this to be so slippery."

Derek shrugged. "It is frozen, after all. You should have been more careful when you came down here."

"I wasn't intending to come down quite like that," Annja said. "Most times, I'm content to keep upright and walk carefully."

"Well, so much for that thought, huh?" He turned back to the shaft as if studying something. Annja brushed herself off and glanced back up toward the surface. Had anyone seen or heard her come down here?

"Derek," she said looking back. "We shouldn't be down

here. There's no telling what Wishman will do if he finds out we came into the burial mound before all of the bodies have been relocated. We were asked *not* to do this."

"So? He doesn't have to find out, does he?"

"It's not as though I'm going to go running to tell him," Annja said. "But we really should get out of here."

Derek shook his head. "I'm trying to get the radar set up so I can see how deep the shaft goes."

"Why are you so obsessed about this?"

Derek eyed her. "There's that word again."

Annja held up her hands. "All right. Sorry about that. I just don't get the rush. There will be time for this when Nyaktuk and his men are done with the bodies of the dead."

"You mean the bunches of bones?" Derek smiled. "The BOBs?"

"You definitely don't want to be making comments like that, Derek. Seriously, that's pretty disrespectful."

Derek glanced around at the numerous branches going off from the main shaft. "Well, really, it's not as though we're talking about the recently deceased, are we? Everyone that's here has been for at least several hundred years. Or more. And the decomposition has reduced them all to bones. It's not like Nyaktuk is going to pop into one branch and see his mother looking at him from behind some rotted-away visage, is he?"

"You're being disrespectful to the culture and also to your promise to them. Not like they haven't already been disappointed with the way this deal is resolving itself, Mr. Bearer of Bad News."

Derek shook his head. "Look, you can go right back to bed if you want. There's no need for you to share in the horror that I'm supposedly committing here. If Wishman finds out, the blame will be all mine."

"And what if he does find out? What then?"

"Then I'll deal with it."

A cold breeze swept down the shaft, making Annja shiver. "I don't get it, Derek. A day ago you were so concerned about letting the Araktak down and now you're standing here flagrantly ignoring their request to stay out of here until they were finished."

"Well, maybe I'm just incredibly curious." He continued positioning the radar unit and managed to set the second probe some distance down the shaft.

"Yes, you obviously are. I am, too—"

"Then help me."

Annja shook her head. "I can't be a party to this. My word has to mean something. And it would hurt Godwin, as well."

"Ah." Derek's eyes flashed at her. "I wondered if that was the case."

"What?"

He smirked. "Godwin."

"What about him?"

"You two. You've got something going on, haven't you? I heard you tuck him into bed earlier. It was all very Florence Nightingale and all, you know."

Annja sighed. "Godwin and I do not have anything going on, Derek. He nearly died today."

"Yes, that was supposedly what happened."

"Supposedly? You think he faked that?"

"Why not? He admitted that the Araktak haven't accepted him as one of their own. No doubt tonight's stunt aided him in that cause to be seen as one of their own. I have to tip my hat to him. It was a genius bit of planning. Took a lot of nerve to pull it off so convincingly, too."

"You're nuts."

"I most certainly am not."

Annja turned to leave. "I'm going to get Wishman. I don't want this destroying everything we're supposedly working for."

Derek prepared a hole and pushed another probe into the ground. "You won't go."

"Excuse me?"

Derek looked up at her. "You won't leave. Despite all your words and demonstrations about what I'm doing, there's a part of you that is desperate to know just how far the shaft goes. You hide it better than I do, and yes, maybe you've got a bit more self-control, but here we are—almost ready to fire up the unit and see what the truth is. All you've got to do is choose to stay."

Annja shook her head. "You underestimate me."

"Do I?" Derek watched her for another moment and then shrugged. "So, in that case, go do what you have to."

"You're not going to come out of here?"

"Nope."

Annja sighed. "You're damned frustrating, you know that? I never knew this side of you existed before."

Derek fiddled with the machine and then got the final probe ready. He scampered farther down the shaft to another fixed point and then drilled a hole and pushed the probe deep into the frozen ground.

He looked back up at her. "Haven't you left yet?"

"Shut up."

He smirked. "You see? It's got you, too, hasn't it?"

"What?"

Derek stood up and spread his arms. "This. This place. The tunnel. You can feel its life even as it bathes in the death of those who were buried here. It's almost a living thing. This shaft and the wind that passes over us even now, it's like something is breathing through this tube. We're on the road to its heart, the beating heart, at which lies an untold vein of diamonds and other precious minerals."

Annja shook her head. "I don't feel it. It's nothing but a mound of earth turned into something sacred by the people who used it."

"And just what do you think they did to make it holy ground?"

Annja shrugged. "I have no idea. They probably consecrated it somehow and that was it."

"Do you think that Wishman has magic abilities? That he could commune with the spirit world and turn this place into something living?"

"Like what he did earlier with Godwin? That was one thing. It was impressive as hell. But I'm still not sure if I'd call it magic."

"Then what would you call it?"

"I don't know. But this and the burial mound's traditions are something else. I don't know if one is connected to the other."

Derek frowned. "You're supposed to be an archaeologist, Annja. Surely you'd be the first to admit that there's always something of a connection. Especially when a secretive tribe like this is concerned. All of their traditions and history are interwoven. One ceremony to save a man's life from the ravages of hypothermia could very easily connect with a ceremony to consecrate a burial mound."

"Perhaps Wishman does have an arsenal of abilities that deal with this type of thing," Annja said. "But I have no knowledge of it."

"Your own sword," Derek said. "Isn't that proof enough of magic for you? Or do you cling to some silly notion that there's a scientific principle at work there?"

"I'm not sure what to make of that."

Derek's eyes narrowed. "You're being ridiculous. If I had such a thing, I would go insane trying to figure out exactly what it was and its origins. But again, if that's not magic, then what on earth is?"

"How about love."

Derek looked at her and then laughed. "Love is something that is lost to me."

"The love of a child is as magical as the love of the opposite sex. Surely you haven't forgotten about your children and their devotion to you?"

Derek stopped. "I miss my children very much. But my wife has custody and I get to see them very little."

"You still love them."

"I do."

"Then there's all the magic you need. Why quest for anything further?"

Derek examined the ground radar. "Because I can."

"If this goes wrong, you could lose your job. Then what would happen to your children?"

"They'd be fine. As I told you before, I've taken great pains to make sure they will always be taken care of."

"And I'm sure that as they grow up, they'll want to spend more time with you and make their own memories and judgments about whatever might have happened in the past—whatever it was that caused your wife to leave you."

Derek took a breath. "It's late. I'm tired and cold."

"Then haul this back to the surface and let's go back to the shelter and grab a few more hours of sleep. Tomorrow's a busy day," Annja said.

Derek smiled. "Maybe…no." He turned and flipped the switch on the radar.

Annja heard the series of beeps sound and Derek's face lit up. "There."

Annja frowned. "You shouldn't have done that."

"But I did." He examined the screen closely. "Now, that's interesting."

"What is?"

He looked up her. "Oh, I wouldn't dream of telling you anything about it. I don't want you to have to compromise your beliefs and your word. That wouldn't be fair to you."

"I could just beat the crap out of you," Annja said. "How would that be, Captain Wiseass?"

Derek grinned. "Curiosity getting the better of you, Annja? Is that drive sparking up in you? That push for answers? You know you want to find out how far this thing goes."

"Show me," Annja said. "Show me the screen."

Derek waved her over. "Come closer, then. I've got the unit perched on a small rise in the ground here and if I move it, I'll disrupt the picture."

Annja looked back up the shaft toward the surface. As far as she could tell, nothing stirred up top. What would the harm be in just taking a look? She could take a look and then get Derek to switch the unit off and haul it back out. If they did it right, they could make sure the shaft looked as though no one had been down here all night. And in the morning, no one would be the wiser.

She hoped.

"Annja, come on."

She turned back to Derek. "I'll take one quick look and then we get this place back to looking like we haven't been here, okay?"

He nodded. "Fair enough. You have my word."

"Oh, please. Like that's good for much."

Derek touched his hand to his chest. "You slay me."

Annja came over and squatted next to him. "Shut up. I'll deal with you another time. Now show me."

Derek pointed on the screen and Annja frowned. She could clearly see that the shaft continued on, but the angle of slope increased dramatically after another several hundred yards.

"Looks like an elbow, doesn't it?" Derek asked.

Annja nodded. "But what in the world is that?"

She pointed at the screen and Derek followed her gaze. He peered closer. Right before where the shaft turned into a steep angle of descent, a horizontal line barred the passage.

Derek shook his head. "I don't know, but it looks almost like…a door?"

19

Annja leaned back from the radar unit. "What in the world would a door be doing down here?"

"Wasn't there one over the burial mound leading down here?"

"Well, yeah," Annja said. "But it also doesn't explain the sudden increase in slope just beyond the door. To look at the display, the shaft goes almost vertical."

"I'd like to get a look at that door," Derek said. "Do you think we have time?"

Annja frowned. "We've pressed our luck far too much already. And I'm not at all pleased you made me stay here."

"I did no such thing. You stayed of your own volition, not due to any pressure from me."

Annja sighed. He was right, of course. Her curiosity had gotten the better of her. Or had it? Maybe Annja was supposed to stay down here for some other reason. The idea that the sword was controlling her came back into her head and she frowned. "Well, we might as well see what's behind the door."

Derek clapped his hands together. "Excellent. I'll rig the lights to extend farther down the shaft."

Annja watched him move away from the radar unit. She studied the screen. The shaft seemed to resemble a missile silo farther on. How far does it go down? she wondered. Does it ever stop? One thing seemed certain—Derek's mining company might have bought itself a huge trough of diamonds.

"Let's go." Derek's voice was a hushed shout. Annja glanced up and then switched off the radar unit. She moved down the shaft, careful of her footing. The ground farther on was dry and she felt a bit more confident, even though it still sloped down.

Derek pointed. "Do you see it?"

Annja did. The door looked as though it had been made from some type of dense wood but she couldn't identify it. It stood about eight feet high and the same width. Crosspieces braced it into position.

"It doesn't look like it was meant to open," Annja said. "Maybe it's not a door after all."

"Then what could it be?" Derek asked.

"Maybe it's a wall."

He frowned. "Why would anyone place a wall here? Why would they close off the shaft from the outside world?"

Annja shrugged. "I don't have any answers for that. All I know is I don't see any hinges and there doesn't seem to be a way to swing it open. The way this thing looks, it's been set into the sides of the earth. Who knows how far those pieces of wood extend into the earth?"

Derek walked closer to the door and ran his hands over the rough-hewn wood. "It feels almost warm."

Annja moved closer and she could feel the heat emanating from it. "I suppose that makes sense, depending on how far into the Earth it goes. We could be talking about some kind of thermal updraft from the interior of the Earth."

"Straight to the core," Derek said, his voice full of wonder. "It's incredible, isn't it?"

"It is cursed."

They spun around and saw Wishman standing there in the dim light of the shaft. He did not look happy.

Annja started to speak, but Wishman held up his hand. "Do not seek to quell my anger with your excuses." He frowned and shook his head. "I had hoped to avoid this, but such is the curiosity of man."

"Avoid what?" Annja asked.

Wishman gestured to the giant wall of wood. "That. The secret that my people have kept for many years."

Annja looked back at the wall of wood. "What is it? It doesn't seem to be a door."

Wishman scowled. "Well, that depends on who you ask. Some people would see it as a wall to keep something back. But from the other perspective, it would be seen as an exit for what lies beyond."

Annja looked at him. "What lies beyond?"

Wishman nodded. "The secret of this land."

Derek moved away from the wall. "What is the secret?"

"You would desire to know that, wouldn't you?" Wishman sighed. "Perhaps I am at fault in this, as well. I know well that when you forbid a child from doing something, they want nothing more than to run right out and do that very thing. So it was that I watched you from the woods this night. The spirits told me this would be the time you chose to seek your answers."

"But you didn't stop us," Derek said.

"Until now," Annja said.

Wishman leaned against the wall of the shaft. He

seemed to be breathing harder than usual. "What good does it do to stop the curious? Sooner or later they will seek their answers. And then they will have them. One way or another."

"Are you all right?" Annja started forward to help him. But Wishman raised his hand.

"I am all right. Probably the time I spent waiting in the cold of the woods, seeing if you would discover what you have."

"How long would you have waited?"

He smiled. "I heard your talk of going back to sleep. I prayed you would be successful in that, Friend of Bear. But you then gave in and wished to see what he wishes. And then I knew that as soon as your machine drew you the picture, you would need to investigate further. That was when I came down here."

"I slipped and fell," Annja said. "How did you manage such sure footing?"

Wishman waved his hands as if dismissing a mosquito. "I did not get to be my old age by being a clumsy oaf," he said. "My feet have known far more treacherous surfaces than the likes of this burial mound."

"I wasn't exactly clumsy," Annja said. "The ground was slippery is all. I'm usually quite good on my feet."

"I'm sure you are," Wishman said. "However, you were not tonight. I should thank you for the brief humor I enjoyed listening to you attempt to sneak up on him."

"Glad to help," Annja said. "Now, tell us about this curse or whatever this thing is."

Wishman beckoned Derek. "I should ask you to come away from that area or your presence may draw it closer to us. Probably even now it senses our flesh and would like nothing better than to do away with that wall once and for all."

"'It'?"

Wishman nodded. "The creature that lives beyond the wall."

"What creature?" Annja said.

"A terrible thing. In my youth we hunted it mercilessly, but still it eluded us until we found this burrow. We guarded it with armed warriors, poking our spears into the entrance to keep it at bay. The shaft of the tunnel was far too narrow for it to escape and engage us in the open."

Wishman shook his head. "We summoned a shaman from a faraway village to come and use all of his magic to set the thing back deep within the shaft so we could imprison it within. For five long days, while we kept it inside, the shaman stood here in a trance and he chanted his most powerful magics, using a variety of spells to drive the creature back."

The old man shivered then. "It howled as we drove it back further into the shaft. Its pain was evident, but we had seen too many of our people taken by the creature. Never would we find any trace of them save for a spare item of clothing. They were dragged down here and consumed whole."

"But what is it?" Derek asked. "Some kind of animal?"

"At one time," Wishman said. "Now it is probably more an angry spirit than anything tangible. It has been locked here for years. Imagine our horror when we found that it had made a burrow out of our burial mound. It lived in our most sacred ground, adding more death to the numbers we stored here, unknowing of its presence."

"So what happened?" Annja asked.

"The shaman forced the creature back further and further until it slunk down the deepest part of the shaft. Then he made us construct the wall you see there. We toiled hard and fast to make the wall. None of us thought it would be enough to hold the fury of the creature back, but the shaman bade us do as we were told. And when we had finished its construction, he ordered us back to the surface. He alone stayed down here in the shaft. And then he called out his magics again, using them to mystically seal the creature behind the wooden wall. No amount of strength would ever free it from its captivity. As long as the wall remained in place, the creature would never again bother the Araktak people. Or anyone else for that matter."

Annja took a breath. "But now…" Her voice trailed off as she started to realize the implications of the wall.

Wishman nodded. "So, you do see the problem after all, Friend of Bear. Then perhaps you are not as reckless as this one here."

Derek frowned. "I am sorry for going against your word, Wishman. But this land doesn't belong to you anymore. It belongs to the company."

Wishman's eyes twinkled. "And what would you have the company do with the awful truth of what lies beyond that wall?"

"I don't know what lies beyond the wall," Derek said. "And the men I work for are not used to dealing with legends of horrible monsters. They are used to making money."

"And that will be their downfall," Wishman said. "For to disregard what I have told you is far more dangerous than believing it."

"Surely no creature could survive for as long as it has been locked behind that wall," Annja said. "Do you truly think there's still a danger?"

Wishman nodded. "Not a danger of the flesh, but of the spirit. Such a creature as this would never go off quietly to the afterlife. It would seek vengeance on those who imprisoned it all those years ago."

"On you."

Wishman nodded. "I am the last of the original group who hunted the creature. It is why I have become the shaman of the Araktak. I needed to learn the skills of the shaman we originally summoned if I had any hope of dealing with this being."

Derek cleared his throat. "Look, I don't mean to be a real jerk here, but frankly, I'm not sure I buy all of this."

Annja glanced at him, but he kept talking.

"I mean, Wishman, if you're trying to renegotiate the deal, then perhaps this stuff is better saved for the company's lawyers. Fact of the matter is, you were only too happy to sell us this land when we sent Godwin here originally."

Wishman shook his head. "That decision was made by the younger members of my tribe who have no knowledge of this creature. They want the modern life that plagues the rest of the world. Only a few of us know of the horror that lies beyond."

"Nyaktuk," Annja said. "He knows."

Wishman nodded. "Indeed. He has been my apprentice for many years. He is already becoming skilled at certain magic."

"All this talk of magic," Derek said. "I don't know if I can buy into it."

Annja shot him a look. "Now you're just being hypocritical. Only a few minutes ago, you told me about your obsession with things like this. And now, when Wishman tells you that something…otherworldly lies beyond that wall, you decide it's time to be all clinically detached? It's ridiculous."

"Your magic is different than the tall tales that this guy is weaving," Derek said. "I think it's just an elaborate shakedown."

Wishman looked at Annja. "I thought I recognized

something about you when you came into camp. A presence about you."

Annja waved him off. "I'd rather we kept the talk centered around the wall and what we're going to do about it."

"You believe, then?"

Annja shrugged. "I don't know what to believe. I've seen a lot of crazy things in my time. And I've dealt with some unusual animals, as well. Right now, my main concern is making sure we don't open some kind of Pandora's box here."

Wishman nodded at Derek. "You would do well to listen to your friend. She has much wisdom, no doubt gained by hard experience."

Derek frowned. "I don't need to be told what to do or who to listen to."

Annja shook her head. "I don't know that I even understand you anymore, Derek."

Derek smiled. "Well, that's just going to have to be something we work on, I guess." He nodded and looked beyond them. "Did you bring it?"

Annja and Wishman turned. Hansen stood behind them. Annja glanced down and saw that he held something about the size of a book in his hands.

"Right here."

"Hansen?"

He smiled at Annja. "Evenin'."

"What have you got there?"

He smiled. "Just a little something Mr. Wainman asked us to bring up from Yellowknife."

Annja caught a whiff of something in the air. It smelled like marzipan. "Oh, no, not that."

Derek grinned. "You are sharp. I should have known you'd know what it smelled like."

Wishman glanced at her. "What does he have?"

"Explosives," Annja said. "Semtex by the smell of it. Czech military grade, if I'm not mistaken."

Wishman whipped his head around to face Derek. "No. You must not do what you intend to do. Do not blow up that wall. You mustn't!"

Derek reached for the explosive from Hansen. "Well, here's the deal. You can either walk your butts back up top or you can stay down here and be inside when this thing goes. But one way or another, that wall is coming down."

20

Annja looked at Wishman. "I think he's serious," she said.

Wishman kept staring at Derek and Hansen as they placed a ring of explosives around the wall at key points. Derek seemed to be humming happily and the difference in his attitude shocked Annja.

"You've changed."

He smiled at her. "You're cute, Annja, but terribly naive."

"Oh?"

Hansen chuckled. "I think she'd love to know what you're talking about."

"No doubt. Too bad she's not going to find out anything right now. We've got work to do."

"We could kill them both right now and no one would know. It would just be one of those terrible little accidents that happens in mining," Hansen said.

Derek looked as if he was considering it, a fact that made Annja's blood boil. She could rip the sword out now and kill them both.

Derek pointed at her. "Don't even try it, Annja. You make any gesture like you're going to pull that damnable sword of yours out and I'll hit the detonator and kill us all. And if you think I'm bluffing, go right ahead and try me. See how wrong you truly are."

Annja stopped. She knew he would do it. At this point, the safest bet seemed to be to assume that whatever Derek had told her up until this point was nothing but a pack of horrible lies.

Hansen, however, eyed Annja carefully. "What sword?"

Derek laughed. "Oh, you should see the little blade our girl there has. Quite the trick she can do, pull the thing out from nowhere and put it back again. That's what she used to dispatch Leon."

Annja frowned. "Who is Leon?"

"He was my friend, for one thing," Hansen said.

Derek's smile grew even further. "Leon was driving the truck that nearly ran us over."

Annja shook her head. "That was a setup?"

"Of course."

"But you were in the truck, too. You could have been killed. It doesn't make any sense."

Derek sniffed. "I was never in any real danger. And even if I was, death isn't something that I particularly fear to any great extent."

"I'll remember that when I run my sword through your worthless guts." Annja bit her lip. "And Godwin? Is he a part of this charade, as well?"

"Godwin was never anything but a pawn to me," Derek said. "He has no idea what he has been a part of. And I think he's probably still sleeping off that near-death experience anyway, so why don't we just leave him be?"

Wishman held up his hand. "My men will kill you for your treachery."

"Your men are all sound asleep and will be for some time," Hansen said. "That little party we had last night saw to that."

"You drugged them?" Annja asked.

Hansen nodded. "Yup. You left early so I guess you managed to avoid any of the effects."

Derek fixed the detonation cord on the last package of explosive. "There. All set with that lot."

Hansen checked the wiring and then nodded. "Looks good."

Derek wiped his hands on his jacket. "Now, then. What to do with our Araktak shaman and the mystical swordswoman. Choice, choices…"

"What will be most interesting," Wishman said, "is what will happen to you when you open up that wall there. I have warned you of the consequences of your actions and yet you choose to defy it. I will take great pleasure in seeing your reeducation once that wall is destroyed."

Derek smiled. "Yes, you have indeed warned me, old man. But you should know that I have known of what lies beyond that wall for many years now. And long have I sought to find this place. Now, at last, we have the means to free the being from beyond. And when we do, we will be able to use it to further our own agenda."

Wishman shook his head. "The creature will never bend to your will. You aren't strong enough to force it to submit. Only those of a higher power mind may exert influence over it."

Hansen glanced at Derek and chuckled. "I see you've sold them on the divorce story again."

"I'm tired of it," Derek said. "But you know, it does work ever so well given our modern society and all."

"Did you include the kids this time?"

Derek's eyes flashed with glee. "The kids make the whole thing come together all the better. Otherwise, it's just a boring sob story about a man and a woman never meant to be. But the kids, they add a whole new layer of emotional baggage. It's great stuff."

Annja sighed. "If you're going to stand here and sing the glories of your charade, I'd rather go back up top and head to bed."

Wishman glanced at her. "There will be no sleep this night if they blow up that wall."

Derek looked at Annja. "The shaman thinks the creature behind the wall will rampage upon being released."

"Will it?" Annja asked.

"Of course not," Derek said. "Hansen and I have the means to control it. And we will."

"Fools," Wishman said. "Let me go and I will gladly flee from this place. I will walk the countryside and take my chances with the environment. And if that beast comes for me, I will meet it on my own two feet rather than huddled in horror at the back of a cabin."

Hansen smiled. "I love the way you speak. Reminds me of an old horror film."

Wishman's expression was almost sad. "You, my son, shall be the first to die when the beast is freed from its cage. You think you have the means but you do not. And tonight, you will learn how very awful that truth is indeed."

Hansen looked at him for another moment and then turned back to Derek. "Can't we just kill them?"

Derek shook his head. "We still need them for appearances' sake. And besides, I will take great joy in seeing the shaman realize how wrong he is when we successfully control the creature."

Annja looked around. "Does this have anything to do with diamonds at all? Or was that just another one of your stories?"

Derek shrugged. "There are plenty of diamonds here. But their value is inconsequential to what we truly desire. The company will mine here, yes, but our focus has forever been on the release of the creature."

"Why?"

"Because we answer to a different god."

Wishman's eyes narrowed. "You worship the dark gods."

"Different names," Hansen said. "But I guess you're in the ballpark."

"And your god told you to free this being?" Annja asked.

"Our god is this being," Hansen said. "And when it was imprisoned here, it reached out with its mind until it found a receptive consciousness that could understand it and learn from it."

"Learn from it how?"

Derek flipped up a switch on the detonator. "We live in a world where money is an unfortunate necessity to the greater plans of man. Our god taught us how to realize riches beyond our wildest dreams. Those riches in turn fueled our quest to free our god. When we could buy anything, including powerful members of government, we became better able to realize the goal of freeing our dark master."

Hansen smiled. "And when we used Godwin as our unwitting counterfeit, all the Araktak saw was a half-breed they could despise. Their attention was so focused on him that they never sensed our approach until it was too late."

"And here we stand," Derek said. "At the moment of greatness."

"Shouldn't your corporate masters be here with you?" Annja asked. "Isn't this also their moment of greatness?"

"They're far too old now to be here," Derek said. "Hansen and I were chosen to lead this mission. And when we have freed our god, he will reward us all with immortality."

"Empty promises," Wishman hissed. "He will promise you whatever it is your heart most desires. But he will never give your rewards to you in the way you imagine them."

"Is that so?" Derek said.

Wishman spit on the ground. "Your immortality will be spent as an eternity of suffering in the fires of Hell. Your god will never share his freedom and power with you, but only subjugate you to the lowest pits of the flame."

Derek waved his hands. "All right, enough of this. Let's get out of here and get this done. The sun will be up in an hour or so."

"That will be the optimal time," Hansen said. "According to what they told us back home."

Derek nodded. "Get them out of here."

Hansen pulled a gun out from under his jacket. "All right, you two, let's go. And Annja, no tricks. I even see you move funny and I'll put a bullet into your heart from behind. And this gun is packed with the kind of bullets that will go right through whatever you've got on like it's not even there."

"Fine." Annja walked behind Wishman and her mind raced. Was there really a creature behind the wall? Why did they even need her in the first place?

Derek came alongside of her. "You're here because of

what you represent, Annja. As I said at our first meeting, we know all about you. You helped sell the Araktak on our mission, but you and your sword are also quite the cherry on top of the lovely icy sundae."

Annja looked at him. "I am really going to enjoy killing you. And that's not something I normally do."

"What? Kill people?" Derek laughed. "I beg to differ, given your rather bloody record."

Annja shook her head. "I'm not denying the deaths I've caused. But I've never enjoyed the act. I've always viewed it as a something of a necessity. Lives taken to spare innocents. But you are different."

"I like being different," Derek said. "But you should know that I am not an easy mark. And I will not fall as easily as some of your other victims."

"Victims?" Annja almost laughed. "Those who have fallen because of my blade have all seen the justice they so richly deserved. You'll see it soon enough, as well, Wainman. If that's even your real name."

"My real name needn't concern you," Derek said. "And it's such an inconsequential thing, you won't even remember being concerned about it once we blow the wall in the next hour."

Annja climbed the slope and soon felt the icy gust of the exterior on her face. Wishman kept quiet as he clambered out of the burial mound.

Annja glanced at Derek. "What if you're wrong?"

"Excuse me?"

"What if this is all wrong? What if Wishman is right? That your bargain with your god is just a sham. You could be spelling out your own doom and not even know it."

"Oh," Wishman said, "but they are."

"Shut up," Derek said. He looked at Hansen. "How long until the dawn breaks over the horizon?"

Hansen checked his watch. "Perhaps forty minutes."

Derek nodded. "I'll make a fire to keep us warm until then. No sense freezing to death while we wait."

Wishman smiled. "A fruitless gesture, fool. You'll taste death sooner than you think. Once that wall comes down, this world will be a terrible place."

Annja felt herself slipping away from reality. Where was the truth in these words she heard from both sides?

And would it be too late when she finally found out for certain?

21

Annja watched as Derek gathered a bundle of thick branches, long dehydrated by the pervasive winter winds, into a stout pile over a small bundle of tinder and kindling. He stooped and set a lick of flame to the smallest pieces and then stood back as the fire ate at the dried wood. After a minute, a blaze illuminated the area, spreading only a moderate degree of warmth.

Derek gestured to Annja and Wishman. "You're welcome to move closer to the fire, but Annja, don't do anything to make Hansen put a bullet in you. Any move and he won't hesitate to kill you."

"I don't doubt it," Annja said. She moved closer to the fire listening as the twigs and branches crackled. Wishman stayed back, however, seemingly unconcerned with the fact that the temperature hovered around minus thirty-five degrees.

Derek regarded him. "You're not cold, old man?"

Wishman's eyes flashed. "I'll warm myself with the thought that your bones will soon be cooked off of your pathetic body."

Derek shrugged. "Suit yourself."

Hansen checked his watch, but kept the gun trained on Annja. "About a half hour left."

Derek nodded. "You brought it?"

"Of course." Hansen shrugged. "Not much point in doing this otherwise, is there?"

"Brought what?" Annja asked. She saw Derek glance at Hansen and she sighed. "Come on, guys. Don't you want to prove what big boys you are and let me witness your obvious superior intellect? What's the big secret? Afraid I'll rain on your parade?"

Derek shrugged. "I don't much care what you think, Annja. If you'd rather have me kill you here and now, just tell me and I'll spare you any further discomfort."

Annja shrugged. "Like *you'd* kill me. You'd just have Hansen back there do it."

"I'll kill you myself," Derek said.

"Right," Annja said. "You don't have the nerve."

Derek stepped closer to her but kept the fire between them. In the firelight, his face looked somehow different as shadows leaped and twisted all over his molten visage.

"I assure you that I most certainly do have the nerve, as you put it. And I will gladly rip your heart out through your chest if you'd prefer it that way." He sighed. "Or perhaps you think your god will come to your aid. Perhaps you believe that the sword grants you some type of invulnerability?"

Annja frowned. "Well, it didn't work out that well for the original owner, now, did it?"

"Perhaps she found heaven through the fires of her death," Derek said.

Hansen chuckled behind her. Annja felt herself growing angry at their obvious derision.

Wishman moved up closer to the fire suddenly. Derek

smiled. "A little too cold for you back in the shadows, Wishman? Well, fine, warm yourself by our fire. Enjoy these last vestiges of humanity."

Wishman stared at him, but Annja noticed that he didn't look especially cold. He glanced at Annja. "What he says about this blade you carry. Is it true?"

Annja nodded. "Yes. I'm not sure why I was chosen to carry it, but I seem to have little to no choice in the matter."

"You were chosen to carry it for the same reason that the polar bear did not maul you."

"And that would be?"

Wishman's eyes softened just a speck. "Isn't it obvious? You are a bastion of good in an otherwise evil world."

"I don't want that role."

"We cannot choose our destinies. They are dealt out well in advance of our physical arrival on this earth. Here, we merely play the roles that the gods have assigned to us. Whatever they may be."

Annja watched the flames dance. "I feel like I'm in an old school play with the role that I never wanted."

Wishman gestured to Derek and Hansen. "Even these terrible men have their assignments they must act out on this stage."

"So you're saying I should feel sorry that they were given the roles of evil people?"

Wishman frowned. "I wouldn't dream of telling you to have any sympathy for them. The dark gods have a different agenda from those of the light. As such, these tools of theirs should be dealt with as severely as possible. Mercy and compassion for them would be a mistake."

"That sounds rather cold and heartless."

Hansen cleared his throat. "And he says we're evil."

Wishman glanced at him and then looked back at Annja.

"I realize that runs counterintuitive to many spiritual teachings, but to give these men and any other agents of evil any quarter is to show weakness to them and further strengthen their own resolve."

"So you don't believe people can change or be rehabilitated? You think that what they are is always what they are?" Annja asked.

"I believe what they are is always inherently within them."

"But what if they could control those inherent traits such that they lived a useful and productive life?"

Wishman's smile deepened and showed the massive lines at the corners of his mouth. Annja couldn't fathom how old he must have been to show such enormous canyons. "Your mistake is that you see this battle as only taking place across this lifetime."

"That's a mistake?"

Wishman nodded. "It is when there are many, many lifetimes yet to play out. This epic battle isn't contained to any one of them. It is drawn long against the canvas of an eternity. As such, we are not at battle with the forces of darkness. Rather, we are at war. A long and terrible war." He pointed at Annja. "And you are a soldier in this war."

"Drafted," Annja said. "How wonderful."

"At least you get to fight," Wishman said. "And your purpose seems noble and honorable."

"Seems?"

He shrugged. "I do not know you well enough to judge if all of your actions are on the side of light. Or perhaps you are merely duping me as these others have done so already." He sighed. "I am growing old and weary of this fight in this body. Soon, it will be time to move along. In my younger years, I would never have fallen for the lies they told me. Never."

Hansen suddenly placed the gun barrel against Wishman's skull. "Say the word and I'll be glad to splatter your brains all over the snow, old man."

Wishman didn't flinch. "You think death scares me, boy? Do you know how many times I have done battle on this plane? How many times I have looked into the gaping maw of Hell's fires and lived to tell the tale? Your puny pistol and the death it delivers would be a vacation from the likes of what I've endured."

"Death is death," Hansen said. "One way or another, you'll be done before the sun is fully up."

Wishman chuckled. "If only you knew how wrong that statement is. One death is never the same as another. And to imagine that death by bullet and death at the hands of the thing you wish to unleash are the same shows how truly ignorant you really are. If you understood how the universe actually works, you would run from the place where you stand now and never look back. You would drop that weapon and leave this sacred land. You still have the ability to act rationally. But once you die, you will not have the option to reject the darkness."

Annja could see that Derek was watching Wishman intently. She glared at him. "Are you hearing this?"

"Of course I am." Derek shrugged. "It doesn't matter what he says. The truth of the matter is in about fifteen minutes we will carry out what we've come here to do. And no amount of Inuit psychobabble is going to change the course of events at this time."

"I just hope you know what you're doing. It'd be a shame to go to all this effort just to find out you're wrong," Annja said.

"As if you'd shed a tear. Didn't you just listen to Wishman? No mercy should be shown to us," Derek said with a laugh.

"I don't have to agree with everything Wishman says," Annja said. "I've always considered myself merciful. Not to a fault, mind you, but compassionate enough when the situation demands it."

"That is a fault you will have to eradicate," Wishman said. "Or else evil will eventually triumph over you."

Annja sighed. "You're really bringing me down, Wishman."

"No, these two men are. If they succeed, we are all dead. This place, this countryside, and eventually all the world, will fall into absolute darkness, fueled by the insatiable lust and hunger of the very fires that burn in the heart of absolute evil."

Annja looked at Derek. "That must be some science project you're getting ready to unleash."

He smiled. "Oh, it is."

"You mind filling me in on it? Just because, you know, I've always been really curious about that sort of stuff. And I've seen a lot of weird stuff, but giant monsters are new to me."

"What once was a monster of the flesh is no longer," Wishman said.

"Meaning?" Annja asked.

"Meaning that the creature is no longer visible in this realm."

"But it still exists?"

"Of course." Wishman sighed. "It really is difficult to explain to people who see things so one-dimensionally."

Annja frowned. "Well, sorry."

Derek smiled. "Now, now, old man, I wouldn't piss the little lady off if I was you. She'd be quite adept at kicking your ass."

Wishman sighed. "All this silliness when the gravity of the situation should be entirely evident."

A sudden wind whipped up around them, scattering a few of the smoking branches from the fire. Their burned orange tips glowed and hissed as they touched the snow, suddenly extinguished in a blast of steam.

Wishman clapped his hands. "You see? The spirits of this place know what is about to unfold here." He looked at Derek. "You anger them with your presence and your intentions."

"Tough," Derek said. "They can stand in line if they want to condemn me for what I'm about to do."

Wishman said nothing more, choosing instead to watch as the breezes continued to rise and fall, like some tidal flux against the shoreline. His eyes had narrowed into tight slits. Crow's-feet deepened on either side of his face and his lips were pursed tight to prohibit any sign of emotion.

Annja wasn't sure if she bought into the notion that there was some great evil stored behind the wall in the burial mound. Still, she couldn't deny that the existence of the wall itself was a little odd. It wasn't exactly the kind of place you would expect to find such a thing. But it could have been put there for a more earthly reason. Such as making sure no one fell down the shaft that suddenly went almost entirely vertical.

And that didn't involve some supernatural entity.

But something about Wishman's face made her wonder if perhaps there was something more to this than she realized.

22

The trunks of the trees that surrounded them in the clearing began to take on a subtle yellow glow as the sun started its inevitable climb. The pines started to glow in the bitter light, as if surrounded by a halo, but even with such an idyllic picture forming, Annja could feel something else worming its way up from somewhere far down below them. It was a true sense of foreboding.

Annja wasn't sure if she was cold or hot. She wondered if it was possible to be both.

Next to her, Wishman had started chanting something quietly under his breath. Annja watched him, but his closed eyes barred any conversation. She saw Hansen was still alert from the corner of her eye.

Annja closed her eyes and checked for the presence of the sword. In her mind's eye, it hung there in the other-where between her world and wherever the sacred blade rested when she didn't need it.

The problem was Hansen. With the gun at her back, any sudden movement or even the suspicion that she would draw the sword would prompt an early discharge of the gun he held. Annja would find a bullet in her back before she could pivot and disarm him.

Not an ideal situation by any means.

Somehow, she thought, I need to get Wishman involved in this. Without his help, I'm done for.

But Wishman seemed oblivious to her machinations. The quiet, steady litany of sounds that issued from him seemed to float out of his body as if lighter than air, carrying up into the frozen atmosphere and drifting away on unseen updrafts.

Annja had never heard anything like the language he chanted. And even the scant bit of Inuit that she'd heard spoken around the camp seemed a far cry from the words coming from Wishman now. If they even were words. Annja had to remind herself that Wishman was a shaman, and as such, he probably knew a bunch of long-forgotten languages that melded with myth and legend to form the basis of his expertise.

Annja closed her eyes and willed her thoughts to break Wishman's concentration. She had no idea if telepathy existed or not, but she was willing to try anything. She pictured Wishman in her mind, doing what he was doing. And then she formed a single thought and tried to picture herself speaking the command over and over again, eventually breaking through the barrier of concentration he'd thrown up by his chanting.

"Help me."

She opened her eyes. Wishman continued as if not disturbed in the slightest. Annja sighed and tried one last time. "Help me!"

But again, the chanting merely continued. Annja frowned and looked at Derek, who was studying his watch intently. He did have an appointment to keep, after all. At last, he looked up at Hansen.

"It's time."

Hansen grunted. "What about these two?"

Derek nodded. "Give me the gun and I'll cover them while you finish the preparations."

"You sure?"

"Of course. And I'm not the explosives expert here. You are. Far easier for me to have the gun."

Derek walked over and took his place behind Annja while Hansen went toward the opening of the burial mound and picked up the leads for the explosives and made sure they were attached to the detonator properly.

"Why not just do a remote trigger?" Annja asked.

Hansen shook his head. "We didn't want to chance the possibility of the wires freezing or something that would have delayed or disrupted the signal. That's not the kind of situation you want to be in, having to check things out and get closer and closer only to have it go boom in your face."

"Yeah," Annja said. "We sure wouldn't want anything to happen to you guys. That'd be terrible."

Derek poked her in the spine. "Watch your mouth or I'll make you suffer."

Annja glanced back at him. "I think I'm going to do that to you as soon as I get out of here."

"Who said anything about you leaving?"

"You haven't killed me yet."

Derek grinned. "That's only because we need a sacrificial first meal for what we're about to release. You and the old man over there are first up for nourishment. It's considered to be quite an honor."

"By who? You and the rest of the guests at the Nutjob House?"

Derek frowned. "I should know better than to waste my breath on the likes of you."

Annja shook her head. "So, who goes first? Me or Wishman?"

"I don't know. It's not up to us. Our god will decide who to eat first and then the other will be taken in time."

"Great."

Wishman's chanting increased, for the first time attracting Derek's attention. He frowned. "What's he doing?"

"How the hell would I know?"

"You're an archaeologist. You're supposed to know these things."

Annja smirked. "Yeah, well, he's not in the ground, so I can't dig him up and uncover his secrets. And you should know from my dossier that your group of sickos put together that Inuit culture isn't a strong point for me."

"Yes, I do recall that. But you do have something so much more valuable to us than your brain power."

"If you mention any part of my body next, I'm going to rip your arms out of their sockets."

Derek chuckled. "I'm not into cheap pickup lines."

"Yeah, I'll bet you just play wingman for Hansen there. Let him do all the talking and you pick up the scraps."

"I do no such thing."

"Did I hit a nerve?" Annja smiled. "I'll bet you two are quite the pair. First you spot a potential couple of ladies and then, what—decide who brings up the human sacrifice to the ancient evil god? Yeah, I can see a lot of women being impressed by that approach. Seriously."

Derek jabbed her in the back with the pistol again. "I'm tired of your sarcasm. It's not amusing in the least."

"Well, I was having a good time."

Derek looked at Wishman. "Time to stop your chanting,

old man. There's no help coming to you now. Your destiny is at hand."

Wishman's eyes opened. He glared at Derek. "So, you have made your final decision."

It wasn't a question, but Derek nodded anyway. "Yes. There was never any doubt in my mind as to what to do. We have been searching for this place for far too long."

Wishman looked at Annja. "Thank you."

"For what?"

"Keeping him distracted with that inane chatter."

Annja frowned. "Excuse me?"

Wishman lifted his head to the sky as the first rays of sunshine started to breach the dark blue of night. He smiled as if welcoming an old friend and then looked again at Annja. "I meant no insult by what I said. But it did serve its purpose of keeping his mind occupied for the time I needed."

Derek pointed the gun at Wishman. "Perhaps my god will grant me the right to kill you here and now."

Wishman stared at him. "You aren't that stupid. Your god will demand nourishment such as only a physical living specimen can provide. For you to rob him of that would be to give yourself an even more excruciating death than what is already in store for you."

"Still convinced of yourself, aren't you?" Derek asked.

Wishman smiled. "You are but a boy playing in an old man's world. And I have lived so very many years and seen far too many things that perhaps none should ever see. I have been through life and death before. And I will be here long after this situation passes." His eyes narrowed. "The same, however, cannot be said of you. Or your friend there."

Derek placed the gun barrel between Wishman's eyes. "Are you willing to wager your life on that?"

Wishman's eyes twinkled. "Are you?"

In that second, Annja drew the sword out and immediately spun to slash Derek's gun hand.

But even as she did, Hansen shouted a warning and Derek recoiled, trying to pull back and put some distance between himself and her blade. At the same time, he started to jerk the pistol up, getting the sights onto Annja, who came rushing right at him.

The gun exploded; its sharp retort broke open the silence of the predawn and echoed across the plain.

Annja's body twisted as the bullet came screaming at her, cutting a hot swath through the air. She heard it hiss through the frozen morning and kept pressing her attack.

Derek leaped sideways and again brought the gun up to fire.

Another shot exploded and Annja felt a sudden burn as the round scored a line across the back of her neck. But then Derek was already squeezing the trigger again as she hit the ground, rolling with the sword, slicing for the gun itself.

She felt the impact of metal on metal and then her blade dislodged the gun as another round came hurtling out of the barrel. It tumbled and spanged off a nearby tree, spitting bark and snow into the air.

Annja jumped up and Derek closed the distance, punching deep into her abdomen, driving her wind out of her lungs.

Annja grappled with him and felt his fingers turn into claws as he raked at her eyes. Derek pressed his attack, bringing up a leg to kick Annja in the knee. His boot glanced off her leg, but she felt the impact and grunted, going down into the snow.

From inside his jacket, Derek produced the *shan-nahk* that Annja had seen Godwin take from the two bar thugs back in Inuvik. But this one seemed longer than that knife. Different somehow.

Annja stood to face Derek, aware that her knee ached. He smiled at her. The blade in his hand was at least twelve inches long, and he must have had it concealed in a sheath that ran down his side.

"Brought your knife to play?" Annja smirked. "It's not going to be much of a contest."

Derek grinned now. "You think? It will be fun watching the expression on your face melt away when you realize this is something far more potent than any blade you've ever encountered before."

"Do tell." Annja circled in the deeper snow, trying to put the rising sun at her back. But Derek wasn't as big a fool as she'd thought, and he kept moving to the side, as well.

"This blade has been made more powerful by the spells and curses of a dozen high priests of the Amur Nal."

"Name doesn't ring a bell. Should it?"

Derek swayed back and forth. Annja could see this blade had a long curve and sharp hooked end. It looked like a nasty weapon, the kind that could produce truly horrible wounds. She didn't like the idea of getting any cuts from it.

"They're from a land before our time. So, no, I wouldn't expect someone like you to know anything about them at all. But it doesn't matter. For the magic they embodied, this blade with is far older and more powerful than anything that has ever touched this earth since."

"All this talk of magic," Annja said. "It gets really tiring."

Derek grinned. "Then we should join the battle and be done with it. I have my god to awaken."

"And I have you to stop," Annja said.

"Oh, you won't stop me," Derek said. "You'll never be able to stop the inevitable."

"I've heard that before."

"Have you?" For the briefest moment, Derek's eyes

glanced away and his mouth turned into a wicked smile. "Do it."

Annja started her attack, but in that split second, the ground suddenly rolled as if a great belch was coming from the belly of the Earth itself. A rumble of dust and smoke shot out of the mouth of the burial mound.

Hansen stood close by with his hands on the detonator. There was a pleased expression on his face.

Wishman was on his knees, eyes cast skyward in deep prayer.

Annja glanced back at Derek, who wore the same wicked smile as Hansen.

"It's done," he said. "The wall is now open."

23

Annja waited as the cloud of black dust, dirt and wood fragments came to rest on the white snow around the burial mound. There seemed to be a pause in everyone's actions. Derek still gripped his blade in a fighting stance, but his eyes were with Annja's on the entrance to the burial mound. Hansen looked extremely pleased with himself, but he, too, stared at the entryway. Only Wishman didn't focus on the burial mound, but instead on the sky above him.

Annja figured she'd seen too many monster movies because she partly expected that some giant seething monster too hideous to describe would suddenly heave open the earth and shudder itself free.

No such thing happened.

Annja frowned. Her sword still gleamed in her hands. There was evil present, certainly, but was it something more than what Derek and Hansen represented? She had no idea and could only stand there and wonder.

"Is that it?" she asked.

Derek smiled. "Remember the words spoken by the old

Araktak man over there. Remember that he said that our god would be invisible to eyes like yours."

Annja frowned. "So, maybe then he doesn't even exist, huh? Or you have to be insane to believe that he's here. Could be that, too, right?"

"He is here," Derek said. "And you will soon feel the heat of his embrace. He has long been locked away behind the barriers of magic that we have helped destroy. It is a good time for you to die."

"I thought you wanted that privilege for yourself," Annja said.

Derek snarled at her. "I would never dream of taking something for myself that already belongs to my master. My goal was merely to keep you here until it was time to unleash my master."

Annja smirked. "I'm not sure I believe you."

"We'll soon find out."

Wishman's voice suddenly erupted into an abject cry. His body seemed to rear back and then stiffen as he toppled face-first into the snow. Something shimmered over his body, and to Annja it looked almost like the heat mirage she saw when driving over hot patches of highway in the heat of summer.

Her eyes narrowed and she tried to see deeper into the scene. Was there something there? Or was she imagining it now because of the nonstop litany of propaganda she'd been hearing from Derek and Hansen? Wishman hadn't helped, either, but at least he was supposedly on the side of good.

Derek's voice was low and filled with wonder. "He lives. Our master lives, Hansen!"

Hansen nodded. "Indeed. See how he feasts upon the body of the old Inuit shaman? Truly a wonder to behold. We are indeed fortunate to have lived to see this benevolence."

Annja looked at Derek and Hansen and shook her head. The shimmering haze seemed to have vanished. Annja spun around, searching for it.

Neither Hansen nor Derek said anything. But they both turned to look at her and both men seemed to drift farther away.

"What are you doing?" Annja asked.

They said nothing in reply. Annja brought her sword up in front of her in case either of them launched a surprise attack. But Derek had lowered his blade and was busy putting it back into its sheath.

A wave of pain passed through Annja's body. She grunted and kept the sword in front of her centerline.

As she backed up, she suddenly stumbled and went down on her back in the deep snow. The sword landed next to her and sank beneath the top layer of white. Annja's hands scrambled to find it. She looked around and as she stared at Derek and Hansen, she thought she saw the same shimmering haze only a few feet in front of her.

She found the sword and held it out and in front of her. I don't know what that thing is, she thought, but we'll see if it likes the sword.

Annja stabbed out into the shimmering haze and marveled when it felt as if her blade actually cut into something denser than the frosty air. Her ears suddenly felt as if they were completely blocked and then an unseen force blew her sideways.

Annja toppled, feeling the snow's cold bite into her skin. She scrambled and came up with the sword again, wiping the melting snow from her face. Her eyes ran with the water and a sudden moisture.

She could see Derek and Hansen smiling from the other side of the clearing. How had she gotten so far away from them in such a short span of time? How was that even possible?

Was there really a dark god that she was battling now? She couldn't see anything and now she couldn't hear anything, either. Annja landed hard and the wind rushed out of her lungs again. The sword landed point up, some distance away. Annja scrambled to her feet.

She turned and looked and then saw the shimmering haze again. I'm either crazy or that thing is actually attacking me, she thought. And then she frowned. But why hasn't it attacked like it did with Wishman?

He was old, she thought then. And despite his powers, he was probably weak.

Annja ran across the snow and grabbed her sword as she went. She would need something else if she was going to survive this. But what? What other skills did she have that she could call forth now? She'd never battled a god before. And the sword didn't come with a user's manual.

With the sword in her hands, Annja turned and then closed her eyes. And there in the swirling gray mists of her mind's eye, she saw it suddenly. A heaving, hulking beast that lumbered across the plain, leaving huge tracks in its wake. Sweeping paws or hands or claws dangled by its side and the air around it shimmered as it passed through.

Annja kept her eyes closed and brought up her sword. The creature that she had decided most resembled a giant tree sloth swatted at her blade. In her mind's eye, Annja's blade glowed a bright silver in contrast to the red outline that denoted the creature.

Was this the dark god that Derek and Hansen had called forth from the prison cell that they had opened? Annja felt her blade connect with the red outline and there was a discharge of incredible energy.

Annja grunted and she thought she heard the creature howl.

I've hurt it, Annja thought. The blade can do battle here with it. As long as she stayed inside herself, she could fight it.

One of the creature's mighty limbs swung in from the left, seeking to thunder into Annja again. She pivoted and dropped beneath the crushing arc. As it passed overhead, she stabbed up into the exposed limb and felt her blade slide neatly in. She twisted and cut back and forth before heaving it out. As she did so, a shower of liquid seemed to fall over her shoulders, and she smelled a pungent scent breaking through her consciousness, as well.

The creature's blood must have been a foul and vile thing indeed.

She could hear its shrieks now amid their battle. It was angry and wanted her dead. I'd be angry, too, she thought, if after being imprisoned for so many years, the first person I saw was beating the crap out of me.

She almost laughed but then she felt a sudden explosion of pain in her gut. She was lifted off the ground and flew through the air in the gray mist of her mind. Annja tumbled and struck something she thought was the ground. She rolled, her breath coming out of her in heaves, trying to get to her feet.

The red outline of the creature came at her again and Annja ran to meet it. She swelled with the energy of her blade and her mission, slicing this way and that, trying her best to cut this thing down and be done with it. She saw her edge pierce the red outline over and over again, and the howls that assaulted her ears broke like a thunderstorm over her head, echoing and debilitating. But Annja gritted her teeth and fought on, possessed of a savagery she had not yet known.

Another blow crashed into her head while another slammed into the side of her thigh, and she tasted her own blood for the first time in this fight. Annja whirled and cut a back slash at the creature. Her blade sank deep, cutting as if the creature weren't there, and Annja heard another peal of agony explode from somewhere deep in its chest.

She clambered to her feet and then surveyed the scene. The creature moved slower now. Clearly her attacks and cuts had wounded it. The red outline seemed to drip in places. One of its limbs seemed to hang lower than the other and even its footwork dragged.

But still it came for her, searching, questing for what it demanded. Annja would not give in.

The creature unleashed a sudden volley of attacks, drawing strength from some subterranean pit of Hell to help battle back against this pesky warrior of virtue. Annja parried the first few attacks but then the exertion took its toll. She missed the parry of the fourth attack and felt the blow smack into her shoulder, followed by another low attack against her leg.

That opened her up for the next few attacks and Annja felt herself driven back, battered like a rag doll. If she hadn't had the sword, she might have died from any of the blows. But each time the creature attacked, she felt a sudden discharge of energy and the attack's worst effects seemed nullified.

But Annja was still hurt. And she knew she couldn't keep the fight up for much longer. Her strength was failing fast. And now the creature renewed its attack again. Annja watched as it came for her and she struggled to bring her blade up to meet its advance.

Another thunderous kick slammed into her gut and Annja was again flying through the air. She reached out and stuck the sword, stopping her momentum. She swung over the handle of the sword almost as if she was a gymnast, and then used that to propel her at the creature.

She flew back at the creature with her sword pointed at its head. She felt her blade bite into something hard and then soft, and then she was over its head, behind it, falling back toward wherever the mystical ground was in her mind's eye.

Annja ripped the sword free, hearing another agonized wail fill the air around her. She felt her feet touch down and then she rose up, turned and drove her blade through where she desperately hoped the heart of this thing was. The sword sank deep and Annja used the last bit of her strength to twist the point.

Another flood of acrid stench assailed her nostrils, but Annja hung on, ramming the sword into the beast over and over again. Sweat poured from her body and Annja knew she was at her limit.

But she kept up the attack and the creature seemed to flay about with its back skewered. It couldn't reach her even though it desperately wished to. Annja drove forward now, using her momentum to run the creature faster than its feet could keep up with until it stumbled and fell to the ground.

Annja stood over it and climbed on top of its back. The beast struggled to dislodge her but she used her knees to climb higher on its back until she thought she was astride its head.

She glanced up toward the sky and said a silent prayer. Then she drove the point of her sword down, deep into the skull of the beast.

One more screech jetted out of the creature, and then there was a terrible and sudden stillness. Annja could hear nothing. And she could see nothing, either.

The images ran into a swirled distortion of past, present and future. She struggled to hold on as grisly scenes of death and carnage washed over her. She kept holding tight to the sword still jutting out of the creature's head. It was as if the rapids were tearing at her and the sword was a branch poking out from the shore of stability and life.

Annja would not let go.

She screamed as more and more images came flying at her. She could see the destruction wrought by evil and the innocent lives lost to its unchecked rampage. She didn't know if she was seeing what atrocities had been committed in the past or if this was a potential future.

But she knew that if evil was allowed to continue without those who fought for good, the world would dissolve into a wretched pit of despair and horror.

Annja struggled to hold on, crying out as the worst came at her, over and over again. She could hear pleas to join them, the seductive voices that called at her like a Siren whispering promises of greatness and power into her ears. They cried at her refusal. They mourned her for not giving in. It would all be so easy, they called, if she would just let go and join them.

"No!"

Annja's voice exploded from somewhere deep in her gut, and then the mist seemed to draw back away from her. The images gave way and yielded, shrinking back into the shadowy depths of her subconscious, seemingly content to wait for another chance at some later date. Then they would be back to try to lure her again from her path.

From her destiny.

But for now, Annja still gripped the sword.

And as she did, she finally opened her eyes.

24

The white field of snow looked as though a score of soldiers had trampled through with their heavy boots. Annja could see the forward, backward and sideways movements of footprints, the smear of slips and slides and the impact of bodies hurled to the ground. As she lay among the shallowest of depressions, one thought came to her mind— Was I a part of this?

She rose to her feet slowly and surveyed the scene. No blood speckled the now-dirty snow. No limbs lay hacked off in some grisly manner. Nor were there any bodies of slain figures.

Only Wishman's body still lay where he had first fallen.

Derek and Hansen had vanished.

Annja glanced down at the sword and frowned. It felt heavy in her hands and she struggled to understand what she had just come through. She felt battle weary and battered, but she was unable to comprehend how she had arrived back here intact.

She sent the sword back to the otherwhere and then rushed to Wishman. As she turned him over, he gurgled slightly and she could see the line of spittle and melted snow dribbling from his mouth. Flecks of dirt marred his face, but otherwise she could see no sign of injuries.

She patted him on the chest. "Are you all right?"

His eyes opened and fluttered in brightening sunlight. He looked around and then back at Annja. "Friend of Bear?"

She nodded. "Yes."

"And the demon seekers?"

Annja shrugged. "I don't know. Vanished. Perhaps they left when things turned bad."

"What do you mean?"

Annja sighed. "I think, and it's only a thought, that I did battle with their dark god. And I defeated it."

Wishman tried to sit up and Annja helped push him into a sitting position. He took her hands. "You did battle with the creature? How was that possible?"

"I don't know," Annja said. "But somewhere between this world and another, I fought it."

"And won." Wishman's voice was tinged with wonder.

"I guess so. It doesn't seem to be around here any longer. At least, not that I can see."

"But you did see it? On this plane, I mean."

Annja looked around. Somehow, the sunlight seemed to make the entire scene a lot more friendly than it had been earlier during her fight. "It seemed to be a shimmering haze. Like a mirage."

Wishman nodded. "Yes. Then you have seen it, my child. And to live to tell the tale. Miraculous!"

"Yeah, well, I don't feel much like a miracle right now." Annja smiled. "We should get you back to camp."

Wishman shook his head. "No. We must first go down

into the burial chamber and see what damage was done to it by the explosion those two idiots set forth."

Annja glanced at the burial mound. She wasn't so sure that heading back down into the darkness was what she wanted to do right now, even if she had defeated the creature.

"I could use a cup of coffee," she said feebly.

Wishman smiled. "I know you're tired. I am, as well. When I saw that shimmering haze, I felt it slam into me as if I was only a puppet. Why it did not devour me then I will never understand."

"Maybe it wanted to do battle with me first?"

Wishman considered this and then nodded. "It's very possible that it did indeed see you more as a threat, gifted as you are with such a formidable weapon as that sword of light seems to be."

"Sword of light?"

"You vanquished an evil god with it. Surely, there can be no doubt as to its inherent nature if it enabled you to do such a thing."

Annja helped Wishman to his feet. "Let's get you down into the mound, check out the damage and then hoof it back to camp. I feel like I need a long sleep and a lot of food."

"Supernatural battles always deplete the resources of the brave warriors," Wishman said. "I will be quick. I promise."

"You don't need me?"

"Just your help to the entrance will suffice. I will go down by myself, if you prefer."

Annja smiled. "Works for me." She walked with Wishman over to the entrance and as she did so, she looked again at the ground and the tracks that covered it. "Looks like I was running all over the place here."

"When you fight in between worlds, this is the result. You may not have been here, per se, but in one form, you were. And the proof of your exertions is all around us on this field."

"Shouldn't there be proof of the death of the creature?" Annja asked.

Wishman shook his head. "Not necessarily. The birthplace of that demon has more likely recalled it home. It would not lay on the field of battle as a slain beast might. Better that it is that way."

"No complaints from me," Annja said. She stopped by the entrance and took her arm from around Wishman's shoulder. "You sure about this?"

"I'll just be a moment." And Wishman uncoiled himself and walked down into the shaft. Bits of blackened soot scarred the entrance, and giant pockmarks of dirt and ice still lay fragmented about the area.

Annja looked around. Part of her wondered if everything that had happened was even possible. She had never before given much thought to the supernatural as such, and certainly hadn't battled anything like this before. All of her other fights had been against mortal enemies, both human and animal.

But this was something different.

Very different.

And the realization that she had somehow evolved to a new level of fighting wasn't entirely a welcome one to Annja. What did this event mean was coming down the pike in the future? Would she be up against the worst that the bastions of evil could throw at her from here on out? Was she now expected to wage a war against the minions of darkness? And if so, was the sword enough of a weapon?

None of the possible answers made her feel comfortable. And the longer she misted the air with her breath, the more she felt tired and unsure of herself and her skills. When she should have been feeling confident and worthy of the thing she had killed, instead, fear plagued her. A fear of failure.

Somehow, that didn't seem fair to her. After all she'd been through in her many travels and adventures, after all the heartache and pain and misery, Annja expected something a little more like a feeling of satisfaction. Instead, she felt less confident than before. As if it had all been for nothing. And all that hard-gained experience was merely a figment of her imagination.

I've struck down a god, she thought. And yet I feel like I am completely worthless.

Wishman's head stuck out of the burial shaft. "Perhaps you would like to come down here and see."

No one seemed to be around. And if Wishman had already been down and back without any ill effects, Annja could probably venture down safely.

She picked her way into the burial shaft and saw Wishman beckoning her on. Something illuminated the shaft, but Annja couldn't see what it was. The string of lights the Araktak warriors had managed to put in place had been destroyed in the blast, but there was something that lit the interior.

"How is it that this place is lit up like this?"

Wishman chuckled to himself and urged Annja to follow him onward. They continued to pick their way down the tunnel. Annja could see now on both sides of the tunnel that the branches had been almost entirely sealed off by the force of the blast.

"The bodies in there…" Annja said.

Wishman shook his head. "We got the majority of them out. It shouldn't take us too much longer to finish excavating them and transporting them to the new location. I think we'll be quite happy to do so."

"Quite happy?"

"Indeed."

Annja frowned. "What are you up to?"

Wishman glanced back at her. "I mean nothing intriguing by my statements, I assure you."

"It's just that I expected you to be heartbroken at the sight of so much damage. I'm amazed the shaft itself is even still standing and hasn't collapsed."

Wishman pointed overhead. "The rock that we tunneled into is remarkably strong."

"Apparently."

"I'm sure you'll understand in time, Friend of Bear."

"That would make for a refreshing change," Annja said. "Because right now, I'm clueless."

"About this?"

"About a lot of things."

Wishman pointed at the floor of the shaft. "See there? The bits of the wooden wall that was used to bar the creature from escaping when we originally constructed this tunnel."

"How long ago was that?"

"Far too many moons," Wishman said. "So long ago I feel sometimes as though it was nothing but a dream."

Annja stooped and picked up a piece of the wood. It felt heavier than any wood she'd held before. "What is this? Oak?"

Wishman shook his head. "It is the strongest wood known to mankind. It is *lignum vitae*."

Annja hefted it in her hand again. "Amazing stuff. Is this indigenous to this area of the world?"

Wishman laughed. "Oh, no. That wood does not grow anywhere around these parts. That is part of the reason why it is so potent and necessary for the uses we had in mind for it."

Annja let the piece fall back to the ground. She could see other, larger splintered bits around, embedded in the walls and the floor and even the ceiling. One piece had shattered all the lights in the nearby area.

"Incredible this place still stands," she said.

Wishman led her on. "We're almost there."

Annja followed him and saw they were almost to the wall site. She looked and saw the remnants of the ground-radar unit on the floor of the shaft. The yellow box was demolished and the bits that had been blown apart in the explosion had melted into a swirling morass of circuit boards and wires, meshed with the floor of the tunnel and completely worthless.

"So much for the radar," she said.

"It is unimportant in the scheme of things," Wishman said. "Always, what the universe takes away, the universe also provides."

"That sounds vaguely familiar."

Wishman gestured. "Ahead, see there, where the wall stood only hours ago, barring the creature inside. Beyond, the shaft goes straight into the very depths of the Earth itself."

Annja could see the dark, foreboding hole ahead of her. Her heart hammered in her chest and part of her expected the creature to come roiling out of the cavernous depths and attack her over and over again.

I couldn't handle another battle this soon, she thought. Not now.

"Are you all right?" Wishman's eyes were locked on hers.

"I'm exhausted," Annja said. "The battle. It wore me out completely and I feel like I could fall asleep right here and now."

Wishman smiled. "You need something to wake you up. No wonder after the fight you waged."

"A little pick-me-up would be a good thing," Annja said. "What did you have in mind?"

Wishman smiled a little wider now. "Only that which has been hidden from our eyes for many, many years. Would you like to see?"

Annja nodded. "Yes."

Wishman stepped away and let Annja peek through.

She gasped.

Behind him, at the crook of the elbow where the wall had stood previously, Annja could look down the shaft. The brilliance of what met her gaze almost blinded her.

Diamonds.

Nothing but diamonds as far as she could see.

25

"That's amazing." Annja stared in disbelief at the plummeting shaft and the brilliance contained within. It looked as though the burial mound had truly been located on the world's supply of diamonds.

Wishman smiled. "This kind of good fortune can only be called a gift from the gods for your help in doing away with the creature."

"Yes, but—" Annja stopped. Hadn't the Araktak tribe sold this burial mound to Derek's company? Didn't the evil worshippers now possess this mine? It probably wasn't possible to argue in court that the deal should be struck down just because they'd tried to unleash an ancient demon from its captivity. Annja frowned. Given how the legal systems of the world worked, the court would probably not only find for the demon, but also award it pain and suffering for the countless years in captivity.

Annja pointed back toward the entrance above them. "We should really get back to the camp now. Try to get everyone else awake so they know what has happened."

Wishman nodded. "What about the rest of the miners?"

"What about them?"

"Are they trustworthy?"

Annja thought for a moment. "Well, Derek and Hansen did claim to have drugged them also. Perhaps they don't even realize what they were a part of. It's not going to be easy breaking the news to them."

They turned and walked back up the gentle slope of the shaft. Annja spotted something and crouched down. A tiny sprig of herb lay on the floor and she picked it up. It was too badly burned to recognize, but when she took a whiff of it, she caught a vague aroma that sent her head reeling.

Wishman helped her up. "Are you all right?"

Annja held up the sprig, but as she did so, the herb crumbled into dust in front of them.

Wishman frowned. "What was that?"

"I don't know," Annja said. "But it smelled rather funny. Made me light-headed almost."

"You're tired," Wishman said. "And with great reason to be. Not many would have the courage to face a demon in battle. Let alone live long enough to persevere. Sleep is what you need."

"And some food," Annja said. "Maybe coffee, as well."

They walked out of the burial mound and back through the pines. The sunshine seemed brighter than it had since Annja had arrived.

"They'll never believe us, you know," Annja said as they passed under the canopy of the pines.

"My men will believe what they want, although some will see the truth immediately. The others will come around in time."

Annja nodded. "I was thinking more about the remaining miners. And Godwin."

"The half-breed," Wishman said.

Annja glanced at him. "He's tried to do more for your tribe than anyone else. Can't you at least give him some quarter? Allow him to be able to call you part of his family? Is that so difficult?"

"For the Araktak it is."

"But why? You've seen what sort of trouble this secrecy can get you into. Godwin would have stood there and gone toe-to-toe with the demon just as readily as I did. His bravery and strength make him a perfect addition to the tribe."

"But his mother—"

"So what? Look, I know the loneliness that he feels. I'm an orphan. I never knew my mother or father and I've struggled with the idea of what family truly is for many years. You've got the chance to make a good man part of your tribe, and I think you should do so."

"It would unwrite years of traditions."

Annja smiled. "The youth of your tribe will do that anyway."

Wishman nodded, a vague smirk playing across his face. "There is much truth in that statement."

"So, why not? If you want the Araktak to continue on and perhaps even prosper, you will need warriors like Godwin to take their rightful place among the ranks of the other men."

Wishman looked at Annja. "I promise you this, Friend of Bear. I will think on it and if I decide the wisdom is there, then it shall be."

"Well," Annja said, "if that's the best we can get for right now, it will have to do, huh?"

Wishman pointed. "They must have awoken from their slumber. The cooking fire is started."

Annja caught the scent of cooking meats on the fire and

her mouth fairly drowned under the deluge of saliva that flooded her mouth. "God, I'm starving."

Wishman guided her to the main lodge and opened the door. The crowd of Araktak men looked up. Godwin was among them and he stood when he saw Annja.

"What happened to you? You look like hell."

She frowned. "Good morning to you, too." She pointed at the sizzling meat. "Is that almost ready to eat?"

Godwin glanced back at the cooking griddle. "I guess so. I mean it was supposed to be my breakfast, but—"

Annja stepped forward. "Would you mind? It's been a really long night and I am starving."

"Where were you guys? I woke up and felt like I'd lost consciousness last night. Your bed was empty. So was Derek's. What gives?"

Annja got a fork and speared the meat out of the griddle, plopped it on a plate and settled herself on a log nearby. The meat still hissed and sizzled on her plate, but she was beyond caring. Wishman pressed a mug of steaming coffee into her hands, and Annja tore into the minor feast, not caring how much of a pig she might have resembled.

No one said anything while she devoured the food. Wishman stood nearby, almost as a protector, and she was grateful to have the moment to eat in peace and quiet. When she had finished her food, she set the plate down and drank the coffee, which had cooled somewhat in the meantime.

Godwin squatted next to her. "You okay?"

"Friend of Bear is exhausted," Wishman said.

Godwin glanced up at him. "You look as though you could do with a meal yourself."

Wishman smiled. "In truth, I could."

Godwin turned back to the fire and got another plate for both Annja and Wishman. This time, he piled on some scrambled eggs along with more meat. When he handed them back, Annja and Wishman started eating immediately.

The remainder of the Araktak warriors watched in silence. Perhaps it was their experience that when their shaman entered in such a fashion, he must have had something happen and they would wait for him to tell them rather than immediately press him for details. Annja found it a quaint throwback to a time when things weren't instantly dispensed at light speed over the Internet via blogs and message boards.

Annja finished her second plate and leaned back against the wall of the lodge. It was still cold but somehow, she didn't even notice. Her stomach rumbled a quick thanks and then set to work on the food. Annja sipped her coffee and watched as Wishman finished and handed his plate back to Godwin with a hearty thanks.

Maybe there was progress happening there, Annja thought.

Nyaktuk came forward and spoke to Wishman in low tones. Wishman nodded several times and gestured toward Annja twice. Nyaktuk stared at her, disbelief showing across his face until it was replaced by admiration. He must be telling him about the battle, Annja thought.

And to Wishman's credit, Nyaktuk seemed to readily accept what the elder told him as truth and not fantasy. That was one fewer person they would have to work hard to convince. Annja hoped he would help them with the others.

Godwin came back over. "What happened, Annja? The Araktak men are quiet and that means something."

"Oh, you know that, do you?"

He shrugged. "I've picked up a few things since I've been here. And some of it comes from what my father taught me about this tribe."

Annja smiled. "Well, something did happen. I still can't quite believe it, but apparently there was some kind of evil creature trapped in the burial mound. Derek and Hansen wanted to free it and Wishman and I intervened."

Godwin shook his head. "What? What are you talking about? Evil creature? In the burial mound? Where?"

Annja took a breath. "Derek slipped out of the lodge last night and I followed him to the burial mound. He was setting up the radar unit up and we found a wall, a wooden wall. Turns out that was the focus of their quest all along. The company—your company—is run by some type of evil people who worship dark gods from times long past. Derek and Hansen were sent here to release the entity and control it, so it would do their bidding."

Godwin looked at her. "You're joking."

"She is not," Wishman said. "She speaks the truth. Every word of it is so because I was there to witness it." He turned to the room. "Listen well to the words that Friend of Bear speaks. It is as she says it was."

So Annja told them the rest, trying her best to keep the fact that she had the sword out of the story as much as possible. The less people who knew about it, the better.

One of the Araktak men wore a smile that mocked the entire story. He laughed.

Wishman's words were harsh. "Be quiet! I told you she speaks the truth. Or don't my words count for anything these days?"

She felt Wishman's gaze on her and he was apologetic. "They are younger than me and take little on faith or, apparently, the strength of the words I speak."

Annja nodded. "It's all right. It's a pretty unbelievable story."

All Annja wanted was a warm bed to sleep in for a few

weeks. She got to her feet, helped up by both Wishman and Godwin. Godwin's strength hoisted her quickly.

"Thank you," Wishman said. "I know that you have secrets you wish to keep. I will help them see the truth for what it really is."

Annja nodded. "Forget about it. All I really want to do right now is sleep for a very long time. If you don't mind, I'll leave you guys to sort things out here while I vanish into my dreams."

Wishman nodded. "Of course. I think we have a lot of things to discuss here while you rest."

Annja turned and started for the door when it opened suddenly and the remaining miners rushed into the lodge. Annja recognized one of them as Hansen's second-in-command. She sighed. The last thing she needed now was another fight, and judging by the expression of hatred on the man's face, that was exactly what he was looking for.

"Where are they?" he demanded. Seeing Annja walk toward him, he held up his hand. "Where do you think you're going?"

"To bed."

"Where are Mr. Wainman and Hansen? They aren't around and we have some stuff to talk to them about."

"What sort of stuff?"

"We were drugged by these Araktak. We want justice! We're not going to take this. If they don't sort this out, we're going to call the RCMP and get this whole project shut down. We didn't come up here to be drugged by the likes of these people."

"Derek and Hansen are gone," Annja said. "And the Araktak had nothing to do with it."

26

Hansen's second-in-command, who went by the name of Dufresne, stood with his arms folded across his barrel chest and a grim expression plastered across a face that sported a day's worth of stubble. He listened as Annja filled him in on the story, trying to minimize the supernatural elements as best she could. When she'd finished, she stood to one side so Dufresne could see that the Araktak tribe was in agreement with the story.

Dufresne looked Annja up and down as if deciding whether she was actually from this planet. Finally he took a deep breath and blew it out in a whiskey-tinged stream of air that made Annja blanch.

"An evil god." He turned to the rest of the men, who clearly took their cues from him. "You hear that, guys? There's an evil god on the loose here and Mr. Wainman helped set it free."

"It's the truth," Annja said. "We were there in the burial mound and we saw the entire thing happen."

"Now, was that before or after you slayed the evil crea-ture, because I can't quite recall that particular detail?" Dufresne's grin underscored the disbelief and sarcasm.

Annja felt her blood surge. She didn't like being called a liar. By anyone. And Dufresne had been passed out in an alcohol-induced slumber tainted with drugs administered by Hansen. As far as Annja was concerned, Dufresne had no right to call her account of things into question. But she had to admit the whole thing sounded ridiculous.

"Well, why don't you tell me what you think happened, then?" Annja asked, fixing her hands on her hips.

Dufresne nodded. "Be glad to." He gestured around the room. "Someone, I'm not sure who, put some kind of drug in our drinks last night, causing me and the rest of the guys here to pass out until just a few minutes ago."

"It was Hansen who brought the whiskey," Annja said. "Not the Araktak."

"As I was saying, these Araktak must have had some kind of drug that they slipped into our drinks and caused us to pass out. While we were asleep, they took Mr. Wainman and Hansen to parts unknown and did some sort of ritual sacri-fice to them, killing them and then hiding the bodies."

Annja's eyebrows shot up. "How in the hell do you go from missing persons to homicide?"

"Well," Dufresne said, "where are they?"

"I don't know where they are," Annja said. "But odds are they're dead."

"Exactly."

"But the Araktak didn't murder them. Hansen and Wainman took it upon themselves to resurrect an evil god. It probably backfired."

"And what got them killed in the process? By what?"

"What do you mean?" Annja shook her head. "You're not making any sense."

"Well, you said you killed this—whatever it was, right?"

"Yes."

"Then what was left to kill Hansen and Mr. Wainman? And where are the bodies to prove it?"

Annja stopped. It was a decent question. And one her exhausted mind hadn't had time to fully process yet, either. If she'd been rested, she would have thought of it immediately. But as it was, her fatigue slowed down her thought processes.

Where were Wainman and Hansen? Annja had killed the evil creature, which left nothing behind to kill the two company men. So where were they?

"You see," continued Dufresne, "what I think we got ourselves here is this little conspiracy."

"A conspiracy? Oh, please," Annja said.

Dufresne held up his hand. "Seems to me what has happened here is when Mr. Wainman and Hansen came up to check things out, these Araktak here got wind that they were sitting on a lot more than they originally thought when they sold the land. So they dreamed up a rather unusual way to try to renegotiate the contract. And in the end, Wainman and Hansen got shivved for it."

"You realize that sounds insane," Annja said. "The Araktak wouldn't stoop to murdering Hansen and Wainman over a piece of land. That's crazy."

Dufresne looked at her. "Didn't you just stand here and tell me a story about an evil creature who had been imprisoned until our bosses freed them?" He chuckled. "And I'm the crazy one."

The men behind him started to guffaw, as well. Annja shook her head. She had to try to make sense of what had occurred. She needed time to try to figure out what had become of Hansen and Derek. But standing here verbally sparring with Dufresne wasn't going to help the situation.

"I need to sleep," she said. "You guys can sort through this mess."

Wishman came up to her. "But how? We need your help to convince them that we are not the savages they think we are."

"You don't need me," Annja said. "You just need someone impartial to help sort through all this junk. I don't know what happened to Wainman and Hansen. For all I know they slipped in a sinkhole or got swallowed up by a giant anaconda or an asteroid came out of the sky and hit them. I have no idea. In fact, I don't know much of anything right now beyond the fact that I am completely exhausted. I am going to bed because I am no use to anyone like this."

"But—" started Wishman.

Annja held up her hand to cut him off. "Like I said, you don't need me even though you think you do."

"But who will help us?"

Annja looked across the room and pointed. "He will."

Godwin looked up. "Excuse me?"

Annja smiled. "There's your impartial judge. Godwin's got no stake in things either way. Part of him is with the Araktak and part of him is with the company. As far as I'm concerned, that makes him the perfect man for the job of sorting through all this madness."

Wishman looked at Godwin. "Would you be willing to try?"

Godwin shrugged. "I suppose. If Dufresne and his men are willing to let me act as the mediator."

Dufresne eyed him for a moment and then shrugged. "Yeah, all right, then. We can deal with Godwin. I know he's good people."

Annja took a deep breath. Now if she could just manage

to make her way back to her bed, all would be well. "Good night, everyone. Don't kill each other while I sleep. Or if you decide to, try to be quiet about it."

Annja pulled on the lodge door and stepped out into the morning air. Sunlight rebounded off the snow, almost blinding her.

She walked back to her shelter and opened the door. She lay down on her bed, falling immediately asleep. Her thoughts drifted away from her as she plunged into slumber. She felt the inexorable reach and pull of sleep dragging her down into the depths of her subconscious like an anchor attached to her waist. Down and down she fell until she thought she could go no further.

But she kept plummeting down through veils of sleep and dreams. And when she finally lost track of how far she had fallen, Annja was deeply asleep.

FROM WHERE SHE RESTED on a bed of dreams and soft visions of tranquillity, Annja's subconscious tugged at her, trying its best to locate her and wake her. Annja resisted fiercely, determined to stay where she was, lost on some tropical-paradise shoreline, feeling the waves lap at her feet and the sun warm her golden body from high overhead.

Annja reluctantly allowed her consciousness to rise back to the surface and her eyelids fluttered. She expected it to be bright when she opened them, but instead, darkness had fallen again.

How long have I slept? she wondered. It must have been at least eight hours since her run-in with Dufresne. She thought about Godwin and wondered how the young man would take to playing the role of mediator between the Araktak and the mining company.

She'd lied, of course, when she had suggested that

Godwin was impartial. He had a lot to gain by playing his cards right. Wishman might be willing to accept him into the Araktak. And she knew that would make Godwin very happy indeed.

But what about the miners? How would they react if they felt things didn't turn out properly?

In response to that question, Annja's stomach seized up and she came fully awake, her eyes scanning the darkness for what had woken her.

Nothing moved in the shelter. Annja could detect nothing out of the ordinary among the shadows that inhabited the room with her. She used the corners of her eyes to try to catch any movement, but after several minutes of keeping still, Annja wasn't convinced she was in any danger.

She frowned. She stifled a yawn and thought about how nice it would be to drift back to sleep.

Annja shifted in her bed and then heard something outside.

She strained to hear it again and relaxed her jaw to further open her ear canals so she could allow more sound waves to enter.

She waited.

Minutes crawled by. And then she heard it again. A shuffle. A crunch. Footsteps. Somewhere outside, close by the shelter.

Someone was approaching her lodge.

Annja slid out of the bed and stole smoothly across the floor to the door. When it opened, she would take down the stalker and see what was going on.

She paused next to the door, feeling her heart hammer inside her chest. She calmed her breathing, fighting back the wave of adrenaline that sought to galvanize her muscles. She would allow the torrent to come when she needed it and not a second before. If she gave in to the adrenaline too soon, it would burn through her replenished stores of energy in no time.

And Annja didn't think she was one hundred percent restored yet. She had to use her strength carefully.

She summoned the sword and held it up in front of her, ready to swing and slash if need be.

Another sound reached her ears and this one was much closer. Whoever, or whatever, approached the shelter was doing so very cautiously and stealthily. The footsteps were all placed so as not to mimic any set rhythm, but to appear more naturally chaotic, as if an animal was poking around outside.

But Annja knew that even the most determined nocturnal animal would not have wasted so much time on these horribly frozen nights. They would have scampered about, rather than meandered the way these sounds seemed to.

No, someone was deliberately trying to make her think that he was not a threat. When, in fact, he was.

Annja figured it might be Dufresne. But then again, she didn't really know the man. Perhaps he wasn't as bad as he seemed. Maybe he'd been honestly concerned about the welfare of Hansen and Derek.

Annja heard another slight noise. It was right outside the door. She looked down at the doorknob and saw it start to turn. She steeled herself and waited as the knob turned all the way in one direction and the latch clicked open.

They paused then, probably waiting to see if Annja responded to the sound of the click. She counted off thirty seconds and then she felt the creep of cold air enter as the door opened a crack.

She could feel the draft and a shadow fell across the door frame.

Annja reached around, grabbed the person and shoved him to the floor in one smooth action. In the next instant she was astride him, jabbing the tip of her sword under his chin.

27

"Stop!"

Annja paused for just a second. She wouldn't have killed him anyway. At least not until she found out who was underneath her. She shifted and allowed a shaft of moonlight to break across the door of the shelter, illuminating the man.

Dufresne.

She frowned. Something hadn't felt right about him when she saw him come through the main lodge doorway earlier today. And now, here was the proof that he was up to no good.

"Should I just kill you now and save myself the trouble later?" she said.

He shook his head. "What? No, don't kill me. I meant you no harm. I just came to check on you."

"Check on me?" Annja smiled. "Is that what we're calling it now? How utterly nonthreatening."

Dufresne tried to buck her off of him. "Let me up and I'll prove it to you."

Annja held him fast. "You move and I'll run you through. Why in the world would you be checking up on me? Does it look like I need a nursemaid?"

Dufresne nodded. "You do. You've been unconscious for two days."

Annja leaned back as if she'd been struck by a solid jab. "Two days? I've been asleep that long?"

"I wouldn't call it sleep and neither did anyone else. Wishman tried to explain to us the exertion you underwent but I don't know how many of us believed it." Dufresne looked at the sword. "However, I must say the presence of that blade is quite convincing."

Annja frowned. Damn. She hadn't wanted to brandish the thing unnecessarily. She got up from Dufresne and switched on the light. The miner pointed next to her bed and Annja could see that there were bowls of some sort of stew that sat untouched.

"We tried to wake you up with food. It didn't work."

"So, how come you're the one checking up on me now? Why not Wishman or Godwin or someone else?"

"It was my turn to pull a shift. Figures I'd be the fool who got you on the wake up. Guess I'm lucky to be alive."

Annja nodded. "Actually, you are. Very lucky. I didn't trust you when I first saw you."

"And now?"

Annja shrugged. "We'll see." She looked around the room. "I don't feel as if I've slept for two days." But she did feel remarkably well-rested. Her limbs felt loose and ready. It felt good to be back and refueled.

Dufresne shook his head. "Like I said, it didn't look like sleep to any of us. Coma was what we thought. The agreement was that if you didn't wake up in another day, we were going to drive you to the hospital and take our chances with the docs."

"Let me guess, Wishman said to wait."

"Yup. And he was right." Dufresne sighed. "I don't understand much of what these people do or say, but they seem to know about stuff like this. Creepy as it is. I mean, evil gods? How do you even begin to process that?"

"Did you grow up Christian?"

"Well, yeah. But I'm not really sure what I am now. Does that matter?"

Annja shook her head. "No. The important thing is that if you recognize that there's some sort of positive force in the universe, then you've also got to accept the idea that there is an equal and negative influence, as well. A lot of people can't do that. And some of the fanatics would argue against it, as well."

"Guess that makes it all the easier for evil to take root, huh?" Dufresne rubbed his head. "Can't say I ever thought I'd be involved in something like this, though. How did you do it?"

"I have no idea," Annja said.

"And that…thing?"

"The sword?" Annja frowned. "I'd really appreciate it if we kind of kept that between us, okay? The less people who know about its existence, the better off I'll be in the long run. I don't need the publicity, if you know what I mean."

"Yeah, yeah, sure. No sweat." Dufresne nodded. "It's our secret. You got it, Annja."

"Thanks." Annja thought about the stew nearby. She was ravenous. But the bowls looked old and she feared she would get sick if she ate any of it. "What time is it?"

"Almost supper time."

Annja smiled. "Excellent. At least that means I can get some grub in my stomach. I'm dying of hunger here."

"Wishman has arranged a big meal. I think he knows you're going to be waking up—er, he knew you would be anyway. I don't know how. I don't know much about what he knows."

Annja nodded at the door. "Let's go."

Dufresne led her outside. She caught up with him and they walked side by side through the snow, which had fallen again in Annja's absence. "Did you guys work everything out?"

Dufresne nodded. "Yeah. Wishman and Godwin working together were quite persuasive, actually."

"They worked together?" Annja smiled in the looming darkness. "That must have been something to see."

"Yeah, they seemed to get along good, all right. At one point, Wishman actually clapped Godwin on the back. And from our end, Godwin ain't a bad guy at all. We've known him for some time, so we took his words seriously."

"Glad to hear it."

They stopped in front of the main lodge and the door opened abruptly. Wishman's smiling face beamed out at Annja. "So, the mighty warrior has at last awakened." He bowed to Annja and then looked deep in her eyes. "Welcome back, Friend of Bear, Slayer of Gods."

Annja almost blushed. "You know, 'Annja' will really suffice. The other thing there you've come up with is far too long and complicated to say."

"But it's the truth."

"Yeah, but it's also embarrassing as hell," Annja said. "Slayer of Gods? Could you make me sound any more like the Terminator?"

Wishman shrugged. "As you wish." He stepped back and allowed Annja to enter. The main lodge was abuzz with noise and laughter. It was a far different sight than when Annja had last left it. Back then, the tension was palpable. Now, it was nowhere to be seen.

"Things have certainly changed," she said.

Wishman nodded. "I am sometimes surprised that I still have so much to learn despite my advanced years. Sometimes it takes a moment of strife and upheaval to drive the lesson home."

"We've certainly had plenty of that." Annja smiled. "But I hear things have worked themselves out?"

"Yes," Wishman said. "Your suggestion about Godwin was perfect. The young man worked out exceedingly well. And his objectivity was obvious to both sides. He made for the perfect bridge between our two people."

"What did you come up with?"

Dufresne cleared his throat. "We're willing to accept the notion that the deal was designed to get Wainman and Hansen into the burial mound and was never about the diamonds at all. In exchange, the Araktak have agreed to renegotiate the deal and enter into a partnership with us for ownership and exploration of the mine."

"Equal ownership?" Annja smiled. "That wasn't something I expected to hear."

Dufresne shrugged. "Well, you never know unless you try, right? And we were the ones who suddenly found ourselves unemployed."

"What do you mean?"

"We called back to company headquarters, or what we thought was company headquarters, only to be told the entire board of directors actually consisted of Wainman and Hansen. And no one seemed to know where they were."

Annja frowned. "The entire company was a sham?"

"We don't know. What we do know is that without a

board, the company has no real future and will most likely be dissolved."

"Yeah, but what about the deal already in place?"

Dufresne pointed at Godwin. "Turns out the young guy there has some powerful connections in the legal world. He made a few phone calls on our satellite phone and in turn, his friends got us out of the original deal. The Araktak will pay back the money and we're free to enter into a new agreement."

"It was that simple?"

Dufresne shrugged. "Well, not quite, but at the end of the day, Godwin managed to get it all worked out. Me? I'm a miner, not a lawyer, so I'm not clear on all the conditions and whatnot. But what matters is that we have a new deal and a new reason to celebrate. The guys and I have better jobs now doing what we do best—digging rock."

"And we will still benefit from the mine itself," Wishman said.

"Once the remainder of the bodies are properly transported to the new burial area closer to the Araktak community," Dufresne said. "That was a mandatory part of the deal."

"Good," Annja said. "So that gives us plenty of time now?"

"It should," Wishman said. "We would like to get started as soon as possible, obviously, but traditions come first. And thankfully, Dufresne and his men seem willing to work with us on that."

"Well, sure. We've all got family we've buried before. We wouldn't want someone rushing us if we suddenly had to move them."

"That's the understanding that was missing from the original deal," Annja said. "Nice job, guys."

"It was Godwin mostly," Wishman said. "He really has proven himself incredibly valuable."

"You can tell me all about it over dinner," Annja said. "I'm starving. I hear I've been out for two days."

Wishman smiled. "Well, you did have a lot of resting to do. I alone was unconcerned. But the men insisted on caring for you. It was quite touching, actually."

"Big bunch of softies, the lot of you."

Wishman led her over to the main table that had been set with a wide range of fresh meats. Annja looked around and whistled. "You've been busy hunting, haven't you?"

"Well, someone had to be ready for when you decided to grace us with your presence again," a voice said.

Annja looked up into Godwin's face. He smiled at her and Annja felt a warmth come over her. "Hey, you."

"How you feeling?"

Annja shrugged. "Rested. Good. Overall, pretty damned glad I checked out for a forty-eight-hour furlough."

"Leaving us completely worried, mind you." Godwin winked. "Wishman was most concerned out of all of us."

"You speak lies, Godwin," Wishman said with a slight smile. "I alone had the faith to know Annja would be fine."

"If you call nonstop pacing in front of her bed 'faith,' then yeah."

Annja looked at Wishman. "You held a vigil over my bed?"

Wishman shrugged. "Just for a few minutes."

"Hours," Godwin said. "We finally managed to pry him away from your side and set up shifts. But it seemed to be touch and go there for a while. I thought you'd manage to make it somehow. After all, I saw how you handled that raging rig on the river."

Annja eyed him. "You saw that? I thought the tire had blocked your view."

He laughed. "How could I have missed that? I just

didn't say anything since it seemed like you didn't want the attention."

"I didn't." Annja paused. "Thanks."

"Forget it. Let me get you a plate." Godwin handed her one and Annja heaped a pile of meats and assorted fixings on it until it felt heavy on her hands. She made her way to sit down and all the men smiled at her. She noted that the Araktak warriors and the miners all seemed to be back and in good spirits again. Although, this time, no one was passing around any whiskey.

They had indeed learned from the last time.

Annja sat down and started to eat when Godwin came over and sat next to her. "I'm glad you're all right," he said quietly.

"Me, too."

Godwin pointed at the plate. "Eat your fill. Then we have other things to discuss."

Annja frowned. "Things? I thought I'd be leaving soon."

Godwin shook his head. "Oh, there's a lot more that we need to talk about. A lot more."

28

Annja finished her meal in quiet, wondering what Godwin had mentioned about there being more stuff to talk about. What could he be referring to? she wondered as she chewed thoughtfully on the piece of game. After all, she'd expected to wake up, perhaps party a little with the boys and then figure out a way to hitch a lift back to Inuvik and from there head back home. Right about now, Brooklyn was looking like a fantastic place to be.

But Godwin had other plans apparently. And as Annja sat there munching away, she watched the flow and energy of the room. Something had changed and it was palpable. Godwin's natural charisma seemed to have taken over. It put people at ease and endeared him without a lot of effort on his part.

He was now a much different person than the quiet driver who had trucked them north to this point. Out from behind the shadow of Derek Wainman, Godwin was very much his own man. And one to be reckoned with, Annja thought. She found his presence slightly intoxicating and wondered if she was infatuated with him or just another victim of his beaming personality.

He glanced over at her a few times and in each instance, a sly grin winked out for a brief second before being withdrawn again. It was like someone dangling a piece of yarn in front of a kitten. Every time Annja tried to smile back, he would be just out of reach.

The hell with it, she thought. He'll be over here soon enough. No sense looking like a silly schoolgirl trying to flirt with him.

She finished her plate of food and got up to throw the scraps away. As she crossed the floor, she spied Wishman holding conference with Nyaktuk. They were deep in conversation and the expression on Nyaktuk's face seemed far grimmer than the environment warranted.

Annja sidled over and nudged Wishman. "Is everything all right? You two look like you're holding a war council or something like that."

Wishman smiled. "It doesn't concern you anymore, Annja. After everything you've done for us, we wouldn't dream of burdening you further with our problems."

"What problems could you have? Last I checked you had a brand-new deal, still owned this land and have nothing but a bright future ahead of you. How could there anything troubling about that?"

Wishman shrugged. "There are…loose ends."

Annja paused. Derek and Hansen. That had to be it. "They're gone. I don't know why you'd even waste your time trying to find them now. Maybe the woods got them. It's not exactly friendly out there, you know."

"None of the trucks were missing," Nyaktuk said. "Which means they have journeyed elsewhere on foot."

Annja eyed him. "Let me guess—you want to go after them."

Nyaktuk nodded. "We cannot let them escape."

Wishman held up his hand to stop Annja before she could protest. "I know what you're thinking, Annja. And you're right. We have a wonderful thing here and should do nothing to jeopardize it. But we cannot let those two men escape. If we do so, they will simply come back another day and try their luck with us again."

"Is this more about being proactive or another useless act of machismo? If this is going to be one of those jaunts, you can count me out right now."

"After everything you've witnessed about the Araktak, do you really believe that we would conduct ourselves like that?" Wishman smiled but it was cold. "We must find them and take them if we are to have the peace we so richly deserve."

Annja frowned. "We'll see."

She turned and found Godwin approaching her. He nodded at Wishman and Nyaktuk. "Do you mind if I steal her away from you for a few minutes?"

"As if I belong to them," Annja said. She elbowed Godwin and got him to walk with her. "What's on your mind?"

They walked toward an unoccupied corner of the lodge and Godwin folded his arms. "Are you in a hurry to get out of here?"

"I'm thinking yes, but I know you have something else in store for me. Don't you?"

He smiled and Annja found herself drawn to him as if

seeing him for the first time. "It would be nice if you could hang around for a time," he said.

"Why?"

He looked into her eyes. "Do you really need the answer to that question?"

"Maybe."

He smirked. "You've got a real playful side to you, don't you?"

"Doesn't everyone?"

Godwin shrugged. "Not necessarily. I've known plenty of people who couldn't have fun if their lives depended on it. They're so locked into these molds they think society wants them to be in that they forget how to be human, how to have fun or just generally be entertaining to be around."

"Well, I've found that brushes with death are a real good cure-all for that kind of behavior."

"Is that so?" Godwin rubbed his chin. "Perhaps I should look into that kind of action. Get the old blood flowing, huh?"

Annja patted his chest. "You know, part of me thinks that there are a lot of different sides to you and you're very careful about what you show the rest of the world. And that underneath whatever exterior you project, there's something pretty special happening there."

Godwin smiled. "Maybe you're right."

"I think I am."

Godwin cleared his throat. "Yeah, well, if you happen to feel like sticking around, who knows? You just might find out if you're right or wrong."

"I've been wrong before," Annja said. "Being right feels a whole lot better to me."

"Yeah, I thought you might say that."

"So, for chuckles, why don't you tell me what's so important that you want me to hang around for?"

Godwin looked around the room. "We've got a good thing going on here. But I'd be a fool to think that it's absolutely secure."

"You think someone wants to sabotage it?"

"No, it's not that. These are good men. Any one of them would stand on the word he gives. But I feel like we might be threatened from an exterior influence."

"Meaning what?"

"We need to find Derek and Hansen." Godwin looked around the room again. "As long as they're around, we have a potential problem. A big one at that."

"You think they'd try to take the deal into the courtroom and battle it out there?" Annja sighed. The prospect of having to go after those two didn't exactly warm her over. She wanted to go home and be away from all of this craziness. She needed to figure out how she'd managed to defeat a dark god—if that's what she'd done. Tracking people across the frozen tundra didn't sound like a lot of fun.

"They might," Godwin said. "Or they might try to get up to their old tricks and start some sort of evil again."

"But their god...I killed it, I guess."

Godwin nodded. "Wishman filled us in on what you accomplished. How you did that, I don't think I'll ever know."

"Join the club."

"But the idea of it worries me. If they could somehow... resurrect that thing, then what's to stop them from trying again with some other long-forgotten deity?"

"How many more are there?" Annja asked. "I was hoping that would be the only one."

Godwin looked at her. "You're not that naive. You know as well as I do that the universe is rife with evil. Wherever good exists, there's the counterbalance. And sometimes, it's unbalanced."

"And you feel that leaving Hansen and Derek to their own devices would unbalance things in their favor, right?"

Godwin nodded. "We've done a lot of work here. A lot of good things have been ironed out. And to just take our chances at this point would be an insult to that work. We've got to make sure that we can have a lasting deal that will provide for the future generations of the Araktak. Not to mention the welfare of the miners and their families. For this thing to work, we need to find those two before they unleash something else against all of us."

"And you feel strongly that they will."

"Very much so."

Annja sighed. She felt eyes on her and glanced up to see Wishman and Nyaktuk watching them intently. She frowned and glanced back at Godwin. "I see this was a tag-team recruitment, huh?"

He smiled. "I won't insult you by suggesting otherwise. Wishman came to me and said he felt like it would be easier if I spoke with you about it. When you interrupted them over there, that was just coincidence."

Annja shook her head. "No such thing as coincidence."

"Well, it was unintentional on our part. The fact that you expressed an interest, though, that makes me feel like you might be willing to come along with us."

"Us? Who's going on this little adventure?"

Godwin shrugged. "Well, me for one."

"That's a good start."

He smiled. "And Wishman says he must come with us. Nyaktuk will be there, as well."

"Four of us?"

"We mentioned it to Dufresne, in order to give him the option of accompanying us. It was mostly out of respect, but we'd welcome another hand on the mission. God knows what those two might be up to out there."

Annja sighed. She could tell that what they told her was the truth. Leaving Derek and Hansen alone would probably only produce a greater threat in the near future. And if Annja thought about the sword as part of her destiny, then she had to be willing to accept the notion that she had the sword for a reason—to help thwart evil wherever it might manifest itself.

And evil had certainly manifested itself here in the frozen Arctic. Despite her stopping the evil creature that Hansen and Derek had summoned forth, the simple truth was they still lived.

Unless they had succumbed to the environment.

But somehow Annja didn't think so. She'd seen enough evil to know that it would burn hottest in the hearts filled with hatred and rage. The two of them would survive out there, wherever they were. Most likely, they would even find a way to thrive in the inhospitable environment, fueled by their rampaging quest for personal power and glory.

If a line was to be drawn in the war against good and evil, then now was the time. Whether Annja felt like drawing it or not. She didn't feel that she had much of a choice in the matter.

Destiny.

Annja waved Wishman and Nyaktuk over. She watched them move quickly as if they had been waiting for the signal for hours.

Wishman smiled at her. "I am sorry that we've had to put you in this situation, Annja."

"At least you're calling me by my real name. That's a start, I suppose." She smiled at him. "You feel strong enough to make the trip? We might have to journey a long way. They have a head start of many miles on us. They could be headed anywhere. And there's been fresh snow while I was unconscious. That means their trail will be a hard one to follow."

Wishman smiled. "We have traveled these lands for millennia. We know every branch and stone for hundreds of miles. If we listen closely, the spirit of the land will tell us exactly how to find them."

Nyaktuk grunted. "I can track them anywhere. I have had many good teachers who have schooled me in the ways of tracking men."

Annja looked at Godwin. "And you? You're up for this?"

Godwin nodded. "I'm looking forward to it. It will allow me to feel closer to the roots of my heritage."

"Godwin is ready to undertake this journey," Wishman said. "And in fact, it will be necessary for his personal destiny."

Annja shrugged. "Well, I guess there's no way I'm getting out of it, huh?"

Godwin grinned. "Is that a yes?"

"It's not a no." Annja looked at them as one and sighed. "When do we leave?"

29

The next morning dawned white and frosty again as the cold winds swept over the plain. Annja was up earlier than she expected, feeling as though she'd stored almost too much energy during her two-day impromptu vacation. She could feel the restlessness in her spirit and knew she wanted to get on with the journey. In reality, it was more likely a hunt than anything else.

She stood atop the burial mound and waited for the others to arrive. As she scanned the surrounding countryside, she wondered which way Derek and Hansen would travel. The wide, gently sloping plain spread in every direction for at least a mile, hemmed in by swaths of snow-frosted pine trees. Every now and again, the winds would send shuddering waves through the boughs, giving the area a strange atmosphere of desolation and loneliness.

As Annja stood there, she cast her eyes north. Beyond this point, the land receded as the Arctic Ocean swelled inland, breaking the masses into islands and peninsulas.

Travelers who did not know the lay of the land could easily find themselves trapped on an outcropping that would be nothing but a dead end.

Still, Annja wasn't worried. With Wishman and Nyaktuk as her guides, they would be able to follow the landmasses and track Derek and Hansen. That was assuming they were even still in the area.

But Wishman seemed to think they were.

To the east and west, the landscape changed to include hills that grew to mountains covered by rocks, lichen and stubby trees. She could clearly make out the snow-covered craggy peaks that jutted out of the earth at odd angles. Perhaps Derek and Hansen had trekked that way. Given that their first goal was not achieved, Wishman felt they might have a backup plan. Was there some evil denizen lurking in the ancient mountains they would seek to call forth?

Annja shuddered. There was something inherently desolate about being in such a frozen environment. Life seemed scant and restricted to the few hours that the sun tried to reclaim its dominant position in the sky. Otherwise, darkness and the cold reigned supreme, forcing life into hollows and tunnels beneath the frigid crust.

Even the dead had to find solace under the earth, Annja thought. And they weren't safe. What chance do we have out in the open, as we'll be, hunting two avowed evildoers intent on causing mayhem and destruction?

But she wouldn't lose herself in the uncertainty of the situation. What was the use in that? As she took a breath, she caught a whiff of something on the air and turned instinctively toward the entrance of the burial mound. The delicate perfume scent seemed to emanate from inside.

Annja stooped in front of the entrance and sucked another breath in through her nostrils. The smell was there and she reeled back. She felt light-headed and almost swooned from the scent. What was that smell? It was the same as the one from the herb she'd found the other day in the wake of the explosion. But that had crumbled into dust as soon as she picked it up. Unable to identify it that quickly, she would never know what it was.

"Annja?"

She turned and saw Wishman coming through the trees toward her. She stood and greeted him. He nodded at the burial mound.

"Reliving the victory?"

Annja shook her head. "I smelled something."

"What?"

She shook her head. "I don't know what it is, actually. But the other day when we went down to see the damage, I found something. It looked like an herb or a plant or something. But it was so badly burned that it crumbled in my hands. Only the scent remained. The same as I just smelled. It caused me to go light-headed."

"Are you all right?"

"Yes. Now. A bit of fresh air is all I really needed. But it's got me thinking that something like that would be a powerful sedative if applied properly."

Wishman smiled. "Most likely, it was a bundle of sacred plants used to help seal the wall. When the explosion happened, the plants, now dried and fragile anyway, would have pretty much vaporized. Perhaps that is what you smelled."

"What sort of herbs would have been used to seal the wall?"

Wishman shrugged. "Strong medicinal plants most likely. Belladonna, oleander, assorted other varieties."

"Some of those aren't indigenous to this area."

"No, but as with the *lignum vitae* wood, we bartered for the more exotic plants. The goal was to use enough of a magical combination to ensure the creature inside did not have a chance to escape."

Annja raised her eyebrows. "So, you borrowed magical techniques from other places?"

"One of the foundations of the Araktak tribe is that we will always use what works best for our cause. If we are in need of material, or even knowledge, then we will do whatever it takes to obtain such things. In this case, our shamans determined that what we needed were more powerful herbs than we had access to."

"I never realized that the trade routes of the Inuit were as well-established as they seem to be."

Wishman smiled. "One of the great unknowns, but yet, we did remarkably well before the modern age. For hundreds of years our kind spread out into five distinct areas, trading with Europeans and Norsemen who settled parts of Greenland and Labrador."

"It's all fascinating," Annja said.

"It is our history," Wishman said. "And now we have the opportunity to write yet another chapter of our on-going saga."

"The war between good and evil," Annja said. "And I suppose I'm one of those things that you go out and obtain if it helps your cause. Is that right?"

Wishman's smile grew larger. "You see? You are becoming much more accustomed to the Araktak way of life than you realize. That is indeed what you might say we are engaged in now."

"So, I'm a tool?"

"You are a friend, Annja. Never forget that."

Godwin came through the trees, followed by Nyaktuk.

Nyaktuk drew two sledges behind him, with deep runners that sliced into the fresh snow. Atop the sledges, several packs of provisions lay along with three rifles.

Annja nodded at the sledges. "Three guns only?"

Godwin smiled. "Well, you do have that sword. We felt giving you a gun might be unfair to our enemies."

Annja smiled. "Good morning to you, too."

Nyaktuk brought one hand up and shaded his brow with it. He looked to Wishman. "Which way do you think they have headed?"

Wishman closed his eyes and chanted softly under his breath. After a minute of this, he opened them again and turned slightly to the right. "East. To the mountains. They will make for the Ragjik Pass."

"What's the Ragjik Pass?" Annja asked.

Nyaktuk frowned. "A place of despair."

Annja sighed. "That doesn't tell me much."

Wishman held up his hand. "We must start now. The pass lays a solid thirty miles to the east. And they have a head start on us."

Annja frowned. "No dogs for this leg of the journey, huh?"

"We will take turns riding the sledges to conserve our strength," Wishman said. "And on the downward legs, we'll be able to ride, as well. But I fear most of our journey will be a climb."

Godwin smiled at Annja. "Still up for this?"

"If I try to leave, will you let me go?"

"Not a chance." He smirked. "Not that I'm kidnapping you or anything. But you know, we need you on this."

Annja held up her hands. "We did the recruitment thing last night. It's fine. I'm in all the way on this." She turned to Nyaktuk. "Now, tell more about the Ragjik Pass. Why is it so full of despair?"

Nyaktuk tightened the straps on the sledge. "The pass is virtually inaccessible during the winter snows. Avalanches are common in those parts. It is wise to avoid them at all costs."

"Ah," Annja said. "So this is turning into a suicide mission." She sighed. "Well, as long as I know what to expect."

Godwin rubbed her shoulder. "We're in this together."

"I know it." She glanced at Wishman. "Is there any sort of significance to the pass itself? Why would they head there when they could go someplace more hospitable to them?"

Wishman shook his head. "The pass is supposedly haunted by an evil spirit that seeks to trap climbers and bury them alive. The legend is that the spirit is of a great animal that used to roam these parts but has since fallen extinct."

"What, like a mammoth or something?"

Wishman shrugged. "No one knows. Over the years many have ventured into the pass. None of them have ever returned to tell the stories of their adventures. I have known a dozen men from various tribes who have tried their luck. None of them live this day."

"And that's where we're going. I really need to plan my vacations better."

Annja mounted the sledge closest to her and looked at the others. "So, why are we still here? Let's get going. How long will it take us to cover the thirty miles to the mountains?"

Nyaktuk shook his head. "It depends on the conditions. We could reach it in a day or two. Or it could take us longer. We are still in the grip of winter and the snow falls long and hard this time of year. Any bit of travel will have to be cautious. But we know the route to travel and the safest one is also the fastest."

Annja watched as Wishman settled himself on the lead

sledge. Nyaktuk would drive it by running and walking through the snow. Annja hoped he'd had a big breakfast.

Godwin stood next to Annja and she gestured for him to climb aboard. "I'll take the first shift driving."

He frowned. "Are you sure? Something about that doesn't feel right. Maybe I should take the first stint."

"Don't get all manly on me now. Just take the chance to rest. I've got a ton of extra energy I'm actually dying to burn off. Now, let's stop arguing about it and just get going."

She pushed off, following Nyaktuk at a comfortable pace. They slid down the gentle incline of the plain and then in minutes, they were already into the trees at the far side of the plain.

Behind them, the burial mound receded from view. Annja glanced at it one last time and wondered if she would see it again.

"Dufresne turned down the chance to come along, huh?"

Godwin nodded. "He said his place was with his men. I don't know if he has the stomach for what we're doing."

"And what exactly are we doing?"

"Stopping Hansen and Derek."

"By doing what?"

Godwin shifted to look at her. "What exactly are you asking me, Annja? Do you want to know if we're going to kill them?"

Annja shook her head. "I think I know the answer to that question."

"Good." Godwin turned back around. "Because, unfortunately, I don't think that they will give us any option but to kill them."

"It feels weird, though," Annja said. "We're going out to kill them. This is an assassination mission more than anything else."

"It's a mission to stop the evil they intend to unleash." Godwin shrugged. "I don't have a problem reconciling it in my mind."

"Have you taken a life before?"

This time Godwin didn't turn around. "What do you think, Annja? Do you feel like I have?"

Annja shrugged and watched as Nyaktuk altered his course. She followed suit. "I don't know. Like I said last night, there are many parts of you. And a lot of them I haven't seen yet."

"Give it time and you will," Godwin said. "That much I can promise."

"I don't doubt it," Annja said. "But will I like what I see when you do show me?"

Godwin shrugged. "I suppose we'll find out when the time is right."

Annja nodded. That they would. But the tone of his voice made Annja wonder exactly what he would show her. She didn't think that Godwin was a greenhorn when it came to violence. She had already seen how he'd handled himself at the bar in Inuvik. Those unaccustomed to fighting didn't move the way Godwin had.

No, she thought, he knows how to fight.

And to kill.

Part of that realization made her feel safer, given what they were riding toward.

But another part of it worried her.

A lot.

30

They traveled quickly over the thick snow that bulked the surrounding landscape with dizzying depths throughout the winter months. The sledges helped ease the strain of the travel by bearing the heavy loads, but the going was still tough in places where they had to plow through chest-high drifts. Fierce winds blew down from the ocean and through the forests they traveled through. While the trees broke up some of the force, in some places, they only served to intensify the blasts. Annja felt cold even when she huddled in front of the blazing fires they built to ward off as much of the chill as they could at night.

They built snow caves, using what nature had already provided, rather than use wood that could instead be spent on building the fire larger and hotter. They crowded inside and built small ledges so the colder air inside dropped to the floor and the heat rose to warm their bodies. Inside the caves, the temperature soared to an almost bearable forty degrees, but huddled inside their sleeping bags, they survived the bitterly cold nights, only to emerge at dawn to another day of relentless cold.

For Annja, despite her travels to the bottom of the world, this cold seemed far worse. It never stopped trying to find ways to infiltrate the many layers she wore. On the second day of their travels, Annja thought about how nice a long, hot bath would be. She imagined the heat seeping into her sore muscles. The cold seemed to shrink everything about her as her very cells clustered together in a vain attempt to find heat amid the frigid conditions.

Wishman drove them on a course that defied logic. They would travel east for a distance, then south, only to turn west and then head north for a short distance before once again turning east. Annja had questioned him about it the first time he did it.

"Are we lost?"

He merely shook his head once, as if doing any more would cost too much of his body heat. "No. But you must always act as though you are being followed. Then you plan accordingly."

Annja frowned. Who would have been following them through this misery? They were already hunting Derek and Hansen. Was there a chance they had passed them already and now the evil demon worshippers were on their trail instead? Or was it just ancient Araktak wisdom that suggested using trickery to confound potential pursuers even when there weren't any?

Regardless, they traveled on, ever on, toward the mountains and Ragjik Pass. Godwin seemed immune to the cold, even though Annja knew how much he hated it. Or at least, she knew how much he claimed to hate it. Despite the shivering wind chill that sucked every bit of thermal energy away from them, Godwin never once complained.

Even Nyaktuk expressed wonder at his seemingly calm demeanor. Nyaktuk himself had started complaining about the ever-present wind.

Wishman called it a spirit and Annja remembered that the Inuit belief was that every living thing had a soul. Probably, she reasoned, they would have gifted the environment with spirits of its own. And when the wind blew as hard as it did, it only made it seem as though they had aroused the wrath of a vengeful, blustery deity.

The sledges carried them far across the forest and tundra of the frozen north. At night, Annja swore she heard the howls of wolves in the distance. Godwin always volunteered to take the first watch and stayed poised by the entrance of the snow cave with his rifle in gloved hands while the others slept.

On the third day of travel, Wishman stopped frequently. Annja found herself wondering if the old man had it in him to push the pace as he was. God knows how old he is, she thought. And he really ought to be at home resting in front of a blazing fire instead of out here in the wilderness.

He glanced at her then and she saw the familiar twinkle in his eyes. It was as if he had read her mind but only shrugged as if to say, What's the use of being alive if you choose to hide inside all the time?

Wishman turned back to consulting the small bones he carried with him in his jacket. Instead of casting them on the ground, he now cast them on the backpacks on top of the sledges. Each time he threw them, he bent close and seemed to study them carefully for minutes on end.

Annja grew frustrated. Each stop was costing them time. And time meant that Derek and Hansen might get closer to their next destination.

She frowned. If they even were headed in this direction.

As much faith as she had in Wishman, she had to wonder if they were on the right track or not. Wasn't it possible that the two evil ones had simply fled the Arctic and journeyed back home to regroup? Couldn't they even now be enjoying a hot cup of coffee and planning their revenge?

The thought of it didn't exactly make her happy, but it also underscored her own concern that they might simply be wasting their time on a fruitless and extremely taxing journey.

Still, Wishman led them and on the afternoon of the third day, as the sun started its descent, they at last spotted the mountains in the east.

Annja caught her breath at the sight of them. Their craggy peaks rose like proud, weathered faces turned into the wind, accepting all the abuse the icy gales heaped upon them without uttering a word of complaint. She could see the thick snows that blanketed them and the exposed rock that ran through the blanket of white like gray-and-black veins. The entire appearance gave the area a very strange look.

Wishman pointed at the mountains. "That is our destination. And there is where we will find our prey."

They set up camp that night in the shadow of a nearby hill, positioning them so they were on the leeward side out of the wind. Nyaktuk and Godwin constructed the snow cave while Wishman fed long sticks into the fire. Annja found that her sword was quite useful in chopping down dead branches of nearby trees and she carried a heaping bundle in her arms back to the camp.

Godwin had also constructed a heat wall to throw some of the precious heat back toward the snow cave's entrance. It didn't work quite as well as they'd all hoped it would.

As night fell, they ate by the fire, chewing on the meat that had frozen over the course of the day, their jaws working on the freshly defrosted meal. Annja found herself working twice as hard to ingest enough calories. Her body seemed to be burning through the food she took in at an alarming rate.

They drank hot coffee as soon as it boiled, knowing that it would cool rapidly. Annja's breath stained her face and then froze there, giving her a sheet of frost on her skin.

When they crawled into the snow cave that night, Wishman laid out their plans for the next day.

"Tomorrow, we will make for Ragjik Pass. It should take us most of the day to reach the mountain and then from there, we will have to leave the sledges and climb up the narrow trail that few know about."

Annja looked at him. "And how do you know about it?"

Wishman smiled. "Because I have climbed Ragjik once before."

Annja frowned. "I thought you said no one ever comes back from there."

"I did," Wishman said. "I climbed but did not have the courage to enter the pass itself." He frowned and looked down at the floor of the snow cave. "I pray that tomorrow I will be able to forego my former cowardice and enter it as I should have long, long ago."

"Well," Annja said, "we'll be with you. You won't be alone this time. That should make it a little easier at least."

Wishman sighed. "I was not alone before. In my youth, I traveled to the pass with my best friend. He and I set out determined to climb and enter the pass. We would camp there a night and then return home having proved that the pass was safe and not haunted. For us, as boys, it was our chance to test our bravery against the legends that had haunted us for many years."

He shifted, trying to get more comfortable in his sleeping bag. "But when we approached the mountain, some kind of fear gripped me like never before. I was young, true, but this felt like an old fear. It was almost a living thing. I had already started my studies into the mystical rituals of the Araktak, so perhaps I was more attuned to such things. But for my friend, he could not understand my sudden lack of resolve."

Annja found herself holding her breath as Wishman continued his tale. "Of course, my friend challenged me to climb with him. He taunted me, trying to galvanize me into action. But it would not work. I told him I would not climb the mountain and I would not enter the pass."

Godwin watched from where he sat wrapped up by the entrance of the cave. "You do not have to relive this tale," he said.

Wishman shook his head. "No, I should. It may help me tomorrow when I once again face that dreaded place." He paused and then took a breath. "At last, my friend was able to convince me to at least journey up the mountain with him. He would then enter the pass while I returned to our camp at the base of the mountain. As much as I did not want to go, I agreed and we set out that next morning.

"The winds blew ferociously that next day as if the very spirits of the north were trying to keep us away. I saw it as an omen, but my friend did not. He was determined to press on and dragged me with him, urging me ever forward despite the growing fear in my belly.

"The trail we took only allowed passage one at a time so we climbed single file up the treacherous pathway. Everywhere there was the chance for a misstep and a sudden plunge to death. The higher we climbed, the less sure the footing became. We contested with snowdrifts that blocked the trail in sections. And there were loose bits of shale and slate that cascaded down the mountain at us when we managed to find parts of the trail not covered by snow.

"The day grew long and our feet never stopped moving. I had not realized that the mountain would stand as tall as it did. From the base camp we'd made, it looked as though we could climb it in a matter of hours."

"But that wasn't the case?" Annja asked.

"You will see tomorrow."

Annja turned back to her bag and nestled herself down as Wishman continued his story.

"We pressed on and a blizzard came down on us, tearing at our exposed skin and clothes with equal ferocity. I found that for every step I took going forward, the wind would push me back two. My friend urged me on. I sometimes think he needed to hear his voice yelling at me to help steel his own nerve. I think he had also begun to falter, but he would not give up the quest as readily as I.

"At last, we drew up to a secluded section and the wind abruptly died. Overhead, a giant boulder acted as a roof and we paused in our travel to have a small meal. The wind had died and the snows had stopped falling. This brief interlude should have caused us to reconsider our plans.

"I pleaded with my friend that we should descend the mountain and go home, but he wouldn't hear of it. He took the lull in the storm as indication that we should press on. He told me that the pass was just a mile further ahead and that we would be there in no time.

"I tried one final time and then told him I would not go any further. He was welcome to taunt me all he wanted, but I had had enough. I hated the thought of leaving him there, but my own sense of self-preservation demanded that I get myself back down the mountain."

"He didn't go with you?" Annja asked.

Wishman shook his head. "No. He stayed there. He said he would rest and then journey on to the pass by himself. He was angry with me for not coming along. I think part of him believed that if he was able to get me to climb that I might forget my fear and agree to go all the way. But that wasn't the case. Each step of the climb only served to convince me more that we should not have been there."

"What happened?" asked Godwin.

Wishman sighed. "I somehow managed to get myself back down the mountain to our base camp. I was ragged by the time I made it. My nerves had left me long ago and my strength dwindled to the point of sheer exhaustion. I made myself a fire and tucked in to try to rest. I was hoping that my friend would appear at any moment and we would be together again before starting for home."

Wishman took a deeper breath. "At midnight, I heard an awful shriek such as I had never heard before and have never heard since. It tumbled off of the mountain and I heard it plain as day despite the howling wind. I knew in my heart that my friend had managed to make it to the pass. What had happened to him then, I had no idea. But I knew he wouldn't be coming back down the mountain to meet me.

"In the morning, I packed up and headed back to our village. I told everyone that we had gotten separated on the way in a storm and I had managed to find my way back. They sent searchers to try to find him, of course, but no one would ever go near the mountain. And so he was gone. And I alone survived. Perhaps I shouldn't have."

Annja glanced at Godwin, but his face seemed hardened to stone. Annja saw Wishman turn over and drift off to sleep. Nyaktuk had already fallen asleep at some point during the story, but Annja felt certain he already knew the tale.

She dug herself deeper into her sleeping bag and

thought about what was coming tomorrow. And then she thought about Wishman's story for a long time until sleep mercifully claimed her.

31

The snow fell deep that night, caking the cave in a fresh layer of six inches of fluffiness that belied the frigid nature of the landscape. Annja blew through the last bit of snow and then clawed her way out of the snow cave to stand in the gray light of the day. Overhead, thick clouds blotted out the sun and flakes continued to spiral downward.

Wishman stood next to her. "It will snow for the remainder of the day. Perhaps several days," he said.

He looked at the sky and the deep crevices on his face caught the daylight and turned them into shadowy trenches running the length of his countenance. He's seen a lot of life, thought Annja. His wrinkles tell their own tales of battle.

"I've never forgotten the sound of my friend's scream," Wishman said. "The way it carried out over the mountain and fell into the deepest parts of my soul. It has remained there for many years. It haunts me. And I think I've known ever since that night that my destiny would one day bring me back here to face my fear anew."

Annja faced the mountain. In the wake of the story Wishman told them, it looked even more imposing than when she'd seen it yesterday for the first time. She could make out no sign of a trail winding its way up the boulders and slick runs. But she knew it would be there. Most likely it was an old game trail used by goats and the like as they prowled the nooks looking for something to eat.

Now it would lead them up the mountain toward the pass.

"How long will it take us to climb?" she asked.

He grunted. "With the weather? I don't know. Conditions down here are pleasant enough, but on the mountain, they'll be far worse. The winds alone will reduce our mobility."

"So, how long?"

Wishman looked at her. "We arrive when we arrive. To plan otherwise would be foolish."

Annja nodded. Nyaktuk was readying his sledge, while Godwin made sure the packs were tied down tight. Annja walked over and pointed at the back of the sledge. "I'll take the first shift."

Godwin didn't argue. He'd insisted on spending the majority of the night on watch. Annja had seen how he gripped the rifle.

Annja wasn't sure what was going on in his mind. Perhaps there was something in Godwin's own past that drove him on like this. Another aspect of his being that Annja had not yet glimpsed.

She felt no sense of danger from him in terms of a threat, but there seemed to be a new cloak of intensity that had settled about his shoulders and emanated from his pores. Godwin the shy driver was forever gone. Whether he was embracing his inner Araktak, Annja didn't know. But she did know that she felt much more comfortable knowing that Godwin was on their side.

They set off from the snow cave after reducing it to a scattered pile of snow. They extinguished their fire and buried all traces of their passage. The deep welts left by the runners of the sledges would frost over with the fresh fallen snow and soon only the trees would know of their passage through this part.

By midmorning they had reached the base of the mountain. Wishman hopped off the sledge and took his time scanning the nearby area. Godwin watched him.

"He's looking for the way into the trail," Nyaktuk said.

"Is this the first time you've been here?" Annja asked.

Nyaktuk didn't take his eyes off Wishman but nodded. "The stories are ones we've all heard. But Wishman's willingness to share his personal story with you last night is something I've never seen him do before. I know that he feels very strongly about stopping those two men."

Godwin gripped his rifle. It was never out of reach now. "Once we get onto the trail, we'll have the leave the sledges here, huh?"

Nyaktuk nodded. "We will hide them for the return trip." He shrugged. "If there is one."

Annja glanced at Godwin, who had no reaction to that possibility. Annja frowned. She intended to come back, one way or another. The thought that this would be some sort of one-way ticket didn't sit well with her. Of course, part of her wondered if the sword would even let her come to harm.

But every time she had tried to figure it out, the sword usually had its own ideas. So Annja gave up trying and watched as Wishman continued to poke among the giant boulders that littered the ground close to the base of the mountain.

After an hour spent scanning the ground, Wishman's

head finally poked out from behind a particularly large boulder and he waved them on. "It is here."

Godwin wrestled the packs free of the sledge and they all took one on their back. Annja tightened the straps so her hips would take the majority of the weight. She moved over to where Wishman stood and looked.

He was in a small valley between two boulders. The smile on his face looked sheepish. "It has been many years since that fateful trip. I apologize for taking so long to find my way back to the trail."

Godwin waved it off. "What matters is that we found it." He looked up the mountain. "It is a gradual incline."

Wishman nodded. "At first. The way for the first thousand feet of ascent is easy enough, even with the packs. From there we will have to be very careful. There are many dangers along the trail. Take your time and we will not hurry."

Annja shielded her brow and looked up the mountain. Far up, she thought she could see some sort of overhang. "Is that the pass?"

Wishman followed her gaze and grunted. "That is the overhang where we huddled before my friend journeyed into the pass by himself."

Annja looked at him. "You're sure this is where Derek and Hansen have come?"

Wishman shook his head. "No. I am not. But the spirits have told me it is so. I must have faith that they would not lead me astray. The time for me to return to the place that haunts me is at last here."

Godwin shifted under the weight of his pack. "Who wants to take the lead?"

Wishman stepped forward. "I have been here before. I will go first."

Nyaktuk frowned. "Is that wise?"

"I know the ground," Wishman said. "And with each step I will feel more familiar with it, whereas none of you have seen this place before."

Nyaktuk bowed. "Very well."

Godwin looked at Nyaktuk. "Do you want to follow him or bring up the rear of our train here?"

Nyaktuk considered the options and then said, "It may be better if I follow Wishman directly. If he stumbles, I can help him."

"All right," Godwin said. "After you, we'll put Annja and then I will bring up the rear." He looked at all of them individually. "If I yell for you to get down, please do it without hesitation. I will need to get a clear shot with the rifle."

Wishman seemed as if he wanted to say something, but then thought better of it and merely nodded. Godwin gazed at him and then Nyaktuk. Unspoken words seemed to pass among them, but Annja could fathom none of it.

"Let's get going," Godwin said.

Annja fell into the line and watched as Wishman, who had also insisted on bearing the load of a pack on his back, led them up the start of the trail. As they walked, Annja grew more and more amazed that the trail was virtually invisible to anyone looking at the mountain. But she could see how mounds of dirt and rocks obscured the outside edge of the trail blending it in with the rest of the mountain. No wonder she hadn't been able to see their way up from down at the base.

The snowfall increased as they climbed ever higher. Annja felt the wind stinging her face and she glanced back at Godwin several times searching for a smile to help keep her warm.

He had none to give. Godwin scanned the ground every

minute or so. Otherwise, his eyes remained fixed well ahead of them, constantly roving over the landscape and above them as if he expected an ambush. His feet gripped the ground with certainty and there seemed no hesitation in his movements.

Annja was far less sure of her own footing and turned back to concentrating on where she placed her feet. Twice, she had almost rolled her ankle on loose stones that went skittering down the trail toward Godwin. His response was always the same. By the time the rocks reached him, he had directed his body out of the way and they flew past him oblivious to the man they might have otherwise struck.

Wishman kept up a good pace, pausing only every hour to gather his wits about him. Annja could see that the clouds overhead showed no signs of moving on, as if the peaks were a magnet for their presence.

As the slope of the trail increased, Annja felt the strain on her back and tried to adjust her load. She had started this trip feeling overly energized and was now starting to question how much juice she had in her cells.

She imagined the sword and felt a small drip of extra strength that propelled her up the slope a bit better. Behind her, Godwin's footsteps were mere whispers in the afternoon air. His stealthy tread skirted the ice and rocks that now littered the pathway.

Annja stepped over them, careful of what she came down on. She knew that one misstep on a slippery patch of ice could pitch her headlong over the side of the mountain. She risked a look down and saw that they were now almost five hundred feet up.

The path seemed to corkscrew around part of the mountain. In other places it seemed to go straight up, carving chunks out of the mountain. There was no order to the trail, and Annja supposed that was yet another reason it was so difficult to pick out from far below.

They ate a late lunch of jerky. Annja felt her jaw muscles tighten as she worked the bits of dried meat. Wishman would not permit a fire and Godwin wouldn't have allowed it either if anyone had suggested it.

By three o'clock, they had made their way up half of the mountain. The overhang that Annja had spotted from the base of the mountain still seemed to loom an impossible distance away.

Wishman caught her gaze and grunted with a vague grin. "It will not take us forever to reach it, even though it may seem like it. Things look different on this mountain. You will see when we get there."

They stood with aching muscles and shouldered their packs again. Annja's legs felt as if they had already borne the brunt of the trip and her quadriceps burned like molten iron. She refused to complain about it, though.

Godwin held a huddled conversation with Wishman only to return to his place at the end of the train, rifle always shouldered and at the ready.

Annja looked at him and he seemed to notice for the first time all day. He grinned and there, for an instant, was the old Godwin. "Sorry. How are you doing?"

"I'm tired," Annja said. "This is a hell of a haul."

He nodded. "It's not easy, is it?"

"You don't seem affected by it much."

He shrugged. "I did a lot of climbing with my father when I was younger. I guess I'm sort of used to it by now."

"You did a lot of mountain climbing?"

He nodded. "Mountains, hills, trees, buildings, whatever we could find to climb, we climbed."

Annja smiled. "Well, it's serving you well now."

"If only that was the only skill I needed on this venture," he said. But his voice was quieter and more of a mumble to himself than a statement to Annja. He looked at her and smiled again. "We should keep moving. Wishman has already started up again and we don't want to lose him."

Annja turned back to the trail. Wishman and Nyaktuk were a hundred yards farther on. She hastened to keep up and had to consciously slow herself from rushing when she almost slid off the side of the mountain. Only Godwin's sudden hand on her back had saved her from certain death.

"Thanks."

"Don't worry that they're ahead of us. It's a straight shot for now and we can make up the distance easily. Just keep slogging along and we'll cover it in no time."

Annja nodded. "Yeah, you're right. Sorry about that."

"Forget it. I'm glad to be here."

They walked for another two hours and as the gray clouds overhead turned a darker shade with the coming of night, they rounded a corner and Annja caught her breath. They had walked into a valley of sorts, with two parts of the mountain shooting up on either side of them, one the mountain itself and the other side sprouting up a hundred feet before it sloped back in the opposite direction. Overhead, a giant boulder formed an impromptu rooftop.

And Annja knew they had at last arrived at the place where Wishman and his friend had shared their final meal together.

32

A subdued hush fell upon all four of them as they went about preparing to rest. The gray daylight finally gave way to deepening blues that heralded the onset of night. The wind, which had been their torment throughout the day, fell away as they nestled under the massive boulder.

Annja tried a little levity to lighten things up by pointing at the rock that loomed a few feet over their heads. "You sure this thing won't crush us tonight?"

But it fell on deaf ears. Not one of them broke a grin.

From the packs they drew out their sleeping bags while Nyaktuk and Wishman scavenged bits of bramble to make a small cooking fire. They leaned their packs up against one side of the rock to cover their fire from any eyes that might be ahead of them looking down from on high.

Snow still continued to fall, and the gentle white flakes that drifted slowly down only served to reinforce the dreaded sense of isolation that Annja had felt upon entering this nook in the mountain.

Still, she felt grateful for stopping. It had been a hard day of nonstop walking and the drain on her senses after having been so keen and alert for missteps had left her feeling empty. The food she ate, a reconstituted portion of the delicious stew they had eaten back at the burial mound camp, felt wonderful and warm and she ate greedily. The others did, too.

Finally, after the meal, Wishman huddled them all together and spoke in low tones that Annja could scarcely hear. "We are not far from Ragjik Pass. It is but another thousand yards ahead and the climb falls away to reveal level ground if the original directions my friend and I followed were accurate." He hesitated a moment, looking into each of their eyes before he continued. "Sound is our biggest enemy now. I have little doubt that our prey rests beyond us in the pass."

Annja held up her hand. "And what lies beyond the pass?"

Wishman didn't blink. "Legends say that beyond the Pass lies the entrance to a massive cavern inside the mountain. That is where we will find Wainman and Hansen. There they are even now prepared to unleash yet another dark creature from its slumber."

"Which entity?" Annja asked.

Wishman frowned. "I know it only by the name my people gave it aeons ago—Onur. He is an elemental god with a wrath as fierce as any, and this is his land we are said to be treading upon. As with the other dark gods, he demands sacrifice, in order to come into this plane."

Annja frowned. "I don't recall that Derek or Hansen sacrificed anyone back at the burial mound. How did they unlock that creature then?"

Godwin frowned. "It wasn't them who sacrificed. It was you, Annja."

She whirled. "Excuse me?"

Godwin held up his hand. "You had no idea you were doing it, of course, but that is exactly what Derek wanted. The two idiots who attacked us in the bar were working for him. Later, they chased us in the rig. And when you used your sword to cause them to sink beneath the ice river, I distinctly heard Derek chanting something. I thought it was a song at that time, but I know now that he was offering their souls to the creature at the burial mound."

Annja sighed. "I thought you had to make the sacrifice at the location of the demon you wanted to bring on to this plane." She shrugged. "Of course, I don't exactly study the occult, so that information may be wrong."

Wishman nodded. "If Derek is powerful enough, he can give over those souls how he sees fit. And since they were evil men to begin with, in Wainman's employ, then he had the right to offer them up, according to the old ways."

Great, Annja thought. Here I was thinking I was saving the day and instead, I end up facilitating the destruction at the burial mound. Way to go, ace.

Wishman's hand rested on Annja's. "You could not have known at the time what you were doing. No fault lies with you."

She frowned. "Yeah, well, I'm not feeling good about it. And what about here? Who will they have to sacrifice here to call forth this demon?"

"I imagine they will use one of us," Wishman said.

Annja looked at him. "What?"

He shrugged. "They will know by now that we hunt them. And they would most certainly expect us to, given the damage they caused back at the burial site. They know that Araktak law dictates their pursuit and that justice be wrought upon the criminals. I think they'll use that to their advantage."

"They know we're coming," Annja said. "Wonderful."

"Well, perhaps they don't know you or Godwin here," Wishman said. "But they know that I would come along with Nyaktuk. Since we are both the Araktak who would have to follow this through to the end."

Annja leaned back against on the packs. "So, we start for the pass in the morning?"

Wishman nodded. "It is too late to try for it now. We need every bit of light to aid us in our quest if we are to be successful. The wind and the snow will fall hard tonight and the way will grow even more treacherous by the morning. So sleep well and be prepared for the coming day."

With that, Wishman rolled himself into his sleeping bag and started to snooze. Annja watched him sleep and looked at Nyaktuk.

"Is all of that true?"

Nyaktuk nodded. "If Wishman says it is true, then it must be so. I have studied with him a very long time and know of his ways. He must ready himself for tomorrow now. Not only because of what we three will face, but also what he must face. And I feel that what he will face may well be worse than our own destinies, joined though they are."

Annja slumped down some more. "Who wants first watch?"

Godwin shifted. "I'll take it. You guys get some sleep. I'll wake you first, Annja, and then Nyaktuk."

She nodded. She rolled into her sleeping bag and, despite the frozen ground beneath her, she descended into her dream world. Her limbs relaxed and the knots of tension that had wound themselves throughout the course of the day slowly untied. She yawned once and then drifted off into a perfectly dreamless sleep.

GODWIN NUDGED her awake. Annja wanted to moan but she remembered that Wishman had insisted on as much silence as possible. Reluctantly, she got out of her sleeping bag and took up her position where Godwin had been sitting for the past three hours.

He slid into Annja's sleeping bag, grateful for the heat that remained there, and instantly fell asleep.

Annja watched him doze and smiled. He was the one bright spot of this trip, although she still questioned exactly what his motives were. He seemed even more driven the closer they drew to the pass, almost as if he was the one with the karmic debt to repay and not Wishman.

Annja looked out at the terrain. The moonless night kept everything hidden under a blanket of darkness. No stars shone through the clouds and the only bit of ambient light came from the snowdrifts that continued to build up around them. Annja heard the flakes falling and had to pinch her thigh to keep her eyes from drooping back into the slumber she'd just woken from.

Her eyes sought to pierce the pervasive darkness, but she could see little beyond the realm of their small huddle. They had scattered the cooking fire as soon as they were done making their meal earlier. In the blackest of night, the flames, small though they were, would have been a magnet for anyone keeping watch on the approach to the pass.

Annja sighed. She'd been in combat many times and the one thing she always relied on was the element of surprise. Now, according to Wishman, that was already compromised. Derek and Hansen knew that they were coming.

That meant their enemies would take great pains to attack before they could get into proper position.

Annja shook her head. It somehow violated everything she'd learned about defending herself and protecting others. If it was up to her, she might have suggested they travel back down the mountain, head home and maybe take up the chase some other time.

But she also knew that Wishman had a destiny to fulfill and the time for fulfilling it seemed to be now.

Would have been nice to be consulted first, she thought with a wry grin. At least then she might have known better what she was getting herself into.

Godwin's form rose and fell in time with the other men. There seemed a languid, relaxed danger about him as he dozed. But somehow, Annja knew that if trouble arose, he would spring to her side in a flash, ready with his rifle or the knife she'd seen him attach to his belt.

She'd asked him about it, but he'd drawn his jacket on over it before she could see much of the detail. From what she saw, it looked long and deadly.

Annja shifted her position and then heard the noise.

She froze.

Was she imagining it? She let her jaw relax and tried in vain to again pick up the sound she'd heard, but nothing reached her ears. It had been there, though; she felt sure of it. Just the briefest scuff out of time with the rest of the ambient noises that surrounded them.

And now it was gone.

Was someone headed down here to attack them?

Annja frowned. She could wake any of them to help her, but what if it was just a false alarm?

She rose from her spot and, using all of her skill at remaining quiet, crept out from under the boulder. She scanned the area above them, but could see nothing beyond the snowflakes that continued to drift down. They'd been beautiful before, but now they were an annoyance that clouded her vision. Every time Annja thought she saw something that needed closer scrutiny, the snowflakes fell into her eyes, making that impossible.

Maybe Wishman was right, she concluded. Maybe Onur was the demon of this mountain and knew all the ways to confound travelers.

She walked a little farther away from the camp, her boots light on the fresh snow. Carefully, she picked her way across the whitened landscape, searching for any signs that they might be coming under attack.

But she found nothing. There were no footprints. There were no depressions in the snow where a man might have squatted to ready himself.

Nothing.

Annja was just about to turn back toward her camp when she thought she heard the noise again.

Another scuff.

She could feel her heart start to hammer away at the inside of her chest like a drum. The steady beat brought a surge of warmth to flush her skin with blood as it did the same to her muscles.

But Annja didn't move.

I need to be sure, she thought. I don't want to look like a hysterical fool crying wolf.

One more time, she thought. That's all I'll need.

But the sound didn't come again. Annja cast a long look around at the walls looming over them. Any one of them could sport positions from which to attack, but to try to climb them in the darkness would have been sheer madness. And Annja would have died in the attempt anyway.

She stalked back to the camp. It must be close to the time when Nyaktuk would take his turn at watch, she thought. She was suddenly gripped by the taste of cold that made her shiver. The thought of crawling back into a sleeping bag was a pleasant one.

The camp loomed ahead. Annja made her way through the same footprints that marked her exit from camp and followed them back to the comfort of the overhang.

She paused at the entrance of the camp and placed her hand against the massive boulder that shielded them from the night weather. Nice to find an unlikely ally out here in the midst of hell, she thought. And she patted the ancient stone with reverence. Her way, she supposed, of thanking it for its shelter.

Annja ducked beneath the overhang and froze.

The camp was deserted.

Her spirits plummeted as she tore through the camp, but each sleeping bag was empty. Did they leave me here? she wondered. But just as quickly, she dismissed that idea when she saw that all three rifles were lying about the camp.

She studied the ground and saw tracks that suggested all three had been dragged away.

Annja shook her head. There was no way that any of them would have gone without a fight. So if they hadn't fought, that meant that they had been subdued from the first moment of attack.

But how?

Annja felt certain she knew who was behind it. Derek and Hansen must have trusted their instincts or the whims of their dark masters to know that Wishman and his company were already on the mountain. They had acted first and scored a deep victory.

Did they know that she was among the hunting party?

There were only three rifles in the camp. And while there were four sleeping bags, Godwin had slept in Annja's, leaving the fourth packed.

Perhaps, she reasoned, they believe it was a trio that hunted them and not a quartet.

She smiled, but there was no mirth in it. They may not have known that Annja was a part of the hunters right then.

But soon enough, they would.

33

Annja considered what to do. Should she wait until morning, when she could see her way through the darkness? Or pursue them right now?

She scanned the ground leading out of the makeshift camp. There were clear tracks in the snow that might be ruined if she waited until morning. Plus, she had no idea of how to get into the mountain even if she made it all the way to the pass.

No, the answer was an easy one. She would follow them now.

She left the camp the way it was. Annja figured that the distance would not be as far as she thought. Dragging captives was exhausting work for anyone. And anything over a few hundred yards would tax them to exhaustion.

Perhaps there was a secret entrance that Wishman did not even know about. Perhaps it lurked close by.

Time ran short and Annja crept out of the camp, following the tracks in the snow. She was more than acutely aware that she might well be walking into an ambush.

The urge to take her sword out was great, but she reluctantly denied herself its security. The blade might catch light from the moon and in the darkness, that light might compromise her position.

She would have to walk blind, content to follow the tracks that curved away from her around a bend on the trail. Annja slowed her gait and listened. She heard nothing to suggest a trap and walked on.

Around the bend, the trail straightened again and the deep furrows in the snow led Annja on her way. She felt even more certain now that they did not know she was with the party. If they had suspected she was, they might have taken the time to conceal the tracks.

Or at least leave someone behind to deal with Annja.

But she saw no signs that they were hurrying. And the trenches were easy to follow as the incline increased. Annja felt her legs groan and complain as the renewed exertion taxed their muscle fibers again. It was too soon, they seemed to be saying. Too soon to be starting a hike again.

But Annja's mind forced compliance and her body responded. She'd been taxed to exhaustion before. She'd recovered in every instance. The price was a high one to pay and her recent two-day sleep proved that.

Annja felt a blast of wind whip into her, making her lean into the side of the mountain for support. The snows whipped up a frothy frenzy of flakes that assaulted her face at every step.

She kept her eyes focused on the ground, willing herself to step forward with each breath of ice she inhaled. The tracks kept her concentration although Annja tried her best to maintain some degree of alertness for the possibility of ambush. She doubted they would bother with it on this night. It genuinely seemed as if the ancient spirits were out and Wishman's story came back with a fresh gusto. Annja fought back the fear she felt welling up within her soul and kept on the trail.

And then, in front of her, she saw the pass. There was no sign that this was the place, but somehow, she knew. The side of another mountain, unseen until now, sprang up alongside the trail Annja walked. The sheer face of it was a stark contrast to the craggy face of Annja's mountain.

And the trail went right between the two giants as if it had been flossed through by someone's unseen enormous hand.

Ragjik Pass.

Annja bent her head to withstand the sudden massive blast of wind that charged into her like a bull. The pass acted like a giant wind tunnel, funneling and accelerating the already impressive wind gusts that haunted the peaks. Annja bent herself almost parallel to the ground and managed to take another few steps forward.

What lay beyond the pass? She shielded her eyes and tried to see. But then she realized that the ferocious wind was already destroying the tracks she was following.

I need to keep moving or I'll be lost, she thought. She bent farther and willed her legs to keep moving. On and on she walked, until at last, the second mountain fell back away from the first and Annja moved out of the pass.

The wind abated slightly, but was still a force to be reckoned with. Annja's eyes never left the ground and she could see the tracks better now.

The trail curved and kept winding up the mountain. Over the wind, she thought she heard sounds. They were distant but distinct. Voices? Annja paused and then felt certain she heard someone talking.

She squatted down on the trail and tried to peer through the snowy dark. Ahead, the trail took on a more vertical climb.

The noises she'd heard suddenly stopped. Silence returned to the area and Annja rose and kept walking.

The ground swooped upward and Annja bent forward again, trying to use other muscles to help her aching legs. But each step relied on her feet to keep moving and Annja sucked in breaths to try to keep the muscles replenished with fuel they could burn.

Her heart thundered in her chest, pumping furiously to keep up with the demand. She had to find the destination soon or else she would need to rest and recover out here, not exactly the best idea given the harsh conditions.

The tracks suddenly changed.

Instead of deep furrows showing the way, there was a mass of footprints that showed the captives must have regained consciousness and were now walking on their own. Annja frowned. That probably made their captors happy.

Annja bent once to study the tracks. She could only count three distinct impressions among the mass of overlapping tracks. She knew there would be more than three of them, but given the narrow trail and the snowy conditions, discerning three was a challenge enough.

She slowed her pace. For every step she took, she rested a few seconds, trying her best to regulate her inhalations so she could keep moving without collapsing to the ground, where she would most likely die.

The ground continued to slope upward, forcing Annja to bend forward some more, resting her hands on the tops of her thighs. She was sweating, strangely enough, and that sharpened her mind, aware of how dangerous that was.

Sweating in these conditions would bring about hypothermia that much quicker. As she sweated, it would freeze, thereby accelerating the reduction of her body temperature. If she didn't get out of this mess soon, she was going to die.

Annja forced herself to keep walking. Ahead, she could see that the trail seemed to level off and almost disappear.

Was the climb over? Was this the top of the mountain? She didn't know. From her vantage point on the trail, she couldn't see anything except clouds and snow. The wind continued to whip around her and snowflakes felt like tiny lances of ice.

Her face felt shrunken and tight. She was certain that the ice had caused several cuts, but even blood refused to flow in these damnable environs. Annja took another breath and then stepped up and the trail suddenly leveled off.

She paused and went down to one knee. Around her, she could feel the immense mountain watching her. It had tested her to the extreme limits of her endurance, and only the anger that flowed in her blood had kept her alive this long.

But Annja was dangerously spent. She closed her eyes and tried to draw some energy from the sword. She opened her eyes and felt the hilt of the sword in her hands.

She looked around quickly, fearful that she would be seen, and returned the sword.

Annja searched the ground. She could see the tracks in the snow, but then they simply stopped.

She scanned the walls of rock around her. This was it. There had to be some type of entrance into the mountain itself. This was where they had taken Godwin and the others.

All Annja had to do was find a way inside.

Annja's gloved hand brushed snow from the rock face and probed each nook and cranny for some sort of sign that it would open to the interior of the mountain.

It took her fifteen minutes to find it, but at last her fingers traced their way along a narrow indentation that formed the crude outline of a doorway. Annja traced it until she had the entire dimensions outlined in her mind.

But how did it open?

She stepped back from the doorway and studied how it was formed in the rock. Did it slide inward and then to the side? Or was it hinged somehow? Perhaps it just moved aside on unseen runners.

Annja tried pushing at it until she collapsed against the wall, heaving for breath. It didn't make sense. The climb up to this point had been a massive effort. Why make the door that much harder to get into? There had to be a simpler method for opening it.

Plus, with the extra burden of captives, there had to be a release mechanism.

Annja crouched down and studied the base of the doorway. It seemed to bleed right into the trail itself, but then her eyes caught a glimpse of ground that had been scarred free of snow and ice. It almost looked as if the rock slid back on a track.

Annja stood and searched over the top of the doorway and then felt something out of the ordinary. A piece of twisted metal jutted out of the rock. Annja stood on tiptoe and looked at it. The aged metal had to have been ancient and of some special ore to withstand the conditions up here on the mountain.

Annja summoned her sword and then pressed the metal.

A grumble sounded from the mountain as if it was upset that Annja had succeeded in finding a way inside. But the rock slid back to reveal a dark opening just wide enough to permit one body to pass through.

Annja took a breath and stepped inside.

The rock slid back a second later, almost catching her as it did so. She jumped forward and held her sword aloft.

She could make out that the cavern led into a tunnel of some type that seemed to descend into the mountain. Annja leaned against the wall of the mountain, willing herself to catch her breath. Just holding her sword made her feel better.

No noises reached her ears, although the sound of melting snow dripped all around her. The air temperature was at least forty degrees now, a welcome change to the blizzardlike conditions outside on the mountain's exterior.

Time to move.

Annja crept over to the tunnel entrance. She studied the terrain. The pathway was dry rock, pockmarked with enough depressions to ensure she wouldn't slip on it and tumble to her death.

On either side of the path, the ground fell away for thousands of feet. That was the quick way down, she reasoned.

The tunnel opened farther ahead and Annja thought she could pick up some degree of ambient light. But from what, she had no idea.

She moved forward, slowly. The last thing Annja wanted was to announce her presence before she was ready.

She moved down the tunnel and then out onto a type of stairway. She blinked and immediately put her sword away.

Up ahead of her she could see something moving.

Squinting in the dim light, she could make out the two torches that cast light over Derek and Hansen.

With them were Godwin, Wishman and Nyaktuk.

Everyone looked angry.

34

Annja crouched in the darkness on the stone stairs that led down toward some point far below. There was no way she could attack right now. The stairs were only wide enough to permit one person at a time, and any attempt she made would likely result in the death of Godwin, Wishman or Nyaktuk.

Instead, Annja trailed them down the steps, using the ambient light from their torches to help find her way. The flames appeared like small fiery orbs dancing as they descended ever farther into the bowels of the mountain. Annja couldn't help but wonder when they would stop. Wherever it was, she hoped it was flat ground that she could fight on without worry.

Her breathing had calmed and the more she descended the stairs, the better she felt. Her time on the mountain had drained her, but she could feel her strength starting to return. Her pulse throbbed a steady beat, and she knew that when the fight came, she would be ready.

Around her, the walls of the mountain rose, and the

whole place reminded Annja of a pumpkin carved for Halloween with its guts scraped out. The mountain actually seemed hollow, and once again, Annja thought about the dwarves of modern men who toiled away in the mines and deep caverns beneath such places.

Who was the demon Onur and what was his history? Annja had never heard the name in all her travels or studies. Still, she wasn't that surprised. There were many things that had been lost over time—traces of culture, whole languages and the religious and spiritual customs of countless tribes and ethnicities. Just because she hadn't heard of Onur, it didn't mean he didn't exist. Or that he wasn't a very dangerous foe if allowed to come onto this plane. She knew that wasn't the most rational thought but nothing made sense anymore.

The party ahead of her seemed to pause on the stairs. Annja froze in place, tensed and waiting for them to continue on. Had they spotted her?

But then she heard them urging Wishman to move faster. She couldn't hear their exact words, but the urgency in their voices was evident even at this distance. Most likely the trip had been hard on the old man and he was in need of rest.

If Hansen and Derek had their way, Wishman would be at rest soon enough—terminal rest.

She moved again as the party continued down the steps. Annja was getting closer to them. She was only one person whereas they had five and could not travel as fast.

Gradually, Annja carefully picked her way down the stairs. She remained in a semisquat position.

She believed that there was no way for them to see her unless they looked at her at the wrong moment and caught a glimpse of her movement. She watched them closely and whenever they paused, so did she.

Their scuffles and footfalls rebounded and echoed in the great cavernous passage. Annja had to be especially careful now as she drew ever closer. One mistimed step would alert them and then her element of surprise would be lost.

Right now, that was her most precious weapon.

And if I blow it, she thought, they'll all be dead.

At last, Hansen and Derek led them off the stairs and their torches were level. Annja stayed where she was, still two hundred feet above them, perched like a great jungle cat.

She could hear Derek's voice. "Everyone in good shape?" He laughed. "Well, good, we're so happy about that."

Godwin seemed to be eyeing him. Derek thrust his face at him. "Something you'd like to say?"

Godwin paused and then his words made Annja's hairs stand on end. "I will enjoy seeing you die."

Derek leaned back and laughed. "You first, my friend. And when I drive my blade into your heart, I will feast on your blood."

Godwin was silent and Annja wanted to jump right then and there, but a sudden movement caused her to stop. Another torch came into the flat area from somewhere unseen. There must have been another tunnel that connected to the cavern.

"All is ready."

That voice. Annja recognized it even though she hadn't heard it in days. She tried to ease closer to the ledge and then in the flickering torchlight, she caught a glimpse of the rough-hewn face and knew who it was for certain.

Dufresne.

Annja felt her heart beat faster. The traitor! He'd insisted on remaining at the camp by the burial mound, but here he was. And how had he beaten Annja and the hunting party to the mountain?

Annja thought back to their journey and Wishman's in-sistence that they do their best to set a trail that would delay pursuers. Did Wishman know that Dufresne was a traitor or did he even suspect it?

Yet somehow, Dufresne had reached the mountain first. Annja shook her head. What had become of the Araktak men who had stayed behind at the burial mound? Were all of Dufresne's men evil, as well? Was this entire company hell-bent on sacrifice and resurrecting demons?

Annja wanted to know what had happened, but Du-fresne wasn't alone. There were other men with him now. And these faces, Annja did not recognize. Dufresne spoke to them in French, and they hustled Godwin, Wishman and Nyaktuk away, leaving Dufresne, Derek, and Hansen alone at the foot of the stairs.

Derek cleared his throat. "Who shall we deliver first?"

"The old man is one of the ancients. He has battled the forces of our master for many years. His death will bring him great pleasure," Hansen said.

Derek nodded. "Excellent point. But what about Godwin? He has changed since I met him at the company. Where I once saw a young man who was shy, now he holds himself differ-ently. I was no doubt deceived by him, but to what end?"

Dufresne chuckled. "We could torture him. Find out everything we need to know before we kill him."

"He claims to be a half-breed Araktak, but there is some-thing about his nature that speaks of his past. He's tried hard to conceal it. Hell, he fooled the woman. And he fooled us, as well. But there is something about him, some-thing deadly. I want to know what he's about."

Dufresne bowed once. "I will see to it personally."

Derek smiled. "Make sure he's still alive when you're

done. Our master does not like sacrifices that are already dead."

"On my death I swear it," Dufresne said. He withdrew from the chamber.

Hansen eyed Derek. "Are you sure that's wise?"

Derek shrugged. "Godwin has a story. I would like to know it before I kill him. Did you see the way he looked at me? He knows how to kill—of that I have no doubt. But where did he learn? And has he killed before?"

"I'm certain of it," Hansen said. "But we could find nothing of value in his records. It's almost as if he's some sort of ghost. His claims of being a half-breed don't add up, either."

Derek smiled. "Dufresne will find out his secrets. I've never met a man who could hold out against his technique."

Hansen coughed and the sound echoed up to Annja. "What about the others? Wishman and Nyaktuk must be sacrificed soon. The hour of our master's rebirth grows near."

"We will sacrifice the ancient first. Then Nyaktuk. After that, Dufresne should be finished extracting all the information we need from Godwin. He can then join his fallen friends in the pits of Hell."

"Excellent."

They walked out of the chamber, the fires from their torches receding as they strolled down the unseen tunnel.

Annja crept down the last few steps and paused. In the darkness, she could see the tunnel entrance as a vague outline. The torchlight grew fainter in the distance. She took a breath and stole down the tunnel.

The mountain seemed to be honeycombed with a variety of tunnels and branches that shot off in unknown directions. Some of these, she imagined, might contain dead ends or traps. She'd been in enough ancient tunnels to know that their construction was simultaneously as devious as it was utilitarian.

But somewhere ahead of her, there had to be a room used for the sacrifices that Derek spoke of. That was where she would find Wishman and Nyaktuk.

She had a bigger problem, though. If she freed Wishman and Nyaktuk first, Dufresne might hear the commotion and simply kill Godwin. Likewise, if she freed Godwin first, Hansen and Derek would kill the others.

Annja hesitated at a fork, trying to decide which way to go. She could take the left option, which sloped upward toward some other destination. Or she could go to the right and continue on the level floor. Down that avenue, she could just make out the last of the torchlight from Derek and Hansen.

That would be where they would sacrifice Wishman and Nyaktuk.

Annja frowned and weighed the options. At last, she came to her decision and started up the slope toward the left. She would free Godwin first, trusting in his ability to fight and help her free Wishman and Nyaktuk.

She just hoped they would be able to take on the rest of the people in the mountain. Annja had no way of knowing how many of them there were. She would have to assume there were many more than she had seen so far.

She crept up the tunnel and paused every few feet to listen. Annja knew she was running out of time, but she needed her stealth in order to preserve her advantage for as long as possible.

As she climbed up the slope, she could see flickering torchlight ahead. They lit this area of the mountain. That must mean that there was more activity in this section than in other places.

Annja crouched by the turn and waited. She heard the scuffle of footsteps and noted their rhythmic quality.

A guard.

She would have to take him out before she could progress any farther. She listened carefully, judging when the guard walked closer to her position and when he moved away.

He seemed to be on a three-minute cycle, covering a wide section of the hallway. Annja risked a glance around the bend and saw the torch was fixed in a bracket in the wall of the mountain. At least that would work in her favor. She would have to stalk the guard when he turned his back to her.

She waited until he had come close to her and then turned.

Annja crept from her hiding place and padded down the corridor toward him.

His back was huge and Annja frowned. She never got the small guys to take out. She made sure she was lower than he was and just as he was about to turn back in her direction, Annja snaked an arm around his throat and threw herself backward, rolling back and jerking her arm toward her.

She felt his trachea give way and he started to retch, but Annja kept the pressure on as he fought desperately to clear his airway.

Annja wrapped her legs around his waist for better support and clenched her teeth, listening to him drown on his own vomit as he struggled to get free.

It took almost a full minute for him to pass out from the lack of oxygen to his brain. Annja slowly crawled away from him.

She took a breath as she untangled herself.

She crept up and beyond the range of the torchlight. The

tunnel intersected with another and she had three new options to consider.

She could see more torchlight far off in the distance. Did that mean there was another guard down there? And if so, would she be able to get the jump on him as she had with this one?

She decided to move down the tunnel.

That was when the screaming started.

35

Annja no longer worried about the second guard. All she cared about was reaching Godwin and stopping whatever madness Dufresne had unleashed upon him in his torture chamber. She swooped down the corridor, her sword already unleashed.

The second guard she expected to find by the torch was also running down the corridor, but away from Annja toward the sound of the screaming. He had a gun out and as Annja caught up to him, he started to turn. She simply cut him down with a strike from her blade. She didn't stay around long enough to watch his body twist and fall to the floor.

She came to a stop at the entrance to a large cavern that had been rigged with electrical lights. She could hear a generator humming, and the sight of the interior of the room made her blood run cold.

Hospital gurneys stood side by side. All sorts of equipment was stocked in the room and at first, it looked more like an infirmary than anything else. But then she saw chains and long troughs cut into the sides of the room. The floor was also pitched slightly so as to allow the blood that invariably ran from the victims to be channeled into a bucket positioned underneath a spout at the far end.

It wasn't an infirmary at all, but a place to enact all manner of evil upon chosen victims.

Annja shuddered, but something grabbed her attention. At the far corner of the room, two people struggled and in the dim light, Annja could not see who they were.

She figured one of them was Godwin. He proved her assumption correct when, in the next second, he pivoted and sent Dufresne flying across the space with a terrible crash. He whirled and Annja caught a glimpse of his face. It was set and firm, with no hint that he would give Dufresne any quarter.

Godwin reached into the tangled mass of machinery and hauled Dufresne out. Blood streamed out of cuts to the torturer's face and Godwin peered into his eyes. "Have a fun time in the afterlife, you sick bastard."

He wrenched Dufresne's head. Annja heard the crack of bones and Dufresne went limp in Godwin's hands.

Godwin let him slide from his grasp and saw Annja standing there with her sword in hand. She caught her breath. "You okay?"

"He was going to give me electroshock treatment." Godwin shook his head. "Well, he's in no position to do anything now." He looked at Annja. "I'm glad to see you. We were concerned you'd die out on the mountain."

"I heard a sound," Annja said. "And when I went to investigate, I couldn't find anything. I came back and you guys were gone."

"They knocked us out and dragged us out of camp." Godwin shook his head. "I've still got a terrible headache and I don't think they were too gentle with us."

"I came back and saw the tracks. Figured then was as good a time as any to follow. With the snow coming down, I would have lost you if I'd waited. And then I would have died. For certain."

Godwin nodded toward the doorway. "The guard?"

"Dead."

He glanced at her sword, but little of the guard's blood remained on the blade.

"When we came to, they made us walk the rest of the way. Wishman is in a bad state. Probably the beginning stages of hypothermia. Plus, he's angry with himself for letting them get the jump on us."

Annja frowned. "I don't know if I believe that. He's been under the impression they knew we were coming all along. It's not like they had to work at it or anything. We basically came to them."

"For Wishman, this isn't just about stopping their evil. I think it's about coming full circle on something he should have done years ago."

"Which is fine," Annja said. "But I'm not happy that the rest of us were dragged along."

"Speaking of which," Godwin said. "They're due to be sacrificed soon."

Annja led them out of the torture chamber and back down the sloped hallway. She whispered into Godwin's ear, "Let me take point. If we come across any more guards, I can deal with them."

"Be my guest."

Annja led them back to the fork and gestured for Godwin to take the other tunnel with her. They traveled the length of the dank tunnel and came out at the other end.

The wide-open expanse startled Annja for the briefest of moments. Her stomach ached and she could see why. A line of men in black robes filed out of the open room down a tunnel toward a distant flickering light.

Annja glanced at Godwin and pulled them both back into the gloom of the tunnel. "Well, that explains the lack of guards we've encountered so far."

Godwin nodded. "They're all waiting to see the sacrifice. But who are these guys?"

"That's the company you worked for, apparently," Annja said.

"Not the company I *worked* for," Godwin said. "The company I *infiltrated*."

Annja eyed him. "What's that supposed to mean?"

He grinned. "I'll explain later. For now, we need to get ourselves some robes and join that procession. Otherwise we'll never reach Wishman and Nyaktuk in time."

"How do you know they're not already dead?"

Godwin shook his head. "They won't start the ceremony without all of those guys present and watching. Sacrifices like that need an audience."

"And you think they're really going to resurrect this demon Onur?"

"I have no idea. But I do know that I can't let them kill Wishman or Nyaktuk. Not while I still breathe." He patted Annja's arm. "Stay here for a moment. I'll be right back."

Annja watched him slink out of the tunnel. She knew what he was going to do, but even still, as she watched from the dimly lit tunnel, his speed and skill surprised her.

Godwin stole up on the last two robed guards in line and knocked their heads together so hard they both collapsed instantly. He waved Annja on and she rushed to grab one of them.

"Hurry," he whispered. "They'll be starting soon."

"What about the bodies?" Annja asked as she stripped the robe off the guard and slid it on.

"No time," Godwin said. "Pull the cowl down over your face so they won't see you and come on."

Annja hid her face and then followed Godwin down the tunnel. They fell into place behind the other guards and then filed into a new room at the far end of the tunnel. Annja counted at least forty men in total.

Bad odds for any sort of action.

She and Godwin maneuvered closer to the raised dais in the center of the room. Annja could see that in the middle of the dais a large hole was cut into the floor that apparently ran right into the mountain.

Where did that lead?

She didn't have time to consider the options because Derek and Hansen appeared at the back of the room and walked briskly to the dais. Behind them, two guards pushed Wishman and Nyaktuk through the crowd of robed followers.

None of the followers harassed the men, but a low chant started up that reminded Annja of a Gregorian chant.

Derek stood on the dais and held up his hands for silence. The room went quiet and Annja felt her heart start to hammer in her chest again.

"Brothers."

A murmur of greeting went up from the men who watched Derek with adoring eyes.

He smiled broadly. "Our time is at hand."

Hansen joined him on the dais and then looked out over the sea of followers. All of them had their cowls drawn over their faces. Annja felt reasonably secure where she and Godwin stood. She knew she could draw her sword instantly and be on the dais when the time came.

"We have worked long and hard to arrive at this

point," Derek said. "Many of our brethren have not made it this far."

Another rumbling murmur coursed through the crowd like a wave. Annja did her best to mimic it as it lapped past her.

Derek continued. "But tonight, we have the opportunity to achieve what we set as a goal for ourselves a long time ago—the reunification of the society of Onur."

He gazed at the crowd and then continued. "Long have we struggled as factions of isolated worshippers. And the promise of a more powerful union led us to join each other on this dangerous journey. But we persevered and overcame obstacle after obstacle until at last tonight, we are here. At this moment. In this hallowed place. At this righteous time."

The murmuring increased in volume. Derek held his hands up again, and silence once again reigned over the room.

"I know that many of you thought this day would never arrive. Well, your patience is at last about to be rewarded. We will conduct the ceremony to unleash Onur from his prison and he will join us as our new leader. The promise of power and victory over our challengers is assured as the Age of Onur is ushered in!"

The chanting began again. Annja rolled her eyes. If they snapped their fingers, this could be any Bohemian coffeehouse in the 1960s, she thought.

"A few days ago, I undertook a dangerous assignment. I was helped by the courage and tenacity of my second-in-command, Brother Hansen. He aided me in acquiring the one thing that had eluded us to this point."

Annja was confused. "A few days ago" would have meant the incident at the burial mound. But hadn't that been when Derek had insisted they were unleashing the creature? And hadn't Annja killed it? She could see the battle in her mind's eye. The red outline that had tried over and over to slay her. She could see the fight again, feel the impact of the creature's hits and kicks.

Derek kept speaking. "The Araktak have protected this item since time immemorial. When it was entrusted to them by the Viking missionaries who landed in Greenland and then transported over the ice floes of Labrador and Newfoundland, the Araktak knew only that it was an item of immense power. They had no idea what its true purpose was."

Annja could see that Wishman's eyes were sad but curious. Nyaktuk also seemed to be listening intently.

"They hid it well," Derek said. "And in a place no one expected anyone would find it."

He beamed, milking the moment. "But we kept searching and eventually, we learned the secret of the item's location."

Hansen nodded, smiling as if he knew firsthand how long it had taken and how much it had cost in terms of time and energy.

"The Araktak people were proud of their role, but they were fools in the end. They underestimated the perseverance of the brotherhood. They never knew how close we truly were until it was far too late."

Annja wanted to jump on the stage and cut him down before this went any further, but she was also wondering what Derek was talking about. Her curiosity needed calming. Derek apparently had all the answers, so she would let him finish.

And then she would finish him off.

"Behold!"

From beneath his robes, Derek lifted his right hand. Annja saw the brilliant diamond, larger than any she had seen before in her life. It was the size of a softball and cut in a strange way. Each facet seemed further cut into many lesser facets, each reflecting light out in different directions. Beams of light seemed to pierce the room at every angle.

Derek smiled. "This is the Soul of Onur. It was stolen from him during the last battle over ten thousand years ago. As long as the forces of light possessed it, Onur was trapped in the netherworld. There he has lain for millennia.

"But now, tonight, is our time to free him at last from his slumber. He will awaken and rise to join us on our quest for world domination."

Annja struggled to comprehend what Derek held. If they had been after the diamond all along, then why the talk of unleashing the creature? It didn't make sense.

Derek pointed at Wishman. "This ancient of the Araktak tried to stop me. But he and the woman who sought to aid him were both debilitated by the Breath of Onur. And while this one slipped into unconsciousness, his warrior friend hallucinated and engaged in battle with a fictitious demon of her mind's own design."

The words struck Annja and she almost reeled at the thought. It couldn't be. What was the Breath of Onur? Drugs? It would have to be if she had been hallucinating. But had she? The battle had seemed so real! How could she have possibly been taken out so easily? Shouldn't the sword have protected her?

From the back of the dais, another robed figure hastened to reach Derek.

Derek listened and then turned back to the crowd. "Before we start the ceremony, we have another matter to attend to…."

Hansen frowned. "What matter?"

Derek looked out on the audience. "We have an intruder in our midst."

36

Annja fought hard to keep from panicking. Facing a raging mob of forty cult worshippers wasn't the best prescription for healthy living. And while she had little doubt that she could kill a lot of them with her sword, eventually, she knew the law of numbers would work against her and she'd be taken down.

Godwin wasn't armed, either, at least not that Annja knew of. Unless he'd slipped something into his belt back at the torture chamber that she hadn't seen, he'd be reduced to fighting with his hands. That wouldn't work for long, either.

Their best bet would be to hold their ground and feign surprise just like the rest of the hooded fools who stood close by. Already, a murmur had rushed through the crowd as hooded members turned and looked at each other asking the same question, "Who?"

Derek spread his arms again. "Brothers, please. Hold your tongues for the moment. I assure you, we will unmask the traitor very soon."

All attention turned back to Derek. His smile seemed

to warm them, although Annja found it inherently creepy. His white teeth shone amid the dim light. On the walls, torches flickered and cast dancing shadows on the walls.

Derek at last turned to Hansen. "Dufresne is dead. He was found in his laboratory with his neck broken. There'd been quite a struggle."

Hansen's eyes went wide. "And the prisoner?"

"Apparently, he is free."

Hansen looked at the crowd. Annja felt his eyes rove over her but they didn't stop. Hansen looked back at Derek. "We need to find him. Immediately."

Derek held up a hand to stop him. "In time. He can't get far. Exit from the mountain is secured and he won't know how to activate the door without help."

Hansen frowned. "Help?"

Derek smiled. "Isn't it obvious? Someone is helping him. Presumably because they have their own agenda."

"But who?"

Derek looked out at the crowd and turned to them. "Hear me, brothers. Hear my words and understand what I say." He paused and then spoke again. "I have worked hard to bring you all to this point. To the moment when we can at last realize our goal of uniting behind our god."

He held up a finger. "But the road is not a safe one to travel. At times, we have been faced with struggles. Interlopers have clouded the road, making it difficult to see where we should go. And in the confusion, we have made our share of mistakes."

He smiled. "No one likes to admit they've made mistakes, but is it not through failure that we learn the most? Is it not by challenge that we test our spirits and resolve?"

Hansen shifted. "We should be looking for the escaped prisoner."

Derek stopped him. "No. We need to finish this first. Then and only then will we look for him."

Hansen fell silent as Derek continued his speech. "Many times I have had to ask myself if what I am doing is in the best interests of our organization. We are devoted to the domination of the world under the ancient god Onur. Yet, perhaps our dreams are not those dreams of other people. Maybe we have been mistaken is assuming that all of us are of one mind."

Annja felt her heart beating a steady rhythm under her robe. Next to her, Godwin hadn't moved an inch. But she could sense that he was coiled and ready to fight in the blink of an eye.

Derek turned and looked at Hansen. "You helped him escape, didn't you?"

Hansen managed to laugh at that. "Are you joking? Why in the world would I help him escape?"

"Why don't you tell me?"

Hansen looked at Derek and then out at the robed masses. He shook his head. "This is ridiculous. I've been your most ardent supporter."

"Have you?"

"Of course! Didn't I work with you at the burial mound of the Araktak? Didn't I arrange all the deaths at the mining company so we could step into power? Didn't I pay off the judges and the lawyers and get this mountain into our custody?"

Derek nodded. "Indeed. You did do all of those things. But never have you done any of it without first thinking of yourself."

"That's ridiculous."

"Is it?" Derek turned and from under his robes he took out a sheaf of papers. "Behold the bank statements of our illustrious second-in-command." He riffled through them. "There are deposits here in the millions. And you have five personal accounts that we were able to track down. You probably have many more."

Hansen was livid. "Where did you get that?"

Derek grinned. "I've told many people lately that there is nothing that money cannot buy. Information is perhaps the cheapest of them all. Perhaps you'd like to tell the Brotherhood why it is that you have upward of fifty million dollars in your personal fortune?"

"That's not true—"

"It's all right here," Derek said. "Would you dispute these official bank statements?"

"You could have cooked those up on a computer for all we know," Hansen said. "It proves nothing."

Derek shook his head. "It proves that you don't hold the values of the Brotherhood very seriously."

"More insanity," Hansen said.

Derek barely nodded and two guards suddenly rushed forward to pin Hansen's arms behind him. "Is it really insanity? I don't think so," Derek said as he moved closer to Hansen. "You've been skimming profits from our various transactions."

"Not true!" Hansen searched the crowd for sympathy but Annja felt nothing from them. "He's lying to you! Don't fall for his lies!"

Derek sighed. "Such a pity when power starts to corrupt. You know the rules we have in place. No one member of the Brotherhood is above reproach. And none of us is supposed to hold a personal fortune when the greater good of our organization demands the sacrifice of us all so we might enable our destiny of unleashing Onur upon the world that has imprisoned him for so long."

Hansen struggled but his captors held him fast. Annja could see their grim faces and knew that Hansen would have a tough time breaking free.

Derek shook his head as if weighed down by an awful decision. "Fifty million dollars is a lot of money. When the rest of us are living like paupers so that we might help the cause, Hansen here has three homes around the world. And he also has children."

A collective gasp went up from the group. Annja glanced at Godwin, but his face remained hard as stone. She looked back at the dais, and Derek took a deep breath and let it out. "It's true. Hansen has spilled his seed even though our rules explicitly state that abstinence is mandatory until the coming of our god."

He looked out at the crowd. "Are you willing to endanger our mortal souls for the sake of a quick bout of sex? Are you?"

Shouts of "No!" rose from everywhere. Derek nodded and seemed satisfied by the response. "Well, our would-be leader here certainly is willing to do so. And it's not just his soul in peril, but the souls of all of us who have sworn an oath."

He looked at Hansen, anger flashing in his eyes. "Obviously, our words mean little to you. The oath you swore with the blood of your left hand, the pledge you made to everyone here, it was all for nothing. You didn't care."

Hansen looked down at the ground. "It was an error in judgment. I make no excuses for it."

"An error in judgment? Is that what you call it?"

Hansen looked up at him. "You are not beyond reproach yourself."

Derek waved his hands. "I won't dignify that with a response. Your pathetic attempts to redirect the crowd are nothing but an insult to our intelligence. The fact of the matter is you have broken repeated laws, and for that you must be judged."

Silence fell over the room and Annja could feel the energy change. Derek looked out across the masses. "Brothers, you know the laws that we are bound by. Each of us holds the right to make a decision about another man's life. Brother Hansen has transgressed the laws. He has broken his word to us all. His vows are for nothing. And he has helped a prisoner escape.

"Any one of those infractions on its own could carry the ultimate penalty, but taken in concert, the judgment must be made immediately." Derek held his left hand out and closed it into a tight fist. "I call for death."

Around Annja, the other robed figures shot their left hands out, and repeated calls for death sounded around them. Annja noticed that Godwin's left hand shot out, as well. He nudged Annja and she followed suit, although it felt horrible knowing her fist would help condemn a man.

Derek looked out across the sea of closed left fists and nodded. "So speaks the Brotherhood." He looked back at Hansen. "You have been judged by your brothers. You have been found guilty of breaking the laws that you swore to uphold. For these transgressions, you have been sentenced to death."

"I refuse to recognize the judgment of this court," Hansen said. "And I swear my eternal vengeance upon all of you."

Derek shook his head and then gestured to the men holding Hansen. "Prepare him."

The guards hauled Hansen over to the edge of the hole in the middle of the dais. Derek nodded and another attendant pulled on an unseen chain. Annja heard a groan and then a steady creaking.

Something was opening on the dais. Unseen to Annja

and Godwin, the hole had a cover over it. The attendant pulling the chain now opened it.

Flames shot up from inside the hole. Annja could just make out the highest bits of fire lapping at the edges of the opening.

Hansen started to struggle, desperate to fight off the men who held him fast. But as much as he tried, he couldn't break free of their grasps.

"You can't do this!" he shouted.

Derek looked at him as if he was nothing but a pesky fly. "I didn't do this. You did. And now you must pay for your crimes against the Brotherhood."

The guards holding Wishman and Nyaktuk pulled them away from the hole. The guards holding Hansen moved him closer.

Derek looked at Hansen and then frowned. "The traitor still wears our garments. Disrobe him."

"No!" Hansen struggled and kicked at the guards as they stripped the coarse woolen garment off him and handed it to Derek.

Derek hefted the robe. "You have forfeited your right to wear one of these and call yourself one of us."

Annja could feel the tension rising in the room. Godwin had shifted ever so slightly. Was this it? Would they attack now?

Derek paced the dais. "The flames of Onur demand that all traitors be given over to them for absolute judgment." He looked at Hansen. "Do you have any final words for the Brotherhood?"

Hansen spit in Derek's face. "I will never grovel to the likes of you. Or them. You are all bound to die here in this mountain. Mark my words, I will see to your destruction."

Derek wiped his face and nodded. "So be it."

He walked to the edge of the fire pit and raised his hands overhead. "Great god Onur, in your name we beseech thee. We have aspired for many long years to bring about your resurrection and unleash you from the prison that holds you to this day. And here in our midst we have found one who would not see that done. He is one who has been judged by his peers and found guilty of high treason. We ask that you judge him as he deserves to be judged, that you show him the suffering that awaits all who would keep you imprisoned in the netherworld."

The flames licking the edge of the fire pit grew suddenly higher as if they sensed the inevitable. Hansen had stopped struggling and seemed resigned to his fate. His eyes were dark stones absent of regret or hesitation.

He looked at Derek. "If I am to be killed for my crimes, then at least offer me the dignity of doing it myself."

Derek raised an eyebrow. "And why would I grant you that right when none have ever been granted it before?"

"Because we are brothers."

Derek shook his head. "No longer." He turned to the guards holding Hansen. "Throw the condemned into the flames of Onur."

Hansen smiled at Derek. "I will see you in Hell."

"Not for a very long time," Derek said. He stepped aside and nodded to the guards. They started pushing Hansen to the edge.

In the next instant, Annja had the impression that Hansen was toppling into the fire pit at the exact same moment that Godwin leaped forward and up onto the dais.

"Now, Annja!" he shouted.

37

Annja threw off the robe and brought her sword out as she jumped up on the dais. From the corner of her eye, she saw Godwin collide with Derek, who had started shouting at his followers. Godwin sent a left jab that dropped Derek back and down on the floor.

The two guards readying to pitch Hansen into the fire pit abandoned that notion and drew curved blades that reminded Annja of scimitars. The first came at her with a swinging right-hand stroke aimed at her head. Annja ducked as the blade flashed by and then cut up with her own sword, slicing through the dark robe and spilling blood. The man screeched and then fell into the fire pit.

His comrade backed up after seeing the ease with which Annja dispatched the first cult member. He held the scimitar unsteadily, but Annja saw his resolve strengthen and he rushed in, cutting straight down from overhead.

Annja couldn't go to her left or she'd fall in the fire pit. She had to pivot to the right and narrowly missed the singing blade as it cleaved downward at her. She stabbed in with her blade, but the swordsman recovered and parried it up and away.

It was a tight space on the dais. Godwin was engaged with Wishman's guards, fighting them single-handedly. Hansen had tried to scramble away, but Wishman kicked him soundly in the gut and he went down, clutching his groin. Nyaktuk was struggling with his guards, as well, and having a pretty good time of it. Distraction and chaos reigned on the platform while the fire pit sang for more victims.

Annja's foe came at her with a barrage of slashing cuts aimed at distracting her so he could deal a mortal cut at her midsection. Annja dodged and parried and shot her blade right into his gut. Her blade pierced his robe and then his lower abdomen. She heard a horrible sound, and then he pitched forward and dropped his scimitar.

Annja skirted his body and then slipped in a pool of the blood. She fell back and scrambled for purchase, kicking the corpse into the fire pit at the same time. The flames burned hot as they devoured the body. Blood ran into the pit, dribbling over the edge and cooking in the heat. The acrid smell filled the air along with the scent of charred flesh.

Annja winced at the smell but kept going.

Godwin suddenly shouted and Annja looked over. He had pivoted and then thrown one of Wishman's guards. The guard crashed down onto the edge of the fire pit and gravity took over. The man screamed and fell into the pit, his hands still scrambling at the smooth walls even as the fires melted his flesh.

Wishman's second guard came at Godwin, and Annja watched as he moved with minimal effort, evading the small knife the guard sported. They moved as if dancing and then Godwin shot his fist in at the right moment to disarm the attacker. He got control of the knife hand and then reversed the blade and shot it into the guard's stomach, ripping this way and that as the man grunted. Blood sprayed the dais and Godwin shoved him into the fire pit.

The flames shot even higher and Annja felt their savage heat and hunger. Wishman struggled to free Nyaktuk from his second guard, since the younger Araktak had already managed to knock out his first guard with a well-timed head butt to the bridge of his nose.

Hansen was slow in getting to his feet, but finally managed to get off the ground. He was mumbling something and looked at Annja. "How did you know where to find us?"

Annja held her sword at her side. "I was part of the original team. You only thought there were three."

"Don't kill me. I'm no threat to y—"

But as he spoke, Derek rushed at him and shoved him into the fire pit before anyone could stop him. Hansen teetered for just a moment on the edge, trying to reach for Annja to help pull him back from the brink.

Annja was about to stretch out toward him, but Wishman pulled her back.

Hansen fell into the flames, his cries fading quickly in the inferno.

Annja wanted to scream at Wishman, but in that instant, she saw what he had seen already, that the fires were leaping higher. Had she reached for Hansen, Annja would have been caught in a great blast of flame.

Derek stood on the dais looking at them. He smiled as if he had no cares in the world. "So, you've managed to alter the schedule of things a bit."

Godwin eyed him and Annja kept to his other side. "This is over now," she said.

Derek smiled. "Do you think so?"

"You've got no place to flee," Godwin said. "Give it up."

"Me? Flee?" Derek smiled. "I wouldn't dream of it. You, however, have far more pressing problems than I."

Annja spun around and saw that during the melee on the dais, the robed followers on the floor had sealed off every exit and had armed themselves with all manner of bladed weapons.

Derek held up his hands. "We prefer the bladed weapons to firearms. It hearkens back to a time before such modern tools enabled any fool to be able to kill. These men have all studied their craft well and I would be proud to call any of them a warrior."

Annja shook her head. "Yeah, well, that's delightful and all, but if any of them make a step closer, you're going to die."

Derek shook his head. "As if such a thing even matters. My followers will kill you before you get two steps from the dais." His eyes gleamed. "Whether you kill me or not."

Godwin frowned and spoke to Annja. "Any ideas?"

Wishman stepped forward. "Is this a standoff?"

Derek smiled. "Not at all. If anything, you helped get rid of that pesky Hansen and several useless guards who clearly had not studied their weapons training very much. I should be thanking you for your assistance. However, we do have an agenda to keep to here."

"You won't be calling on Onur for help tonight. I'll die before I let you do such a thing," Annja said.

Derek laughed. "Even if you were able to stop me, it wouldn't be like the other day, Annja. It wouldn't be like that crazy little drug-induced hallucination you suffered through."

"Explain yourself," she said.

Derek eyed her. "You didn't actually think that we were going to unleash a creature from the burial mound, did you? That such a creature would allow itself to be walled up in some grave site? Ridiculous. But Hansen, for all his treachery, was a master chemist and mixed a little something we like to call the Breath of Onur with the explosive charges. When they fired off, the drugs vaporized and turned into a very potent aerosol that was blasted out of the hole and infected you and the old man there."

Annja glanced at Wishman, who had his eyes set on Derek.

Derek kept talking. "The old man simply fainted as soon as he took a deep breath of the stuff. But you—" he smiled "—you gave us a great show, running this way and that, hacking up the field and doing all manner of battle with a figment of your imagination."

Annja shook her head. It wasn't possible that her battle had been nothing more than some bizarre acid trip. Or was it? She hadn't been able to see the creature except in her mind's eye. If her mind was clouded by the drugs, then anything was possible.

"All it took was little bit of suggestion to imply the creature would be invisible to the human eye."

Annja pointed at Wishman. "But he said that the Araktak did have a creature like the one you said was walled up there."

Derek shrugged. "Oh that's just some silly old legend. There's no truth in any of those things. But there is truth in the great god Onur. Now throw down your weapons."

Annja shook her head. "You know I can't do that. It's impossible for me."

Derek nodded. "Yes, yes, good point. I had indeed forgotten that that very real sword is somehow mystical in nature. That will be a bit of a problem." His voice trailed off and then he snapped his fingers. "Ah, I've got it."

Godwin was still staring at him, and Annja wondered

what he had in mind. She turned her attention back to Derek. "Yes?"

"You will simply throw yourself into the flames."

"Excuse me?"

Derek nodded. "Yes. You will voluntarily give yourself over to the fires. Onur will be most pleased with your sacrifice. He craves it. You are a bastion of good and he will feed a long time on your soul."

Annja cocked an eyebrow. "Just like that?"

"Is there another way you'd prefer to go out?"

"Yeah, with your head on a stick."

Derek shook his head. "No, no, that won't do at all. Here's the deal. You sacrifice yourself and I will let your friends go."

"I'm not falling for that."

Derek frowned. "I give you my word."

"What good is your word?" snarled Godwin then.

Derek ignored him. "You can choose to die here, Annja, or you will all die at the merest flick of my hand to my followers."

Annja looked out across the massive room. Derek's followers had them surrounded and there would be no way they could move.

Godwin looked at Annja. "Don't be foolish. We can grab him and use him as a hostage."

Derek shook his head. "My men would kill me just to get to you. It is part of our oath never to allow one to be greater than the others. Strike me down and five more will spring up to replace me."

Wishman stepped forward. "Take me instead."

Derek regarded him. "You are old and worthless to me. Onur would rather have the young one and her vibrancy. You are old and feeble by comparison and Onur would find you an appetizer and little more. But Annja, she would be a feast."

Annja smiled at Wishman. "Thanks. I appreciate the offer to go in my stead."

Godwin frowned. "You can't seriously be thinking about this."

She looked at him. "That's long odds out there. Forty of them against us? I'm armed and you are, too, but what about Wishman and Nyaktuk?"

"We'll be all right."

"You'd die and then that would just be a waste." She looked at Derek. "I want free passage for them out of the mountain. I want your word that none of your men will harm them in any way. Let them get out of here."

Derek smiled. "Of course."

"They leave now."

Derek shook his head. "What promise do I have that you will honor your word to us?"

"You have the same assurances as I. If I renege, then you can go outside the mountain and hunt down the three of them. Most likely they'll be easy pickings for your men. The weather is horrible outside and they'd be easy enough to follow. You've got nothing to lose by letting them go."

"Perhaps." Derek mulled it over for a moment. "Very well. If we have your word on it."

"You do."

He nodded. "Then your friends are free to go. There have already been plenty of bodies thrown into the flames tonight. They are no longer needed." He turned to Godwin. "Take the old man and Nyaktuk and leave. Now."

Godwin looked at Annja. "I'm not leaving you."

Annja shook her head. "We can't make it out of this together. You take Wishman and Nyaktuk and go."

Godwin gritted his teeth. Annja could see the hesitation in him. This wasn't like him to leave someone behind. She put a hand on his arm. "Tell me one thing before you go."

"Anything."

She tried to smile. "Who are you?"

"Canadian Intelligence."

Annja's eyed widened. "Really?"

He nodded, his voice a whisper. "We've been wondering about this mining company for about a year now. I was sent in to find out what they were up to." He sighed. "Unfortunately, it took me too long to figure it out."

Annja smiled. "It's not your fault."

"It is."

"Don't live a life of regret," Annja said. "It's not worth it. There's far too much to do in this lifetime without being burdened by it all."

He looked into her eyes and then bent forward to kiss her on her lips. Annja tasted his desperation and pressed herself to him. Then just as quickly, she pushed him away.

"Go," she said. "Before I change my mind."

Godwin backed away and looked at Derek. "We aren't finished yet. Not by a long shot."

Derek grinned. "I have no doubt." He ushered over a guard. "Show them the fastest route out of here. The exit by the base of the mountain should suffice. Then get back here. We have unfinished business with the woman."

The guard nodded and waved for Godwin to follow him. He held a flickering torch aloft and then, as Annja watched, Godwin, Wishman and Nyaktuk left the dais. The sea of followers parted for them, and Annja watched them walk back down the tunnel. Soon enough, the flickering torchlight died and they were gone.

Leaving Annja all alone with the cult and its hungry fire pit.

38

Annja could feel Derek watching her intently. She glanced over at him. "Something I can help you with?" she asked angrily.

"Are you ready to carry out your end of the bargain?"

Annja looked at the room. Derek's followers had shown no signs of getting impatient, even though they'd been waiting for the better part of twenty minutes since Godwin and the others had left. Annja wondered if Derek had some sort of hypnotic hold on them.

"How long does it take them to reach the mountain entrance?"

Derek shrugged. "Perhaps ten minutes. If you were wondering how Dufresne got here before your party did, that's how. It's significantly more convenient than traipsing up toward the pass, eh?"

"I'll bet."

Derek smiled and then noticed someone entering the cavern. "Ah, your friends' guide has returned. You see?

They are all safe and sound. They've left the mountain, and I have upheld my end of the bargain." His eyes narrowed. "Now it's your turn."

Annja started toward the fire pit, but Derek held up his hand. "Wait!"

Annja looked back at him. "What's the problem?"

Derek shook his head. "We're not ready yet. There is a ceremony to be carried out." He nodded at several new guards who flanked the dais. Each one lit a new set of torches and a waft of incense blew over the room. Annja found her head going light. She blinked back the sensation and bit into her lip, determined to keep her wits about her.

"I see you recognize a bit of the Breath of Onur," Derek said. "We find it helps us achieve the proper mind-set for the summoning."

"Summoning?"

"Our ceremony to bring Onur forth on this plane." Derek held the giant diamond aloft and now spoke to his followers. "Behold the Soul of Onur!"

A collective chorus went up from the remaining men. Annja gazed at the diamond, spellbound by its beauty. Each facet seemed to twinkle and bewilder. She lost her gaze looking at it, and it seemed as if all the light in the room was reflected through it. What an incredible piece, she thought.

"So, that was the whole push to get to the kimberlite, huh?" she said.

Derek shushed her but nodded. "We knew it had to be somewhere where there would be naturally occurring diamonds. When we found the kimberlite, we knew we had it. Our people at Ekati had turned up nothing, so it was a logical assumption."

"Lucky for you."

Derek turned back to his people. "We have the Soul of Onur and now all that remains is to call forth our god from his place of slumber."

One of the guards approached the dais with a bottle of wine. Derek removed the cork and poured much of the wine into the fire pit. The wine barely made an impact as the flames continued to lick the sides of the pit. All of the blood that had been spilled earlier was nothing more than a charred series of stains on the stonework.

More of the incense wafted over the room. Annja struggled to keep herself composed. The effect was a heady one.

I've got to keep it together, she thought. Otherwise, I actually will sacrifice myself.

She'd never intended to kill herself. Not for a freak like Derek. But at least she knew that if she volunteered, then Godwin, Wishman and Nyaktuk were guaranteed to be safe. If she'd opted otherwise, there was a chance all of them would die here in this cavern.

Now, when Annja unleashed herself, it would be one against the many. And she would probably die, but at least she would have the pleasure of taking a lot of them with her. She also wouldn't have to worry about accidentally cutting anyone friendly. She could go berserk and not care.

"Bring me the blood," Derek said.

Another guard approached bearing a container of blood. Annja grimaced at the sight of it. Derek poured it into the fire and started chanting in some unknown language. Annja thought it sounded vaguely Scandinavian, but she was unsure which language it might be.

Derek's voice rose and fell much as Wishman's had when he had chanted over Godwin's hypothermic body back at the camp. But whereas Wishman had helped heal Godwin, there was no doubt that Derek's motives were far different. His voice sang out and cried for a million unintelligible things.

From the dais, Annja watched as his followers moved closer en masse. Their cowls shielded their faces, but Annja could feel the mixture of excitement and fear. What was it they had been promised that would make them forsake a good life in pursuit of the resurrection of an ancient evil god? Annja shuddered to think of what they had given up or promised in exchange for the chance to be part of this.

She frowned. None of these men deserved any mercy. The blood had presumably been obtained by killing an innocent or innocents. That meant they had engaged in murder.

Derek looked at her. "Yes, you see what we are now, don't you? You know that we have hunted good people for centuries and dragged them here to be part of this process. It has taken us years to get to this point, but now we are ready at last."

Annja's mind swam. How had Derek heard her thoughts?

But he only smiled at her. Any answer would not be forthcoming and he merely gestured to the fire pit.

"Look at it, Annja. You see how it grows in anticipation of your touch? It can smell you. He can sense the goodness that flows in your body, the spirit of resolve you possess that separates you from most of humanity. He desires you and wants to feed upon your flesh and make you feel pain and agony such as you have never felt before. And when he is at last finished, he will rise from this pit and reclaim his place on this plane. All will yield before him. He will smite the nonbelievers and allow his faithful to gain the power they crave and deserve."

Annja felt hotter. The heat of the cavern seemed overwhelming. She could smell the incense and it was overpowering her senses. Derek's voice became like an insistent gentle prod in her ear. She felt her mind starting to switch off.

She wanted to die.

"Arise, Onur!"

She wanted to jump into the fire pit.

"Arise and claim your victim! Take her into the depths of Hell and feast!"

She wanted to be with Onur.

"Then join us!"

Annja stepped forward.

The flames lapped at her. She could feel their gentle touch. It didn't hurt. She could step right off the edge and it would be over in an instant.

She looked down into the fire pit and there, amid the yellows, reds and oranges, she saw something else. Something amorphous and black. A shadow that grew as the flames rose and fell. She could sense its presence, coming for her. Wanting her. Its wanton desire unmasked.

The energy of the room throbbed as Derek and his followers started a new chant.

Annja took another step.

It would be over soon.

Come to me....

That voice… It spoke inside her head…. Annja blinked. The scene changed. She was covered in sweat. The heat overpowered her. But still, the black shape in the fire pit seemed to rise faster.

Onur was rising.

"No!"

Annja felt the energy flood back into her body. She whirled and whipped out the sword. Derek's eyes were wide and white.

"You must not deny him!" He drew a wicked dagger from the nearby guard and rushed at Annja, screaming, "You'll ruin everything!"

Annja sidestepped and Derek's dagger slashed through empty air. Annja turned and cut down, cleaving through Derek's body, her sword not even slowing as she did so. The air exploded with gore and blood and Derek shuddered, falling into two distinct pieces.

He toppled forward and fell into the flames, his final screech dying as the flames took him.

The giant diamond—the Soul of Onur—skittered across the dais. Annja picked it up and regarded it for a second and then threw it into the fires, as well. "You wanted this so badly, here you go."

Annja whirled around and stared at Derek's followers. They surged forward, ready to take her on.

Annja grinned. "Well, if this is how it's going to be, cool. Let's get it on, boys. Don't keep a lady waiting."

And she leaped into the closest bunch of them, hacking and slicing. Bodies fell around her, but she hardly registered the carnage. Her sword sang as it cut through flesh and bone alike. For all their supposed skill, not one of Derek's followers could touch Annja.

Her blood coursed through her veins and her heart pulsed and kept her moving as if in another world.

And for all of them, it was the last thing they ever saw— her grim face and the bloodred blade that cut through them as Annja made her way toward the back of the cavern and to the tunnel that led out of the mountain.

She could see the tunnel.

From behind her, she heard something that jarred her out of her state. There was an awful thunderous boom and she risked a glance back. From the fire pit, the blackened shadow that she'd seen with her own eyes rose up, blocking out the light of the torches.

An awful voice sounded across the cavern, speaking

some ancient tongue. Derek's followers clamped their hands over their ears and screamed. Annja kept cutting down more of them as she hacked her way to the back of the cavern.

Three of them tried to bar her way. Others were screaming that Onur had risen. Shadows loomed over the cavern, and as Annja cut down the three men with fierce strikes, she paused to look back again.

Onur, if it was him, had seeped out of the fire pit and was casting his shadow over the few living followers who had remained standing because they'd been too far away from Annja's sword. The great shadow fell upon them and Annja heard a sickening sound of feasting as they screamed. Onur was sucking their very souls from their bodies.

The cavern started to rumble. Rocks started to plummet from the ceiling. More men died under the cascade of boulders that shook loose from the walls. Their screams sent Annja struggling to get to the tunnel.

And then she saw Godwin reaching for her from the tunnel itself.

She threw herself forward. "I knew you wouldn't leave."

He grinned. "Not yet anyway. But I think now's as good a time as any to be leaving."

She stopped him. "Do you see him?"

"Who?"

"Onur. He's risen."

Godwin looked behind Annja and for the briefest moment, his eyes widened. But then just as quickly, he dragged on Annja's hand. "We have to get out of here before the whole place collapses. I don't want to die here."

Annja fell into his arms and then paused one final time to look back at the cavern. The entire ceiling was caving in, burying everything. But the black shadow seemed untouched by any of this.

We'll meet again....

Annja blinked. "Did you hear that?"

"The only thing I hear is my gut telling me to get the hell out of here, Annja. Now let's go!"

They stumbled along the tunnel and then emerged into the other cavern. Wishman and Nyaktuk were there armed with their rifles. Wishman smiled. "So you got her."

"She was on her way out," Godwin said.

Annja looked into Wishman's eyes but something there told her not to speak. Not now.

Instead, she looked at Godwin. "I think I'm ready to go home."

Godwin nodded. "We've got the way out of this place. Let's go!"

They rushed down another tunnel that sloped down and led them to a smaller room beside a massive boulder. Nyaktuk reached up and activated the old switch. The boulder swung back, revealing the dim light of dawn just starting to bleed across the horizon.

Annja stumbled out of the mountain and looked up at it from the outside. She could still hear the caverns starting to fall apart. Soon enough, the interior of the mountain would be completely caved in.

But outside, the new dawn promised a new beginning.

Most importantly, it promised life.

39

The journey back to the camp at the burial mound seemed to take a lot less time than when they had traveled to the mountain. Annja rode most of the way in silence, lost in her thoughts about what had happened. She had a great deal of questions, and as usual, the answers only seemed to prompt further questions to which she had no solutions.

"You're wondering about what transpired at the burial mound," Wishman said on one of their breaks. He had regained his smile and the twinkle in his eyes had come back, as well. Annja guessed that he had had some sort of revelation back in the mountain. Whatever it was, she was certain he would always treasure it, despite the high cost.

"I was wondering if what Derek said was true," Annja said.

"About the drug-induced hallucinations?"

"The Breath of Onur," Annja said. "Yeah."

Wishman looked out across the forest they were traveling through. The pine trees swayed back and forth in the stiff breezes that still tore across the frozen landscape. "I can't say. My first impression was of the shimmering haze that we already spoke about. But after that, I'm afraid my memory clouds. It may well be that my body's reaction to the drug was to fall unconscious."

"So there was no creature," Annja said.

Wishman looked at her. "I don't know, Annja. I simply don't know. I know what we attempted to imprison there a long time ago. But even that I now question. Were we deluded or was there truly a danger back when we walled it up behind the barrier? I just don't know."

"Sure seemed real to me," Annja said. "But at the same time, I can't imagine doing what I was able to do."

"Why not?"

"Because I've never done something like that before. I've never battled a supernatural creature."

Wishman nodded. "And I'm sure that a newborn baby looks at the giants around it and sees them walking and running and says much the same thing as you've just said."

Annja watched him climb back aboard the sledge and they moved off. Annja glanced behind her at Godwin, who had insisted on driving most of the way back to camp.

"Suppose you tell me about your past now. The real Godwin."

He grinned. "Anything in particular you want to know about?"

"Only everything," Annja said. "But suppose we start with the whole half-breed thing. Are you really part Araktak?"

He nodded. "And very proud of it. My father was banished from the tribe for rescuing my mother. What I didn't tell you was that she was the daughter of the head of Canadian Intelligence. When my father brought her back to civilization, my grandfather was grateful beyond belief. He praised my father and treated him with all the respect in the world and was overjoyed when my father proposed."

Godwin smiled at the memories. "When I was born, my grandfather said it was the happiest moment of his life. In many ways, I learned from two men growing up. My father taught me everything he expected his Araktak son to know. My grandfather taught me the world of espionage." He paused as they rounded a bend. "And from my mother, I learned how to never give up hope."

"Sounds like quite a childhood."

Godwin nodded. "It was. I went into the military and found my way into special operations. From there, my grandfather encouraged me to enter the intelligence world. It seemed a natural progression. I took to it easily."

"And the assignment for the mining company?"

Godwin shrugged. "We knew something was going on, but no one knew exactly what. There seemed no rhyme or reason to their pursuits."

"What did they do that even brought them to your attention in the first place?"

"We tracked a large investment that originated in Saudi Arabia, got washed through Liechtenstein and then wound up in their account."

"That was unusual?"

"Given that it came from a family with known ties to several radical splinter terror cells, we thought it prudent to see exactly what Derek and company were up to."

"So you drew the short straw?"

Godwin laughed and then looked at Annja. "I might be inclined to say I got lucky drawing this assignment."

Annja batted her eyelashes. "I suppose you might." She turned around and watched the trees flash by as they drove hard back to the burial camp. "So, what happens now?"

"I don't know," Godwin said. "I've chased things down on this end. Seems likely that someone—possibly even me—will have to go and chase down the start of the money. That would mean a trip to the Middle East."

Annja sighed. "It's a lot warmer over there at least."

"Yeah, but too much sand. It gets in everything and everywhere. It also chafes like a bastard."

"Maybe I'll take a vacation," Annja said. "I could use a change of scenery. I'm kind of tired of all this snow."

"Yeah?"

"Yeah."

They made their way back to the burial camp that night. Coming back up the wide open plain, Annja felt a twinge of déjà vu.

The camp was a shambles and the twisted corpses of the remainder of Araktak warriors lay strewed about the camp in callous heaps. Judging by their wounds, they had been bled almost dry by Dufresne's men. That blood had then been used in the summoning ceremony Derek had started.

Wishman and Nyaktuk wept openly at the loss of life. Godwin's face was hard as he helped them prepare the bodies for burial.

But Wishman shook his head when Godwin suggested they be buried in the mound itself. "This place is no longer for the dead. It has been violated in so many ways that we must use the new location." He looked at the burial mound. "And we will use this as a new mine. It will be our way forward to the future."

"What about all your traditions?" Annja asked.

Wishman smiled. "The money we earn from this mine will help us educate our young. We will teach them the old ways while we prepare them for the new. In that way, the

Araktak will always be a force for good, rather than a dying whisper in someone's memory."

That night, they loaded the dead in one of the trucks. Godwin used the satellite radio to phone in his report and the military showed up the next day to clean things up. By the end of the third day, Annja was on her way home.

SHE'D RIDDEN almost eight hours on airplanes that connected to other airplanes that then sat on tarmacs awaiting takeoff clearances. By the time Annja staggered into her Brooklyn loft, she was as exhausted as she'd been on that frozen mountain in the Northwest Territories.

A hot shower. It was all she wanted. All she needed.

She pressed her voice mail out of habit as she walked to the refrigerator to make sure she had a good bottle of wine already chilled.

"Hi, Annja. I hope you know who this is."

She smiled from the kitchen. There was no mistaking the deep timbre of Godwin's voice.

"I'm going to be in New York for a few hours tonight. I know this is last-minute and everything, but I'd love to have dinner before I have to leave. I'm staying at the Hyatt. Room 615. Call me."

Annja took a healthy swig of wine. Dinner sounded good. But first, she needed to get every last bit of gunk off of her body.

She walked to the bathroom and ran the shower and turned it as hot as she could stand. Steam started filling up the room and seeping out into her bedroom as she stripped off the clothes she'd been wearing for what felt like weeks.

Annja climbed into the shower, closed her eyes and let the hot water soak into her skin. It took her forty minutes before she finally felt clean again. She switched the water off and grabbed the towel hanging nearby.

Stepping out, she rubbed the mirror to wipe the condensation clear. Where would she take Godwin tonight for dinner? The choices in the city were endless, but Annja felt like something spicy. Or maybe that was just how she was feeling in general.

The trip up north had prompted a lot of questions, but tonight, Annja was only in the mood for Godwin.

TAKE 'EM FREE

2 action-packed novels plus a mystery bonus

NO RISK

NO OBLIGATION TO BUY